THE WAR ON DOGS:
IN VENICE BEACH

A Novel

ALSO BY RONALD ALEXANDER

Below 200
The Final Audit

THE WAR ON DOGS:
IN VENICE BEACH

A Novel

Ronald Alexander

Illustrated by Nathan Geare

Hollyridge Press
Venice, California

Hollyridge Press
P.O. Box 2872
Venice, California 90294

Original Cover Art and Illustrations by Nathan Geare
Book Design by Rio Smyth
Author Photo by Cynthia Smalley
Manufactured in the United States of America by Lightning Source

Publisher's Cataloging-in-Publication
(Prepared by The Donohue Group, Inc.)

Alexander, Ronald D., 1942-
   The war on dogs : in Venice Beach : a novel / Ronald Alexander ; illustrated
by Nathan Geare.

   p. : ill. ; cm.

   ISBN-13: 978-0-9799588-0-9
   ISBN-10: 0-9799588-0-6

   1. Dogs--California--Fiction.   2. Fathers and sons--California--Fiction.   3.
HIV-positive gay men--California--Fiction.   4. Police--California--Los Ange-
les--Fiction.   5. Venice (Los Angeles, Calif.)--Fiction.   I. Geare, Nathan.   II.
Title.

PS3551.L35755 W37 2008   2007937589
813/.54

14 13 12 11 10 09 08 07   10 9 8 7 6 5 4 3 2 1

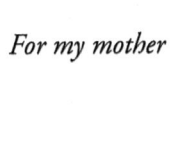

For my mother

My father was a Saint Bernard,
my mother was a collie,
but I am a Presbyterian.
—Mark Twain, *A Dog's Tale*

Skim milk masquerades as cream.
—Sir William Schwenck Gilbert, *H.M.S Pinafore*

Accidents occur in the best regulated families.
—Charles Dickens, *David Copperfield*

The War on Dogs:
in Venice Beach

ಬಿಬಿಬಿ One: Separation

THE RAIN CAME HARDER now, no longer the light but steady drizzle that had transformed Gramercy Park into a study in black and gray at daybreak. Bobby Smelzkoff sat on the bedroom floor, surrounded by boxes of his belongings, listening to his favorite recording of *The Magic Flute*. He had slept poorly, without undressing, and awoke with the taste of aluminum in his mouth.

When Jason and he decided that it was over, Bobby had accepted the decision as best for everyone, but now as he prepared to move out of their miniscule, yet workable, two-room flat his resolve began to recede. If he loved Jason, and Jason loved him, why not work harder on the relationship? Bobby knew the answer: he simply could not allow himself to become another person's permanent responsibility. And, thanks to the cocktail drug therapy, now that a cease-fire was in effect between his body and the virus, he actually could take care of himself, at least for the present. But that didn't mean he could afford the luxury of worrying about someone else.

For the first time in his life he saw something as the end of a chapter instead of a beginning. Ginger lay nearby at the edge of the carpet, head resting on her paws, with her eyes open and watching while Bobby packed, though occasionally when Mozart employed the power of the full orchestra, with horns aroar and strings afire, she shifted her eyes in the direction of the affronting speakers.

Bobby said good-bye to his friends at the party on Saturday, but Jason hadn't attended. He insisted that he had to pack for the family meeting in Hyde Park on Sunday, and he professed that it would be too painful to return until after Bobby had removed every trace of himself from the apartment. Though their association had failed, Bobby argued that he had succeeded in New York over the last several years; he had attended several schools, worked on numerous productions (from spear-carrier in *Aida* to assistant set designer of the Lincoln Center production of *Hansel und Gretel*), and even been in love for a while. And he didn't wish to blame Jason. Jason had his own life, and couldn't afford to be burdened with a partner who might not see forty—or thirty-five for that matter.

Still, to head back home to California—with little money, few possessions, and an uncertain life expectancy, to live with one's mother and her husband was hardly a show of independence. AIDS didn't exactly make one feel like a winner. His dilemma committed him to a role he wouldn't even have accepted in the theater. And then there was the matter of Poppy.

Ginger groaned, pushed up onto her front legs, and barked, two staccato notes which meant that she wanted to go outside; not necessarily to do her business, but because she was bored. Ginger became distraught whenever he or Jason got out a suitcase. They had picked her out together more than two years ago, a rescue dog of indeterminate age and unidentifiable lineage, so timid and trembling they could almost see the boot marks on her head. Bobby believed that Ginger was a Lab and Beagle mix, but that didn't account for her curled tail. One could be so in-tune with a dog. A dog communicated in subtle ways: when Ginger opened her mouth and panted quietly, her water bowl was empty; when she barked twice, she wanted to go outside; when she placed her head on Bobby's leg, she wanted him to pet her; when she nuzzled in his lap and twisted her head, she wanted him to rub her ears. When Bobby first saw her, at the shelter, and reached to rub her head, she had lowered her eyelids and quivered, and he knew that she was remembering her past. For months, after they brought her home, she flinched whenever anyone made an abrupt or unexpected move, she wouldn't eat while anyone watched, and she wouldn't go near strangers. She had hip dysplasia, too, which caused her to limp.

Just before the "Revenge Aria", when the Queen of the Night commands her daughter to murder Sarastro, Bobby reached to turn up the volume. An amazing piece of music: Sumi Jo's voice exquisite as crystal. Many a soprano had been crushed by the two high F's. In opera and musical theater, if the music was beautiful, it could make one cheer the devil. Take *Evita*, for example.

Sometimes Bobby fantasized about Ginger's past experiences, wishing to extract compensation. "Come on girl. Take me to him." And then, a bizarre libretto set to music by a drunken Franz Lizst, Ginger races through the streets and leads him to Little Italy and some unshaven, unsavory brute with grease smudges on his clothes and dagger in-hand. Ginger snarls and catapults off the man's chest and clamps onto his throat and doesn't let go, though the villain, in *basso profundo*, pleads: "Release me from this mangy cur. I did not mean to harm her. Can't you see? She's killing me!" And then Bobby gives the signal: a snap of his fingers and, "Good girl, Ginger. Off."

But her history was never to be revealed.

Bobby stuffed the plastic bag in his pocket, snapped Ginger's leash onto her collar, and waited while she shook her head and ears, violently in a sideways movement. Her mouth was open in an exuberant smile— she hadn't figured out what the boxes and the clearing of the closet meant and for the moment was simply excited to be going outside. Bobby walked down the dark and vacant hallway and entered the empty elevator.

Rain had turned the weather colder; Bobby pulled his jacket tighter at the neck, put up the umbrella, and led Ginger through the door, held open by Samah, who had leapt from behind his desk and a plate of something in curry sauce, to perform his duty. Jason's apartment, a gift from his corporate-executive father, sat at the edge of Gramercy Park, and though the unit itself was at the back of the building with no view of the park (the three windows overlooked a concrete interior space three floors below) as residents of the building they had received a key to the gated park in the center of the square.

Knowing Jason was to dispel the myth that all homosexuals were endowed with an inalienable sense of good taste. During their first year together Bobby had overseen the remodeling of the unit, including the design and installation of a beautiful and functional kitchen in a space so small lovebirds would have been cramped, and then he had furnished it and overseen all the housekeeping chores. He bought freshly-cut flowers weekly, made coffee and squeezed juice mornings, burned incense in the evening, vacuumed, dusted, mended, and solved problems. Take the apartment's three windows with no view: Bobby's solution had been to mount flower boxes on the outside and fill them with impatiens. The area gained direct sun for a few hours a day and that came only in mid-summer but what a difference it made to look through their windows and see color instead of grimy bricks and gray gloom. Jason would miss him. Jason emphasized money as he marginalized creativity.

Ginger squatted every few yards to pee and sniff, oblivious to the rain, which increased in intensity. Bobby's boxes were going by Greyhound; there would be a final lunch with Brandon, a chance to unburden himself on a good listener and a loyal friend, and then off to LaGuardia and on to Los Angeles, by way of Chicago. Cheap fares seldom offered the opportunity to fly nonstop.

His real regret was that he had to leave Ginger.

Taxis splashed by in the street; umbrellas took up space on the sidewalks. Bobby loved dark and damp inclement weather. Rain inspired him. The mere thought of pollen drifting through sun-baked air made his eyes tear and his nose run.

☙•❧

"I found these pictures," said Bobby. "Jason had stuffed them in a shoe box. They don't mean shit to him. I thought you might like to have a few."

"On the deck we built. Two years ago. Right?"

"Three, actually. Jason and I had just met at the Morning Party."

"I wish you would use the house for a while before you go back. I'm not there until June, and even then you're welcome." Bobby had met Brandon, an attorney at a prestigious (that was the word Brandon had used) New York law firm, in a Greenwich Village bar one Friday night after Bobby first arrived in the city. Despite the attraction, nothing sexual ever happened between them. Perhaps that's why they were still close.

"I can't put it off," said Bobby, "and I'm not going to stay with Mom and Tom any longer than I have to."

"Your father is there too, isn't he? Does he know you're coming home?"

"We don't talk, but maybe Mom told him."

"Oh, that's right. He's the cop."

The waiter, a precocious boy with spiked, black hair and eyes that narrowed when he smiled, stood over them with his coffee pot and waited before taking their order, which he always did without writing anything down. After he left Bobby said, "Remind me to ask him to marry me when he comes back."

"Honey, she's an actor," said Brandon.

"From the frying pan onto the pyre," said Bobby. "What I resent the most is how he discounts what I did. I admit, he paid most of the bills, but I worked my butt off until I got sick. Trust me, Martha Stewart isn't half the homemaker I am."

"Jason isn't one to sacrifice," said Brandon. "I'm not saying he's a bad person. He's not made that way, that's all."

"He didn't get me anything for my birthday last year," said Bobby.

"Sometimes I'm sorry I introduced you two," said Brandon, putting his napkin in his lap when the omelets came.

"Jamie, let me take you away from all this," said Bobby.

The boy smiled, the eyes narrowing on cue, and said, "I can't cook. Someone in the kitchen made these."

"You don't have to cook," said Bobby. After the boy left, Bobby looked at Brandon and said, in a low voice, "Just deflower me and leave." Brandon laughed into his napkin as Bobby took a bite of eggs, then added salt, pepper, and a bit of Tabasco. "I can't taste anything. These new meds fuck with everything," he said. He took a few more bites, reached for the catsup, and unscrewed the top. "Let's see who throws him a birthday party this year," he said. He sipped his coffee, three times in quick succession, put down his cup, and said, "When I met him he was wearing Levis," and after two more sips which drained the cup, he added, "Boot-cut."

ಬಬಬ Two: Assignment in Venice

GENERAL SMELZKOFF SWALLOWED THE DREGS of his coffee, coughed up a wad of phlegm, and spat in his waste can. Of course he wasn't a real general (there was no such rank in the police force) but General was what the men at the Pacific Division station house called him, because of the similarity of his name to that other general and because of his assignment in the battle now taking place in Venice.

At the gym, men and women alike called, "Hey, General, how goes the war on dogs?" "Great day for a raid." "How's your prostate?" He should have never mentioned his scheduled appointment to anyone; all he had wanted was a little comfort, a *You'll be fine; you're healthy* assurance.

Smelzkoff's recently assigned office, if you could actually call it an office, sat at the back of the station close to the heating and air conditioning works and near enough to the alley that when his aluminum-framed window was open he could hear each and every scheduled trash pickup. The dumpster landed on the ground with a crash, startling Smelzkoff and reminding him that he'd had more than his daily allotment of caffeine.

Stanley Smelzkoff looked more like forty than sixty. He kept his silver hair cut short; his lean face was tanned and relatively free of wrinkles; and his body was solid and toned. He saw the girls at the gym sit up from their workout benches to look, and he'd never spent a day in the hospital. So why didn't he feel good?

At the doctor's office, he had opened *The New Yorker* randomly, and because white space framed the poem he started to read. He didn't indulge in poetry on a regular basis, but he hadn't been able to banish the words from his thoughts. The narrator looked back over his life and saw things misplaced, outright lost, a field strewn with wreckage of broken promises and relationships and at a point in the poem had turned and called out to strangers: "I'm sorry; I'm sorry." Smelzkoff held the magazine in one hand and rested his free hand on his knee and had to grit his teeth and take a breath when he finished. That night in bed, after Violet fell asleep, he lay awake for hours thinking about the aptness of the lines.

This might be his last chance to make a difference. In his career, he'd spent at least seventy percent of his time on matters not crime-related (locating missing persons and children, dealing with marital disputes, and controlling crowds that gathered when ambulances and fire trucks were present) and in twenty-five years he had been unable to progress past the rank of sergeant. Not that he had wanted to discover a corpse in a canyon instead of the missing child, not that he wished to find a couple lying dead on blood-smeared linoleum instead of screaming at each other over a Formica-covered table full of empty beer bottles, but sometimes he believed he would have seen more action as a security guard in a dime store. This assignment, at least, offered a challenge and a chance for redemption. Stop the arrogant dog owners, and if he couldn't, then he could go to the dogs himself. That's what that officious bitch of a councilwoman had implied. How dare she wag her French-manicured finger at him.

The day was full of sun, but chilly. March brought a few tourists but the rush was yet to come. Smelzkoff pulled open the door of his black and white patrol truck and got in. He rested his forehead on the steering wheel for a moment before starting the engine; he hadn't gotten much sleep. But in the past, back before the time changed, he'd caught that woman allowing her three dogs to run loose on the beach at 6 AM.

At the maintenance shed he parked his police vehicle and switched over to the yellow dune buggy. He had barely gotten the cart moving when he saw her in the distance and he removed his mirrored sunglasses and twisted the focus of his binoculars to bring her in close. She was dumping a plastic bag of dog waste in the barrel, and had left her three canines on the grass and was no longer holding onto their leads. Stanley Smelzkoff pressed the accelerator pedal to the floor, sped onto the bike path, and managed to reach her just as she stepped back onto the grass beside the dogs, but before she had the leashes in hand again.

"I could ticket you for not having control of your dogs," Smelzkoff said.

"You're joking," said the woman, stooping to take up the leather straps. "The dogs aren't allowed on the bike path; I only let go long enough to dump the poop."

"And if your animals decide to run for the beach or lunge at a pedestrian, that would be your responsibility."

"Don't you cops have anything better to do?" said the woman.

"Consider yourself warned," said Smelzkoff.

"Consider yourself an idiot," said the woman, under her breath, but he heard it.

"Next time," said Smelzkoff.

ॐ•ॐ

Tonight would be the first time in five years since he'd seen Bobby, though Carol had seen their son on a regular basis. He had to concentrate to remember how old he was, though he remembered with ease how good he'd felt when Bobby was born.

After the divorce Carol had married—not even a year had elapsed—but then that had saved him a great deal of money. For a while Smelzkoff had enjoyed the opportunity to care only for himself;

his money went so much further, especially after Carol remarried to become Carol Waring-Smith (she had kept her maiden name when she and Stanley married, saying she would honor, love, and obey him but she would never without laughing be able to tell people her name was Mrs. Smelzkoff) and he liked coming and going as he pleased. He had initially frequented strip clubs out by the airport and even gotten friendly with a few of the girls, but they kept long hours and indulged in illegal drugs. One he suspected of being addicted to heroin, because she visited the bathroom frequently and moved in spasmodic jerks, and he had no wish to compromise his integrity. Were he to continue to consort with her and others like her, he would be duty-bound to arrest them.

Carol could have at least hyphenated her name. What was so bad about Carol Waring-Smelzkoff? She'd have to go a long way to match Smith for dullness.

He was mightily attracted to Violet, but the girl was thirty years younger and since he had just calculated his son's age he realized for the first time that she was two years younger than Bobby. His son could use someone like Violet. New York had no doubt changed him—though he had always flaunted his sophistication. Smelzkoff wondered.

For a second or two, after he opened his front door, he didn't recognize him. But who else could it be? He was tall, far taller than before, his head practically shaved, and so damned thin that his shoulders protruded through the bloused material of his shirt. And what in Heaven's name had happened to his eyebrows? Smelzkoff stuck out his hand, but Bobby moved forward and hugged him. Smelzkoff patted Bobby on the back lightly and endured the embrace for as long as he could before pushing away. Smelzkoff's first thought was that they couldn't go to the corner bar for hamburgers and beer. Or anywhere in Venice for that matter.

"You look great, Poppy," said Bobby.

"I'm at Gold's every day," said Smelzkoff.

"I'm into yoga," said Bobby. He glanced past his father, into the room. "I like your place," he said. "Show me around?"

"It's just a one bedroom. A friend helped me pick out the colors. This here is Climbing Rose." He stepped back and gestured toward the couch. "Want a beer?"

Bobby put his hand on his stomach and grimaced. "Do you have any white wine?"

"I could go across the street and get some."

"Don't trouble yourself. What kind of beer?"

"Miller's."

Bobby grimaced again. "In a glass?"

Smelzkoff nodded and headed for the kitchen. "How's your mother?" he said, raising his voice to be heard from the next room.

"She and Tom are going to Greece. He got a company assignment in Athens," said Bobby, raising his voice as well.

Smelzkoff came back into the room with two beers and one glass. "Assignment?"

"To audit operations there. Cheers," he said, raising the glass.

"Right," said Smelzkoff taking a great, long swallow.

"I'm going to house-sit while I look for an apartment."

"Then you're planning to stay?"

Bobby crossed his long skinny legs, left over right, and his shoe slid off his heel and dangled from his toes. "I'm over Nueva York," he said and made a slicing movement with his right hand across his throat, the fingers splayed wide, and Smelzkoff noticed for the first time the length of his son's nails, glossy with clear polish.

❧•❧

Later that night, after Thai food in a deserted restaurant next to the Grand Canal, as Smelzkoff lay stretched out on his couch watching "America's Most Wanted", there was a tapping at his door. "It's open," he yelled, not bothering to get up. Violet pushed open the door and came inside.

"I wanted to see you." Smelzkoff sat up and motioned for the chair. "I'm sorry about last week," she said. She stood over him, her right hand on her hip, and waited.

"It's all right, Violet," Smelzkoff said.

"You're the only one who has the nerve to tell me what I need to hear."

"It's not my business "

"I want it to be. I like you, Poppy." Now, she sat on the arm of the chair and looked at him.

What a tall, gorgeous girl. Except for the implants and the small tattoo, there was nothing remotely stereotypical about her. She never resorted to heavy makeup; her hair was natural brown and cut short; her body was firm and athletic-looking without that masculine stria-tion that made some of those fake-tanned women look like pieces of polished driftwood.

"We're too different. I'm too old."

"Poppy, you're the youngest man I know. When I show friends your picture they guess you in the forties." She slid off the arm and sat in the chair. "I came to tell you that I enrolled in two classes at Santa Monica College. I want to get a degree in physical therapy." Smelzkoff did another calculation: at two courses a semester he'd be seventy when she graduated. The girl got up and came over to sit next to Smelzkoff on the sofa. "Don't I at least get a kiss? How about a high five?" Violet leaned against Smelzkoff and stretched to peck him on the cheek, next to his lips.

"School's a good idea," he said.

She rubbed his leg with her hand and looked at him, but he didn't look back for a while, then finally he tried a smile. "What's wrong now?" she said.

"Nothing," he said.

"It's something," she said. "What? Tell me. Please."

"Bobby's back."

"Your son?" said Violet. "I'd like to meet him."

Smelzkoff looked out into the room and sighed.

"You're embarrassed about me," said the girl.

Smelzkoff sniffed and chuckled.

"We don't have to tell him what I do."

"That's not it," said Smelzkoff "It's him."

"I know lots of gay guys," said Violet.

"He's changed," said Smelzkoff

ళ•ళ

He might enjoy this assignment if it weren't for the golf cart. The sun shone brightly; the surf rolled in with a tranquilizing rhythm, the waves round, large, and shapely enough to attract several surfers. Spring had arrived; for the present El Niño was unobservable.

But the grass was littered with piles of excrement. Tiny brown squiggles, runny piles of mustard-colored soup, humongous black extrusions weighing as much as a small dog. Where were all the conscientious owners, the ones who claimed to pick up after their pets? Did they think the shit fairy came out while they slept and picked up?

Then he saw the drunken woman who let her Weimeraner run loose. And run loose it did. Bounding over the sand and into the water, tearing back for the grass, racing in front of the bikers on the bike path, startling pedestrians on Ocean Front Walk. The woman was an arrogant menace. He'd given her three tickets in the past month yet she persisted in letting the gray beast cavort recklessly. She stumbled down the walk, barely able it seemed to put one foot in front of the other, the dog's unattached lease held arrogantly in her hand, her worn flip-flops dragging on the asphalt. Once she had cut between two houses and escaped down Speedway Street and once he had let her off with a warning, not because she was polite and contrite, but simply because he believed in giving citizens a warning first.

This woman had no intention of complying with the law. The dog made a dash for the sand, and Smelzkoff pushed the pedal of the cart to the floor; he bounced over the rough grass and came to a stop in front of her. "You don't learn, do you?" said Smelzkoff

"Bubba never hurt no one," said the woman. She looked at him, pupils dilated, her hair tangled. "Big dogs need exercise."

"Your big dog is exercising his big bowels on the sand over there. I'll tell you what. I'll write your ticket while you clean it up and then you put your big dog on a big leash and I'll be on my way."

"Aren't you going to read me my Miranda rights? There was another break-in last night. Why don't you try to stop that? People are slaughtered like flies in Venice, but you're only worried about dogs."

"Yeah, and a Pit Bull attacked a police horse on the Boardwalk last Saturday. The more they," he paused, "the more *we* have to worry about abusive dog owners the less time *we* have to deal with serious—" He corrected himself. "*Other* crime."

"Does he look like a Pit Bull," said the woman.

Not as much as you do, thought Smelzkoff. He scribbled the ticket, ripped it from the pad, and handed it to her.

"See you in court," she said.

"Bring Bubba," said Smelzkoff. "The exercise will be good for him."

Smelzkoff headed on toward Washington Boulevard. As much as she had riled him, it was Bobby who dominated his thoughts. It had been four days since he heard from him. Bobby had phoned the day following his visit to tell him that he would like to work in the field of entertainment, but he had refused to give his father the details. "I want to surprise you," he had said.

Smelzkoff thought about the possibilities. Bartender. Doorman. Dancer. The front tire hit a hole in the grass sending a bolt of pain across the top of his head. Bouncer was out of the question. So was Dancer for that matter. After an assignment in Hollywood a few years ago he'd seen enough to know: no matter how much the male dancers moved like girls in those clubs, they had gym-cultivated, muscular bodies.

He pulled the cart up next to the pay phone and searched in his pocket for change. "It's Stan," he said when Carol answered.

Silence before she said, "What do you want?"

"I heard you were going on a trip and I wanted to wish you a good time."

Carol apparently didn't know what to say. "Bobby told you?"

"He stopped by."

"He's staying here till he finds a place."

"Better take your good clothes with you," said Smelzkoff

"Do you want to translate that?" Carol snapped.

"I'm sure you noticed."

"Yes?"

"He doesn't seem different to you?"

Smelzkoff heard Carol's breathing and then the sound of her lighting a cigarette. She exhaled and said, "Maybe if you'd spent more time with him when he was a boy "

"Don't blame me. You were the one who coddled him," said Smelzkoff

"Bobby's a good boy. He's the way he is, that's all."

"Yeah, maybe Tom can take him to a Dodger game."

"He and Tom get along fine."

"I'm sure. He's not blood."

"I don't have time for this. Tom and I are going down to get our passports."

Carol was bragging, and Smelzkoff felt jealousy surge, though he had little desire to travel; a problem they had faced in marriage. Tom had taken Carol all over the United States and now they were branching out to other countries. At home Smelzkoff ate a strictly controlled diet: an egg-white omelet (six eggs) and chicken breast for breakfast, a can of white tuna and spinach for lunch, broiled fish and asparagus for dinner, and plenty of fresh fruit for snacks during the day. How could he do that in some third-world country? Or in Nebraska for that matter?

He had religious sleep habits too. He went to bed by ten and arose each morning at six, except for weekends when Violet kept him up late doing, well, you know what. Then there was the gym. He was losing the battle: his pectoral muscles sagged; he had love handles; and his abs were covered with an ever-thickening layer of fat. He couldn't afford to miss a week or two of workouts. He could improve his abs if he gave up beer. But he refused to give up beer.

"Where are you going to live?" said Smelzkoff

"Tom rented an apartment in Athens," said Carol.

"They eat a lot of lamb, don't they?" said Smelzkoff

৯•ৎ

Stanley Smelzkoff stopped going to Fantasy Mansion after he met Violet. In the past there had been a sufficient turnover of girls that he hadn't had to reveal much about himself; he simply told them that he was a salesman, from Torrance. But Violet was more than a fantasy; Violet was a nice girl. She had moved north from Long Beach to be an actress, but now there was the physical therapist thing.

Driving down Pico Boulevard after his workout, he had seen the purple building. He got bored on days off. He parked across the street and jaywalked to the entrance of the club. Inside, the music (Tina Turner singing "What's Love Got To do With It") was loud, deafening in fact, and his eyes had to adjust to the darkness.

Gradually he could see the girls in G-strings, dancing on podiums around the room, but the girl on the main stage, in particular, attracted his attention. She clung to the pole, shimmied up, did a somersault, and slid back down headfirst. She slithered onto the floor and crawled cat-like to the edge of the stage, where five men sat, clutching drinks and grinning. As if the air pressure in the room suddenly swelled, Smelzkoff felt heaviness in his chest; his breathing became labored, and his heart beat loudly in the darkness. The speakers vibrated in his groin. The girl began to do pushups inches from the men's faces, and as he advanced to see her up close she pushed off the floor in one quick movement, leaped to her feet, and started doing jumping jacks. Her's was an athletic interpretation; she didn't lick the brass or hump it and her body was so perfect: no dimpled globs of unnecessary flesh, no bruises, and the proportions of her legs were perfect, her skin so pale.

The music ended, and the announcer said, "Gentlemen, let's give all these lovely ladies a hand. That was Sabrina on the main stage."

Reeling, Smelzkoff lurched to the bar and ordered a cranberry juice. Several girls walked past him and smiled, but after seeing Sabrina he had no desire to talk to any of them. He looked toward the stage, hoping for her to come out from behind and into the room. He glanced to the balcony where men were being entertained with lap dances and felt a tap on his shoulder. "Excuse me," she said. "May I disturb you to get a Coke?" It was her.

Smelzkoff backed out of her way, taking a quick peek. He wanted to say something, but the tightness in his chest had spread to his throat, but when he looked at her again, she smiled.

"Does your mother know you're here?" she said.

"I ran away from home," Smelzkoff said.

"You're really handsome," said Sabrina. "I noticed you out of everyone. She offered her hand.

❧•❧

"Miss Deacon is waiting in your office," said Linda, when Smelzkoff hurried through the reception area.

"Groovy. Roll up the rug and put on the tunes," said Smelzkoff. His bowels grumbled.

He passed Lieutenant Portman's office and made his way through the bullpen of detective's cubicles, to the back of the building. The door to his room was as inconspicuous as the door to the broom closet, and his allotted space not much larger. Gloria Deacon sat at his desk in her red hat, this one a fedora, her briefcase open, working on paperwork, no doubt something of great importance. She looked at her watch when she heard him.

"Sorry I'm late," he said.

Gloria Deacon looked at her watch again, a tiny band encased in the fat of her wrist, as if she planned to note the tardy section of his report card. No matter how high they rose, thought Smelzkoff, women treated subordinates like children—though to his knowledge, Gloria Deacon had never married and had no children, which now that he thought about it, served as proof that the practice was an inborn characteristic of her sex.

"Sergeant, we're going to have real trouble this summer on the Boardwalk. I need your proposal in ten days. What kinds of things can we do to prevent problems? The tourists need to feel safe."

"How about helicopter patrols and SWAT teams?"

Gloria Deacon stared blankly at him for a moment. "Naturally, we'll have helicopter backup when it's needed." She examined her nails as she spoke.

❧•❧

Smelzkoff went into his kitchen. Violet had several of the cabinet doors open, searching for something. "Need any help?"

"Paper plates and napkins. Why would I need help?" She whispered now. "Go back into the living room and talk to him."

"I need a beer," said Smelzkoff. He started for the refrigerator, but Violet stopped him by placing her hand on his chest. "I'll bring it."

"Help me, damn it. You can talk to anyone. Come in and get to know him. When the pizza comes then you can get things ready."

"All right," said Violet. "All right." She whispered again. "But he's your son."

Bobby was paging through a gun magazine when Smelzkoff and Violet sat down. "Do you still have guns here at home?" said Bobby.

"I'm in the safety business. I got guns."

"Besides your regular issue." He looked at Violet. "Poppy and I don't agree about guns."

"In all my years on the force, I've never had to fire my weapon," said Smelzkoff.

"What are you going to do here?" Violet said to Bobby. The boy screwed his face. "For work," she added.

"I'm a choreographer. I'm getting my resume updated. I'd like to find a show to work on."

"You should choreograph a routine for me," said Violet.

"You're a dancer, right? Poppy says you're a dancer."

"An exotic dancer," said Violet. "I'm sick of it, but it pays my bills and I like to be independent."

"Let's go see her, Poppy. It'll help me get some ideas," said Bobby.

"I was a gymnast. Poppy says I bring an athletic interpretation to my work," said Violet.

"You seem tall for a gymnast. Most of them are absolute midgets," said Bobby.

Smelzkoff, relieved that he didn't have to entertain the two, got up with greater relief when the doorbell rang. The conversation made him uneasy. He pulled out two twenties from his pants pocket and handed them to the delivery boy.

"Poppy, that's enough pizza for ten," said Violet.

"One's for me and the other with meat is for you two," said Smelzkoff. "Mine has chicken, vegetables, and no cheese."

"That's not pizza," said Bobby. "That's a salad and bread."

"It pays off," said Violet. "Poppy has a great body."

"Women have bodies. Men have physiques," said Smelzkoff.

"Do you work out, Bobby?" said Violet.

"I do Yoga," said Bobby. "I love the doggy-down position. Look." And then he raised his arm and flexed his biceps. The muscle was slender and stringy.

"Me too," said Violet. "Let's go together, sometime." She flexed her biceps then and Smelzkoff couldn't help but notice that hers was a bit more muscular.

Smelzkoff sniffed involuntarily then took a paper napkin and blew his nose. Bobby and Violet looked at him in unison, then one at a time took another piece of pizza from the box.

৪৩৪৩৪৩ Three: A Few Routine Tests

D R. ZIEMAN, the urologist referred by his regular doctor, sat at his desk across from Smelzkoff, looking at his file. "So, you're fifty-nine years young. Any blood or puss in your urine?"

"No."

"How's your stream? Strong and steady?"

"It ain't what it used to be."

"Get up during the night to urinate?"

"Oh, yeah."

"How many times?"

"Two or three."

The doctor was white, but wore his black hair in an Afro. The office was decorated with several framed, desktop pictures of the doctor in scuba gear, holding a small naked baby, and the walls were covered with enlarged individual photos of tropical fish. The doctor stood, walked toward the door, and motioned for Smelzkoff to follow.

"Let's go into the examination room." The doctor hurried down the hall and turned left through the first doorway. "If you'll take off your very nice shirt and pants and hang them here, I'll be right back."

Doctor Zieman left, closing the door behind him, and Smelzkoff removed his shirt and trousers and placed them on the hook on the back of the door. He sat on the cold plastic chair and withdrew a magazine from the holder mounted on the wall, this time choosing something safe, a periodical with an aging, blonde celebrity on the cover. Her fame had faded after her role in a TV comedy more than a decade ago and the magazine cover proclaimed: "Lonnie's Back!" Lonnie's picture had been retouched and it seemed to Smelzkoff that she had had a lot of plastic surgery. Her eyes, closer together than ever, angled up at sharp ninety degree angles and her nose was now two small holes. Her smile revealed a row of unearthly white teeth.

Smelzkoff couldn't think of the name of her former husband, who had divorced her and taken up with a new woman half Lonnie's age, but she so closely resembled her that they could have been mother and daughter.

The door came open and Doctor Zieman reentered. Smelzkoff put down the magazine and waited for his instructions.

"Sit here." He patted the paper-covered examination table. Doctor Zieman placed the cold stethoscope on Smelzkoff's back and said, "Breathe deep." He moved the stethoscope. "Again," he said. He moved the now warmer stethoscope. "Again." He moved the instrument one final time and this time Smelzkoff took a deep breath on his own. "Lie down and pull down your shorts," he said. Smelzkoff diverted his eyes and raised his pelvis up off the table and did as the doctor said.

The doctor felt below Smelzkoff's testicles and said, "Turn your head and cough." He reached to the other side. "Again," he said.

"Now if you would stand here," he pointed to a small, rubber-surfaced platform at the foot of the examination table, "and put your elbows down on the table."

Smelzkoff bent over and grimaced when he heard the sound of Dr. Zieman snapping on a latex glove. The doctor inserted his finger to probe back and forth across the surface of Smelzkoff's prostate, and Smelzkoff's eyes began to smart. "You can sit up and put on your clothes. He handed a tissue to Smelzkoff and then produced a plastic cup and handed it to him as well. "Go into the bathroom there," he had opened the door and was indicating to another door across the hall, "and give me a nice full sample of your urine. Then I want you to go downstairs to the lab and give them some blood. I'll write up the order. Come back in my office to pick it up."

ஓ•ௗ

Smelzkoff parked his vehicle in front of Carol's house and shut off the engine. He stared at the front of her house for a while before he got out and went up the sidewalk. He wouldn't have to confront Tom, with Carol and him away in Europe. Tom Smith, a tax accountant in downtown Los Angeles, was the most boring man Smelzkoff had ever met; his stomach roiled with excess acid at the thought of his mindless chatter. Despite his constant babble about the big business deals he was working on and his condescending reference to the ever-changing tax codes and the corporate name-dropping that he engaged in, Smelzkoff knew, that dumpy old Tom was a fraud; he made a decent living, but he was far from a major cog in the machinery of his dinky firm. Smelzkoff stopped and turned toward his car. There was no need for this. He's been through enough degradation for one day.

"Poppy, what are you doing?" said Bobby.

Smelzkoff turned and saw his son standing at the far corner of the house. He had a running garden hose in his hand, was bare-chested, and wore skimpy, lime green tank trunks. His hips were large and woman-like and his chest was as flat and undeveloped as a child's.

"Mom and Tom left for their trip. I was just watering the roses."

"I'm on my way home from the doctor's office. I stopped to see how you were doing."

"You're headed in the wrong direction. Want some coffee. I just made a pot, strong the way you like it."

"Sure. Okay." Smelzkoff stood up straight, squared his shoulders, and walked up closer. Bobby's chest glistened with oil and he smelled like coconuts.

"I'll finish this later," said Bobby. He went over to the side of the house and bent to turn off the water.

Inside the kitchen Bobby took down two cups and filled them with coffee. He handed his father one of them and said, "Let's go sit by the pool."

When Bobby sat down he crossed his skinny legs effortlessly, in his usual fashion, left over right. Smelzkoff's legs were too big to sit like that; it was downright uncomfortable and besides it looked feminine. "So how was your appointment?"

"A few routine tests; that's all," said Smelzkoff. "Did you find work yet?"

"There's a club in Hollywood that may hire me," said Bobby.

"What club?"

"It's called Flo's Floozies."

For the first time since he and his son had reunited, he detected a certain hesitation, a change in the tone of Bobby's voice. "Doing what?" Smelzkoff said, aware that the tone of his own voice had changed too, dropping a few registers due to a burgeoning anger that fermented suddenly and unexpectedly in him.

Bobby took a sip of coffee and looked out over the sun-reflecting water of the swimming pool. "Producing and directing a show," he said.

"What kind of show?" said Smelzkoff, leaning forward and setting his coffee down the small glass table that separated them.

Bobby stood and walked over to the other side to the pool and pulled out a two-foot-tall dandelion from a flower box.

"A musical review," Bobby said, in a barely-audible voice, his back still turned toward his father.

And Smelzkoff decided that he didn't need to know any more.

જ•

Violet suggested that the three of them go out to dinner. Bobby chose the restaurant: *Playa de Jaime*, on Venice Boulevard, close to the ocean. When the two owners greeted them at the door, Bobby made introductions. Smelzkoff recognized the redhead: he had the pink-skinned, Boxer puppy that had run across the bike path in front of a tourist and caused an accident. Smelzkoff had had no choice but to ticket him, even though the biker, a woman from South Dakota, hadn't been hurt and he wondered if his host remembered the accident. The redhead said at the time that he been taking the puppy to doggy training school (those had been his words) and pleaded to avoid the citation.

Smelzkoff looked at the one whom Bobby called Jaime. "We've met," said Smelzkoff "You have the Boxer."

"Officer Smelzkoff," said the man. "It's nice to see you again."

Smelzkoff detected a hint of disrespect. "How's the discipline going?" he said.

"Fine," said the redhead. "How's it going with you?"

Smelzkoff didn't wish to smile, but couldn't help himself.

જ•

Smelzkoff lay down on the bench, lifted the bar off the hooks, and did an easy warm-up set with a forty-five-pound plate on each side of the bar. He got up and put two more forty-five pound plates on, lay back down, and had no trouble getting quick twelve repetitions. He slammed the bar back against the iron support rods and racked it. He stood and grabbed onto the vertical frame of a nearby piece of equipment and stretched out his lat muscles. Weight lifting had saved his life.

As a teenager it had been a matter of vanity: he wanted to be bigger. If he had idled his life away, avoiding physical labor and exercise, he wondered, would he look like his son? Or rather, did Bobby represent how he would look? Or did Bobby look like Carol? Well, it was a mute point. He trained with weights to contend with politics and stress. If he couldn't vent his rage at the gym, he might go crazy.

The bloated, blond wrestler, who performed his contrived acrobatics on television, entered the room with his square-jawed girlfriend. The sight of them revolted Smelzkoff. What was going on with this wrestling thing anyway? The heroes were the ones who sneaked up from behind or ambushed their victim in the parking lot; they kicked and beat shamelessly, four against one, urinated on their opponents' motorcycles in the parking lot, punched each other in the gonads, and all of it in the open as if some glorious gladiatorial confrontation in front of twenty thousand spectators in filled arenas around the country who cheered at all manner of lewd, crude behavior. Forget about sportsmanship. Forget about fair play. Anarchy ruled. And the way they stood in front of the camera, microphone in hand, screaming, yelling, threatening, ridiculing. What in Heaven's Name was the world coming to? Gorgeous George. He was nothing.

At the firing range Smelzkoff had unloaded his 38-caliber pistol into the silhouette target with the hope that he could suffocate his worries with noise. For the most part, during the first fifteen minutes, his shots hit their mark in the center of the outlined head, but then, as if he were in some science fiction thriller, the target morphed into Dr. Zieman and the dread returned. He lowered his aim and fired at the target's crotch, and decided that this wasn't going to work. Smelzkoff dropped the pistol to his side and went to his locker. He removed his earmuffs, took out his bag, and left the range.

Why did Dr. Zieman want to repeat a test and add a new one? Maybe it was just an excuse for the weirdo to use his finger again.

౭౭౭౭ Four: *Salami*

LITTLE SPACE HAD BEEN ALLOCATED for the stars and staff at Flo's Floozies nightclub, housed in the old Olympic Theater in downtown Hollywood. Two boxes of a room, adjoining and off a narrow hallway, and in the one, five mirrored dressing tables crammed together with the other room bulging with costumes and props. The hallway connected them to the areas of the stage. One doorway at one end led to an outdoor courtyard, more a passageway, where theatergoers could mill about between acts or before performances and the doorway at the other end led back stage.

Bobby considered himself fortunate to have landed work so soon after returning to Los Angeles, but then he had the credentials. He had worked on many New York productions during his years there, and though he hadn't actually choreographed any of the shows he listed, like many gays he knew how to puff up a resume. When you're out there on your own and have to survive, you embellish a little. And he'd seen practically every show that played the past five years in New York and he had the confidence to know what could be done and what couldn't, what would work and what wouldn't.

He arrived even before Flo, because he enjoyed the chance to sit at the dressing table and contemplate his reflection in the mirror. He leaned over and unzipped his leather bag and took out the vials and lined them up on the table's scratched, varnish surface. But he refused to talk aloud to himself like Eve Harrington or the drag queen in *Torch Song Trilogy*.

Though it hadn't been his preference to be in LA again, money and his condition dictated that he be closer to his family, such as they were, in case anything happened. Poppy and he were further apart than ever. In New York he could pretend that he loved his father, but here he couldn't escape the differences. He couldn't pretend that there was no estrangement. No telling how Poppy would react if he knew, and though his mother doted on Tom, Bobby celebrated his mother's happiness; after all, who among us wishes to admit they come from a dysfunctional family?

He had gotten the idea for the show at the going away party held at a costumer friend's rooftop apartment. A fabulous view of Times Square: one of those special places in New York that clever, imaginative gays on a budget seem always to find. No counting how many had looked at the place and thought it shabby (no security or front desk or posh lobby) because from the outside the building looked like it housed a slum. The roof area was carpeted in tarpaper; the enclosed space contained but two small rooms. Nevertheless this queen knew how to dress a stage and had fashioned the imperfect unit into a gem of an eclectic penthouse with flowering shrubs and refurbished rattan outdoor furniture.

A brilliant, sunny Sunday, with temperatures in the low seventies, allowed the crowd of thirty-five to congregate outdoors to wish Bobby bon voyage. Brandon had planned the whole affair; the guests for the soiree included some of the most creative behind-the-scenes individuals in Broadway and off-Broadway theater (set designers, make-up artists, costumers) and one very special actress, who had made a name for herself in musical theater and film, to lend a touch of real celebrity to the gathering. She entertained the group with stories of love scenes she had played with a famous actor from Argentina, who prepared himself for each take by pounding his chest and screaming obscenities in Spanish.

Another guest, an outrageous character whose claim to fame (or notoriety) was the fact that he had been Empress of New York a decade or so back, told Bobby about a troop of gay men who had once appeared in a satire of the Saturday afternoon airing called *The Texaco Opera Broadcast*. The men had impersonated women but sang in their own voices, parodies of several famous arias, with the narrator or hostess doing a perfect send-up of Beverly Sills. The heroine of the spoof had been a character named *La Dementia*.

Anyway, that's where Bobby got the idea to do a spoof of Richard Strauss's *Salome*, which he decided to call *Salami*. He sold Flo, an ex-marine who had long enjoyed appearing in drag, on the idea and had been put under contract to write, score, and choreograph the production for her recently-acquired, and underused, Olympic Theater. The prospect of getting such a show together unnerved Bobby, as it represented the biggest challenge he had ever faced, but what did he have to lose? If he failed, they would simply speak ill of him after he was gone; if he succeeded, it would be his legacy, and something to take his mind off his affliction.

He turned his face to one side and tried to glimpse his profile. At least his father couldn't say he was fat. Poppy detested fat people, though Bobby wasn't sure why. He opened the pill bottles and he lined up his medication: bleached, unappetizing bits of candy. He twisted off the cap of his water bottle and began to down the pills one-by-one, swallowing with more difficulty with each tablet. He studied the calendar taped to his mirror; Flo wanted the show ready for previews in four weeks.

⊷•⊶

Coexisting with Poppy wouldn't be easy. At *Playa de Jaime* he had returned his meal (sand dabs on a bed of spinach and mashed potatoes) insisting that all he could taste was butter—and then there was the dog.

Bobby Smelzkoff liked Violet immediately. He understood what his father saw in the nubile girl, though he struggled to comprehend what the flower saw in his reactionary father. Awkwardness characterized the evening at the restaurant until liquor lubricated the skids of conversation. Poppy had beer; Violet and Bobby shared a bottle of Merlot.

Poppy wanted to know how he knew about the restaurant having just arrived in town, and Bobby had explained about the mutual friend from New York and the subsequent recommendation.

They were seated at a table in one corner of the outdoor patio. A retractable canvas roof covered the space; holes had been cut so that two palms didn't have to be uprooted and moved (one actually grew up through the bar, along the wall that separated outdoors from indoors) and the atmosphere suggested Hawaii as much as California. Poppy had been seated with his back to the room, with a view of a heat lamp and one of the elaborate birdhouses that adorned the walls, and didn't notice the diners behind him for some time.

"Now that I'm going back to school I need to find a new job," said Violet.

"I need another beer," said Poppy.

"Exotic dancers make a lot of money don't they?" said Bobby.

"Are you going to drink your water?" said Poppy to Violet. "I need water."

"One of the girls, she's a porn star, made ten thousand dollars on a trip back through Kentucky and Ohio," said Violet. "And she was only gone a week."

"You haven't done pornography, have you?" said Bobby.

"Never," said Violet.

"It's one thing to watch, but—"

"I'm dying of thirst here," said Poppy. He pounded the tabletop with his fist, rattling his silverware.

Bobby raised his hand for the waiter.

"I adore your dress," said Bobby. "You have an absolutely mythical figure. You look like a dancer. A real dancer." He rested his chin in his hand, shook his head, and looked up at her. "I'm sorry. I know how that must sound. That's not what I really meant. A classical dancer. You look like a ballerina. That's what I mean."

"I'm not sensitive," said Violet, laughing. "I studied ballet as a girl, in sixth grade, but I got more interested in gymnastics. I think ballet has influenced my work, though."

"Except for your tits. Ballerinas have no tits. How long did you study?"

"A year and a half. Uncle Collie wanted me in gymnastics and Cheryl thought ballet was pretentious."

"Cheryl?" said Bobby.

"My mother," said Violet.

"They identified with the proletariat, huh?"

Violet smiled. "I suppose "

"What in blazes?" shouted Poppy. He had turned around, possibly to get the waiter's attention, and noticed the man and woman seated directly behind them. The couple's dog, it appeared to be a Retriever of some kind—possibly a Chesapeake Bay or a Labrador; I mean who could tell the difference?—sat on its haunches at the foot of the table. The fact that a dog had been allowed to come into *Playa de Jaime* would have been distressing enough to Bobby's father, but to see the man and woman taking turns feeding the animal from their own plates, and with the same silverware that they used to feed themselves, sent Poppy, a.k.a. General Stanley Smelzkoff, over the edge. The hairs on the back of his neck bristled, like the hackles on an old dog when confronted with the scent of a powerful and more virile rival, and he jumped to his feet and stood over the couple's table.

"This ain't Paris, France," he said. "This is Los Angeles. No shirt, no shoes, no service. And no dogs allowed," he bellowed.

Waiters immediately stopped and looked; the bartenders stopped mixing drinks; the busboys stopped delivering meals and clearing tables; patrons stopped eating. Ned and Jaime appeared at the doorway that connected the inside and outside areas. Jaime jabbed his partner with an elbow, and Ned hurried over. He moved with such haste that his unbuttoned Hawaiian shirt, worn over a white T-shirt, billowed behind him.

"I'm sorry," he said. "Is anything wrong?" looking first at Poppy and then the couple and finally at the dog, which seemed unaware that it was no longer getting fed, judging from the way it stared back and forth between its two owners.

"I'll say something's wrong," said Poppy. Violet reached over and put her hand on his sleeve, but Bobby merely covered his face.

"I think this fellah down here got my meal and I got his, cause mine definitely tasted like Alpo."

"Poppy, there's no point in being insolent," said Bobby.

"Sit down, Poppy. Please," said Violet.

"I'm afraid the dog will have to wait outside," said Ned. "Officer Smelzkoff is correct. We could lose our license."

"Fine," said the woman. "Someone should have spoken sooner and we would have taken our business elsewhere. I'm finished. I'll take Barkley outside and wait for you," she said to her husband.

After dinner, Bobby and Violet stood in front of the restaurant saying their goodbyes. Poppy had gone back inside to use the men's room before making the walk home, and Bobby waited for his car, his mother's station wagon actually. "I might be able to use you in my opera," he said to Violet. I didn't want to say anything in front of Poppy. Why don't you come by the theater?"

"An opera," said Violet. "Wow. I went to see *River Dance* when it was in Orange County."

"You won't be able to support yourself on what we could pay, but..."

After the performance at Royce Hall, Bobby and Violet walked across the campus to the parking lot.

"Are you sorry you came?" said Violet.

"Art should have humor," said Bobby. "Even Shakespeare's trage-dies have humor."

"The colors were beautiful," said Violet. "And I enjoyed the 3-D glasses."

"Pretentious. Pretentious and boring."

Silence for a few moments and Bobby saw her looking at her feet as she walked. "Even when I go to a bad play, I'm never sorry," he said. "I think it's important to know what's being done. As long as you can put it in context.

"What was the deal with the eight-foot tall guy on stilts? And the woman who kept waving her hand through the water in the fish tank? And the other who kept mouthing, 'One-two-three-four-five-six-seven-eight. One-two-three-four-five-six-seven-eight.' Lapping the air with her tongue."

Violet said, "It's sounds funny now, huh?"

"It was funny when the computer broke down," said Bobby.

No one in the entire audience so much as chuckled, until three-quarters of the way through the production when the computer-driven synthesizer malfunctioned. For the first ten minutes the audience watched in darkness and silence as the men in the orchestra pit strug-gled to get the computer running again. Just the eerie, murky image of their heads bobbing from keyboard to computer to keyboard and back again. For a while it seemed an intentional part of the staging and eventually someone in the balcony whispered to someone else, then mumbling and muttering and more whispering until a courageous pa-tron spoke aloud, which prompted a loud "Shhh!" from the main floor. The entire audience of fifteen hundred broke into nerve-calming laughter. That had been funny.

Bobby took out a tube of lip balm from his pants pocket and applied it thoughtfully, while they walked. "I forgot how cold it gets here at night," he said. They came to the circular fountain and the brick-paved plaza and he paused to remember which way they had come and then they continued on. Violet had been quiet for a while now and Bobby thought possibly that he had intimidated her with his comments. "Most of my friends in New York refused to go to movies or plays with me. They said I ruined it for them. My friend, Sam, said I was extra-critical. Is that a word? I don't think that's a word."

"You remind me of Poppy, a little," said Violet.

"Oh now, hush," said Bobby.

"That's a compliment," said Violet. "Poppy makes me think about things."

"My father is a homophobe," said Bobby. "Or haven't you noticed? It wouldn't matter so much if he hated Jews and Moslems, and I've never ever heard him make a racial slur."

Violet didn't acknowledge the remark and he thought about asking what it was she saw in his father, but he was afraid that such a question might lead the discussion in a different direction and he had no desire to know about his father's sex life.

They arrived at the parking structure and Bobby unlocked the passenger door and closed the door after Violet got in. When he got in on the other side she said, "Do you want to get something to eat? I'll treat. We could go to VanGogh's Ear. They're open all night."

"Are you busy tomorrow afternoon?"

"Not until four," said Violet. "I'm on the early shift tomorrow."

"Come into the theater. I'll go over my plans for the show. We'll have lunch and—Wait, I've got an idea. I'll come see you at your work." He put the key in the ignition and took out his lip balm and applied another coat. "Are you familiar with the story of *Salome*?"

Violet shook her head. "I'm not sure," she said.

"It's a biblical story. Oscar Wilde wrote the play. Richard Strauss made an opera of it. Salome was something of an exotic dancer."

The strippers who weren't on stage swarmed around him, but he didn't feel uncomfortable. Women had always readily understood that he was gay; his appearance and his mannerisms said everything. This club, like the gay bars that featured male dancers, amused him. Drag was different. Drag was about costumes and makeup; drag was about illusion, a sleight of hand if you will. Now when it came to those who took it all off the game changed. Evaluate one on the basis of his physical appearance, his body, and you insinuate that the mind and theater have nothing to do with sexuality and that simply wasn't the case. The girls off stage in the crowd and in clothes were far more attractive, far sexier. And many times had he seen a male dancer with a perfect physique who exhibited no sexual appeal, some of them thrashing at the floor with flat feet as if making wine. Violet had sex appeal.

She had a fantastic shape and Bobby imagined she had a better one before the boob job, though her body could handle them, which was to say she was tall and strong enough, and hadn't gone over the edge. The girl standing next to him, for example, was not much more than five feet tall and she had breasts that entered a room before she did. It was an old joke, he knew, but it fit.

Bobby tried to imagine where all these men came from in the middle of the afternoon. Some were salesmen perhaps, taking a break from their calls; others were out of work blokes; still others were drug dealers, gamblers, and sex addicts, he imagined. Some were just lonely. He put Poppy in that category. He tried to picture his father sitting with the others at the perimeter of the main stage and felt sorry for him, because he knew his father had always been something of a prude. How on earth had he and Violet gotten together?

Bobby applied his lip balm, and then he saw Violet come out from backstage and wend her way through the crowd. Several times men stopped her, no doubt for private performances, but after a few words to each of them she continued over to Bobby at the rear of the room by the bar service area.

"You're standing exactly where Poppy always stood," she said. "In the dark."

"I'm a chip off the old block all right," said Bobby. "You're good. You're the best-looking and you're the most provocative."

"Thank you," she said

An endomorphic, but muscular patron, dressed in a T-shirt, which failed to conceal his large stomach, approached. "Excuse me," he said. "I don't mean to interrupt but my buddy would like a table dance and he's too chicken to ask. Maybe when you're finished?" He looked Bobby up and down.

"Sure," said Violet, palming the bills he offered. "Who is he?" The boy pointed.

Bobby saw the friend, tall and handsome with black curly hair, and after the emissary left he turned to Violet and bumped her at the hip with his. "Honey, you must be exhausted. I'll give him his table dance."

Violet laughed. "Kent, my boss, is watching," she said. "I've got to go. Don't leave?"

Violet disappeared with the timid boy up the stairway to a balcony. Bobby wondered: was she the faithful type or did she fool around on his father? Surely opportunities surrounded her. But then he didn't know whether aching or longing figured in the relationship they had. When Jason and he were together, he'd never felt completely at peace.

Violet implied that Poppy had slowed things down, and Bobby recognized that something in his father's manner did suggest that he was unsatisfied—or maybe apologetic about his relationship. Bobby knew that when you're truly into someone you don't care what friends or family think. He himself enjoyed the companionship of older men, but that hadn't stopped him from noticing the boys closer to his own age as well.

He imagined Violet dancing for his father like Salome for Herod. Sex, in the absence of anything else, could be good for only so long. He and Jason had had great sex for a year, good sex during the second (though less frequent), and none during the third. After that, theirs had become an association of convenience, a partnership with Jason making money and Bobby keeping house.

৪০৪০৪০ Five: Seduction

THE CROWD AT THE FORUM interested Violet more than the game; she didn't really understand basketball, though Poppy exhibited patience in explaining things. She had heard of Michael Jordan and Shaquille O'Neal but none of the other players. And Poppy loved to teach her, she knew, and she felt flattered by his attention.

Jordan drove for the basket through a crowd of defenders, twisting his body in one direction and firing off his shot in the opposite. Even the home crowd cheered. Poppy jumped to his feet, thrust his arms into the air. The Laker fans in front of them stood too; one of them rotated his hands, fists around fists (like planets caught in each others orbit) and Poppy yelled, "Traveling, my ass."

Violet put her hand on his shoulder when he sat down. "What happened?" she said, tilting her head toward the fan.

"Traveling is when the player takes steps without dribbling the ball. That's a violation. But he didn't touch the floor. That's why they call him Air Jordan," said Poppy. He reached under the seat to retrieve his beer.

She sipped her beer too and tried to concentrate on the game. She hadn't consciously pursued a relationship with Bobby; if anything he had initiated the friendship. Still, a part of her probably believed that it would solidify her position, make Poppy feel closer to her, but in truth it had had the opposite effect. She could feel the distance. As if Poppy's trust of her had lessened. Did he think she would discuss their sex life with his son? If she had courage, she would ask him, but she knew he would simply deny and attribute his quietness to things at work, to the difference in their ages, to his inability to focus on a relationship with anyone, at this point in his life.

She didn't understand why he couldn't just let go and enjoy what they had.

A commotion under the basket, pushing and shoving, whistles blowing and a fight broke out. Poppy jumped to his feet along with everyone else, except for Violet who by now was completely lost. Poppy shouted down to her in her seat. "Double technical. The Lakers are lame," he said. He sat down again when things quieted.

"Why are you a Bulls fan anyway?" said Violet.

"I grew up in Chicago," said Poppy.

"But you live in LA," said Violet.

"I'm a foreigner here," said Poppy. "This is a different land. No offense, but values are different here. Too much emphasis on looks and money. Everyone wants to be famous. Everyone wants to be rich. In Chicago a handshake means something; here they'll shake your hand and call a lawyer."

The crowd noise had suddenly gotten too loud for normal conversation and though Violet wanted to hear more about Poppy's ideas on California it took too much concentration in noisy surroundings.

"Bulls are on a twelve to two run," said Poppy. "Want another beer before they stop selling?"

"I'd rather have a hotdog," said Violet.

She had met many men who denounced LA: businessmen from Minneapolis and Indianapolis; intellectuals from Boston and New York; politicians from Washington D.C. and The Beltway, wherever that was. The stereotypical view they held of California amused her, but they were so naïve that they came in January expecting beach weather.

"The land of fruits and nuts," Cheryl said, who never missed a chance to whine about how much she missed Ohio, who complained tirelessly that she missed thunderstorms and that too much sunshine made her melancholy. To Violet it seemed that California inspired jealousy in people.

On the drive home from the game Violet said, "Why did you come to LA, Poppy?"

"Carol's idea," he said.

She felt she could push things a bit. The Bulls had won. "You did it for her?"

"We'd only been married a year. I'd have done anything she asked."

"Did you think about going back after the divorce?"

"I don't remember. By that time I'd been here over fifteen years. Guess I thought it was too late. You can't live your life backwards."

"I like change," said Violet. "I'd love to live in New York."

"You've got to be kidding. Sounds like you've been listening to Bobby. Have you ever been to New York?"

"Once," she said. "Is there anything about California you do like?"

"For the first two years I was lost. I might have well as come from China. The weather, the people, the freeways, the gigantic size of things made it seem like my life didn't matter. Carol would see a celebrity, not even a big celebrity, a TV person maybe, and she'd run home and say, 'you'll never guess who I saw today,' and I wouldn't know who the hell she was talking about. We were in a restaurant once and I couldn't get her to look at me while I talked because some goofy, pimple-faced kid with a TV show was having a birthday party in the corner. What a joke. When were you in New York?"

"I was like that when I first moved up from Long Beach. Long Beach isn't the same as Hollywood either."

"Outsiders think all of Southern California is one big Hollywood. Who'd you go to New York with?"

"I think I would miss the outdoors though," said Violet. "You can ski in the mountains and the snow and be at the—"

"And be at the beach in an hour," said Poppy. "Who in the hell did you go to New York with and why are you avoiding the question?"

"A friend. I went with a friend."

"A man friend?"

"Poppy, I did have a life before I met you."

"I suppose he paid for the trip."

"What's that supposed to mean?"

"Where did you meet him? Did you meet him at the Mansion? How old was he?"

"You're taking me home? Why are you taking me home?"

"A girl like you won't ever have trouble meeting a man. That's for sure."

Poppy pulled into the gravel parking area, but he left the engine running and waited for her to get out of the car.

"Did I do something wrong? Are you telling me something?"

"I have a big meeting with the Deaconess in the morning and I have to do some stuff tonight. I'll call you mañana." He didn't move to kiss her, so she got out without looking at him.

"Whatever," said Violet. "I go in at six."

Violet didn't watch as Poppy backed out of the space and drove away. In her kitchen, she opened the refrigerator, moved the applesauce and orange juice to one side, and took out the jar of peanut butter and the carton of milk. She put two slices of bread into the toaster, peeled a banana and poured a large glass of milk, and waited for the bread to toast. The window above the sink was cracked open. Whiskey lay on the sill and watched her and he responded by purring when she scratched his head.

In the beginning Poppy had stayed over, saying her place reminded him of a cabin on a lake back home. Her bedroom could accommodate a double bed and a dresser and little else, and her living room held a sofa and an armoire for her television and stereo. She had purchased an aquarium too, and put it in the corner, but she hadn't as yet bought fish. Few of these original cottages remained. After the canals were deepened and widened, after new sidewalks and footbridges were installed, property values had risen and little places like these were razed and replaced with Italian-style villas.

Violet finished making her sandwich and went outdoors. The moon reflected off the surface of the water; ducks and geese slept all around her on patches of lawn and under the shrubbery that lined the banks of the canal, even on the bottom of her red canoe. She sat on the dock to eat, disturbing a brooding female who peeped anxiously for a moment but made no attempt to move. It was the mating season and many of the females already had babies.

After she first met Poppy she had stopped going to therapy, but Dr. Harvey Young still called her every few weeks to see how she was doing, and though he didn't come right out and tell her she was making a mistake by not coming, she knew what he thought. Age didn't matter to her. She couldn't convince the doctor; he listened without comment, when she told him how youthful Poppy was. Dr. Young's head moved almost imperceptibly (her image reflecting in his tortoise-shell glasses) when she emphasized how they laughed together, how she enjoyed hearing about how things were when he grew up. It wasn't like she had a pattern of dating older men. Poppy hadn't been the aggressor. She had pursued him. She had convinced him to see her.

But the doctor didn't want to talk about Poppy. He wanted to talk about the dancing. He wanted to talk about the abuse. She told him: her dancing was a temporary thing. She wasn't a victim. She didn't do drugs. Sure she had done ecstasy with friends, but she never really gotten into cocaine—and God some of the girls had heroine problems. She knew better. She had never told anyone but Dr. Young about Uncle Collie and that was difficult enough. Analysis. Life was hard for everyone. It had happened to her, but she wasn't going to let it ruin her life. Young pressed. Why did she dance? To feel powerful? She wasn't ashamed of her body. It was her way of expressing herself. It wasn't like she left the club everyday with a different man. She had been an ugly little girl, awkward and clumsy, but she felt beautiful when she danced.

Good people came to the clubs too. Fantasy didn't hurt. She'd rather appeal to fantasy than be a female accountant with a suit and one of those absurd bow ties. The part that dismayed her was when men treated her like she was stupid.

But Poppy said the time had come to think about her future. She knew he'd never propose to her while she danced. Actually he'd never mentioned marriage, even as a concept. But she felt safe with him: he had such strong opinions of things. She understood that he disapproved of her dancing even though he had enjoyed going to the club for a while. It was a way, for now, to make money. She couldn't begin to count the number of times she had been asked to do porno, but she had told Bobby the truth. Never. Sex should be private. For some of the girls dancing had been a stepping-stone to the horny porno industry, but not everyone who smoked marijuana went onto cocaine.

Poppy was different now.

Violet took the last bite of her sandwich and threw the leftover crust in the water for the ducks. She went into the house and into her bedroom. She slipped off her shoes, took off her jeans, and put them on the bed, then searched the closet for the Spandex dress that Poppy liked. The dress was small and black, and the light in this room was weak; she had trouble finding it among all her other clothes. For a moment she wondered if she had left it at Poppy's house and then she located it on a wire hanger, hidden in between two pairs of slacks with the tags still on them. No need to worry about the wrinkles; the wrinkles would disappear when she wore it.

In the bathroom she ran a comb through her hair, brushed her teeth, and dabbed a bit of perfume on her elbows, on her neck below the ears, and behind both knees. She went into the front room and looked in her purse for the key. "Goodbye, Whiskey," she said.

She crossed the footbridge and walked toward Pacific Avenue. She knew she'd have to be extremely quiet. He was a light sleeper and the last thing she wanted was to be met at the door with a gun.

When she got to Poppy's place she saw the light in the kitchen and when she stepped onto the porch she saw him at the table. She tapped on the door and watched as he stood and came toward it. He opened the door and she pulled back the screen and lunged against him to kiss him before he could speak. At first his arms remained limp and lifeless at his sides, but then he took a deep breath and allowed her to nuzzle his face with her hair. She kissed him on the forehead and on both cheeks, the way a daughter would kiss her father goodnight, and then just in case there were any doubts Violet pressed her breasts harder against his chest and kissed him on the lips and gave him her tongue. She held his head in both hands, her fingers spread to take his thick hair and pull back his head and bite him on the neck. Poppy shoved the door closed and pulled her dress off her breasts and she felt his rough hands on them as she pushed him toward his bedroom.

ॐ•ॐ

"The good news," said Dr. Young, "is that you're in a relationship. Violet looked up from her lap at the remark. "The bad news is that Poppy is very judgmental."

"I trust him," said Violet.

"And yet, you met him at Fantasy," said Dr. Young. Remember you told me that working there was the reason you distrust men."

Violet didn't distrust all men, but most of the ones who frequented Fantasy Mansion (and she meant the men who came in two, three, even four times a week) had social problems: either they couldn't get dates or they didn't know how to have a simple discussion with a member of the opposite sex or they simply hated women. Some of the men, those who came in on occasion for a stag party with their buddies were all right. But she knew they married the good girls and leered at the naughty ones.

"I trust him because he's not married. Because he's divorced. He's not cheating, you know, being untrue to someone."

Dr. Young sat with his legs crossed in a wingback chair across from her and nodded. "Uh huh," he said. When he wasn't taking notes, the pad and pen rested in his lap and he drummed on the armrests with the fingers of both hands. At first Violet had taken this as a sign of boredom, as if what she had divulged wasn't valuable, but she recognized now that it was merely his way of displacing nervous energy. "Let's get back to last night," he said "So you went to see him with the intent of having sex."

"Yes."

"And after sex, he started crying."

"Yes."

"Did you stay?"

"Yes."

"Did you talk?"

"I asked him what was wrong—and I held him."

"What did he say?" Dr. Harvey Young picked up his pad and wrote something down.

"He wouldn't discuss it," said Violet.

"What do you think was wrong, is wrong?" said Dr. Young.

"That he's too old for me. And that he's worried about work. I think he's worried about his son, too. His son is gay. He accepts that. But his son is very swishy." Violet was pretty sure that Dr. Young was gay (he wore a wedding band, but there were no pictures of women or children in his office) and she wondered if her description of Bobby as swishy was offensive. "And Poppy has some trouble with his prostate. He didn't tell me at first, but he's having some tests."

"It sounds like there's a lot going on with Poppy," said Dr. Young. He stared silently at Violet for a moment; he put the pad back in his lap and dropped the pen and put his right hand up to his face and began to drum the surface of his cheek with his fingers. "What about you, Violet? Do you want a family?"

"Not right now. Maybe. Someday I'd like a kid." Talking about family, parenthood, made her wary. She didn't want to go there today; Uncle Collie lurked, never far below the surface.

"Do you think Poppy would make a good father? How old is he? Sixty? He might be sixty-five when you're ready and he may not want a child at that age. It sounds like Poppy's in a different place. He's already had a family."

"It's not only that—Poppy disapproves of what I—he disapproves of the dancing. He says, I've got to consider my future."

"Violet, I think it's a distraction for you to simply focus on Poppy and his life and his son. Let's set aside how Poppy feels. I'm more interested in why you do what you do."

Was he scolding her? Something about his tone; urgency registered in his voice. "But he's right. Poppy is right. He's pulling away."

"Right about what?"

"That I need to think about my future."

"How do you feel about your future?"

Hopeless. She felt hopeless, but she couldn't say that. Hopeless wasn't a word she would have allowed in her thoughts a year or two ago. "When I started dancing I felt free. Now I'm afraid." Dr. Young sat straighter in his chair, started drumming his fingers on the armrests again. She shouldn't have said she was afraid. "I mean I'm not really afraid, it's only that I don't want to get trapped at Fantasy, and I'm not sure what to do. Where to go for work. I'm not going to be a waitress, that's for sure." Dr. Young took up his pen again. Violet looked out the window. Young's third-floor office didn't have much of a view, but the sky was shining and the Santa Monica Mountains weren't hidden by pollution. She kept looking outside while she talked; it was easier if she didn't think about Young's reaction. "There are new dancers all the time, and they get the same snow job from the creeps. This one actor (he does those kick boxer movies) thinks everybody is dying for his autograph. And the real turkeys are insulting. They must think we're all so stupid that we don't know when some asshole's lying to us."

"So your sense of power is being eroded by the behavior of the customers?" said Dr. Young.

"I guess so. I think it might be nice to be able to tell guys I was a nurse or a librarian or something."

"When you were a little girl, what did you want to be? A doctor, lawyer, Indian chief? Every child has dreams," said Dr. Young.

Violet sat still, looking at the framed movie poster, *Breakfast at Tiffany's*, on the wall behind Dr. Young. The woman in the poster (Violet had heard of Audrey Hepburn) had a black, floor-length evening gown on and held a very long cigarette holder. So much for Dr. Young's sexual orientation. "I wanted to be ballet dancer. I took ballet for a year," said Violet.

"A year?"

"Cheryl made me quit."

"Why?"

"The lessons cost too much. And she thought ballet was snobbish."

"Did that feel like a loss for you?"

"It was a long time ago. And she didn't bother me about much. She didn't care what time I came home at night or how old I was when I dated. The other kids had rules, but I didn't."

"But she didn't like ballet and you did. Was there anything she wanted you to do, like go to college?"

"She never said anything about college. Poppy said I should take courses at Santa Monica College. Oh I know, Cheryl said I could be a massage therapist. She said it was good money. Or I could be a beautician like she was."

"What about school?"

"I stopped by for a catalogue. I'm too late for the summer term.

"Bobby has asked me to help him on his show and I think I will. It'll be fun. He lived in New York for a long time, working on shows, being with neat people. Creative people. Set designers, costumers, make-up artists, dancers and actors. Legitimate show business, you know? I won't have money to give to my mom. I spend too much on clothes anyway. I can get by. I'll cut down on the dancing."

"You like Bobby, don't you?"

"I can be myself around Bobby. He has strong opinions like Poppy."

"You know there's a difference between being judgmental and having opinions. Have you been spending a lot of time with Bobby?"

"We've been hanging. We went to an opera."

"How does that feel?"

"Good. It's fun."

"What does Poppy think about your doing things with Bobby?"

"I think he might be jealous."

"He has a poorly-formed relationship with his son, and Poppy is an insecure man. You have a friendship with Bobby that he doesn't have. I think it's excellent, for you, your friendship with Bobby. What if you found a straight man like Bobby?"

"He'd only want sex. Young straight guys are only interested in sex."

"You went to see Poppy and seduced him? Why did you want sex with Poppy?"

"I guess I thought it would fix things. Make him stop pulling back. Like a Band Aid on a cancer."

"Why did you think sex would fix it?

"Violet, you're an attractive, intelligent, capable, warm and loving woman. I think you might be over-invested in your sexuality. Are you following me?"

ಬಾಬಾಬಾ Six: A Bold Plan

SMELZKOFF SAT AT HIS DESK, reviewing his notes, with the aquarium, a recent addition to his cramped office, bubbling in the corner. His plan addressed all the issues. No dogs on board-walk on weekends for period from Memorial Day to Labor Day; own-ers must keep dogs east of boardwalk, on leads at all times. *Special meetings to be held with the patrol officers, supervisors, and detectives to brief. On bikes, in cars, on horseback. Animal control involved. Special signs and notices. No dogs allowed. Must work together.*

Violet had given him the twenty-five gallon tropical fish tank, but until now he hadn't set it up. She said she'd read that it would soothe his nerves, instill a sense of well being in him, and so yesterday he'd gone to the pet store on Lincoln Boulevard to purchase several kinds of freshwater fish. The boy with a pierced tongue who had helped Smelzkoff said that they were community fish, which he took to mean that they could all coexist in one tank without eating one another.

Enforcement of the rules would pose a special problem when it came to locals: the Venice residents. There was to be a new dog park at Westminster, but because of the limited parking, many owners were not willing to travel more than a few blocks to get there. Smelzkoff had been to one of the meetings, before the park won approval, and seen that there were two camps. Those for the park (dog lovers) and those opposed (residents who lived in the houses at the perimeter of the park) who envisioned a barrage of cars, dogs, and owners descending on the area.

One old woman (she wore a bonnet and looked like an ad for margarine) said: "My dead husband and I bought the house for the view. Families picnic in the park and they won't be able to with dogs overrunning it."

A dog lover's retort: "All you have now is a view of the homeless living in the trees and doing drugs. What kind of view is that?"

The first woman: "I don't know why we're bothering to talk; it sounds like the park is a forgone conclusion."

"We still have to get California Coastal Commission approval," said the dog lover.

In the end the approval hadn't been necessary. The commission said that the park would be far enough east to be out of their jurisdiction. The problem with the Westminster park was that it was too far away from the ocean to mitigate the problem Smelzkoff had been charged with solving. The locals who lived within a block or two of the beach were the real problem. He would have to send a strong message to them that he meant business.

And he'd done his homework. He knew them all. They gathered every evening in front of the homo's house. The smart ass with the German shepherd that chased the Frisbee; the man never even brought a leash along and immediately resumed playing with the dog when Smelzkoff disappeared, or so he thought, from sight. *Nougats* was the dog's name; the owner gave commands to the dog in French. And the cute couple with the way too cute Dalmatian: *Cuba*. Did they think it was a Spanish breed? They let the pup roam the beach and only called it back when they saw Smelzkoff prowling. The big surfer dude with the Mastiff. The blonde with the Chow mix, who treated her dog as if it were human. Called it *Woo Woo*. Talked baby talk to it. The homo had the chocolate Labrador. He only bent to fasten the leash when he saw Smelzkoff. The young girl with baby in backpack who owned the yellow Lab. Never on a leash. There was Rudolph, Chomper, Donner, and Blitzen. Smelzkoff had files on nearly two hundred different dogs and owners. The tall boy, who chain-smoked cigarettes (he'd seen him but couldn't recall where) let his dog run completely free at all hours of the night and day.

Smelzkoff knew what times they came out with their dogs, how often, how long they stayed, and how they played. There were only a couple of law-abiding owners. The odd lady with the Sheltie, for example, who kept it on a leash and let it run in circles barking.

The plan he would present to Deacon was bold, but not drastic.

Three rapid raps at his office door, and before he could say, *Come in*, Gloria Deacon entered, took three steps and arrived in front of his desk. "Smelzy, baby," she said, and dropped her swollen brief case on a stack of papers on the corner of his desk. "What do you got for me?" she said, dropping into the chair.

Smelzkoff pulled his note pad out from under her briefcase, or giant purse, or whatever it was and grumbled hello. There was only one thing worse than Gloria Deacon in foul humor, and that was Gloria Deacon in good humor.

"My plan is bold," said Smelzkoff.

Gloria Deacon pulled out a legal pad and removed the top from a gold and black fountain pen. Smelzkoff studied her hat for a moment, this one a broad-brimmed straw hat painted, it appeared, with red gloss enamel. He pushed a copy of his proposal across the desk to her.

"Your copy," he said. He took a drink of coffee. "Do you want coffee?"

"I already stopped at the Cow's Ass," she said. "Talk to me."

"We'll mount an offensive that will coordinate police and animal control units. Six cars with two officers "

"Those fish have *ich*," she said, staring at the aquarium. "What are they, platys? You need Nox-ich." She stood and hurdled a stack of newspapers on the floor to get to the tank. "You don't have a plycostumus. You need a plycostumus to eat the algae."

Smelzkoff put his face in his hands and rubbed it. How easily he could push the flesh around to feel the contour of his skull, at the ready to emerge. How short a time we inhabit this planet.

"I'm listening," said Gloria Deacon.

He glanced over at her; she crouched now and pressed her nose against the glass of the tank, knocking her hat askew. Smelzkoff cleared his throat. "Our offensive will include six patrol cars with two officers per car on Speedway Avenue. Three cars will travel in convoy from Washington north toward Venice Boulevard and three cars will travel south from Venice toward Washington. That will cut off the escape routes. On the beach west of Ocean Front Walk, we'll have "

"They're all the same size," Gloria Deacon said. "A couple of angels would add some variety. Angels are docile fish. Don't worry just because they're larger."

Stanley Smelzkoff raised his voice. "Patrols on horseback and in SUV's. On Ocean Front Walk itself, the boardwalk, we'll have bicycle officers. I figure ten on bikes, ten on horseback, and ten in trucks. And maybe another half dozen on foot."

He paused, expecting her to either say something about the fish, or to ask him to repeat himself.

"That's forty-eight men," she said. "Double it." She stood again and went back to her chair. "What about helicopter backup?"

He had expected her to quibble about manpower estimates and he leaned forward in his chair and looked at her now. "The chopper, or choppers, will be equipped with military cameras to record the entire operation, equipment so sophisticated that they can not only show us which dogs are off leash, but also zero in on the collars to see which dogs have licenses and which don't."

"When?" said Gloria Deacon.

"Tuesday, May nineteenth."

"What time?"

"The operation will commence at eighteen hundred hours."

Stanley Smelzkoff envisioned the moment. With everyone in place, swords would be drawn and the soldiers could capture the prisoners. Tickets would be issued for any number of offenses: improper licensing, no certificate for vaccination, off leash, on the sand, in the water; the fines would be plentiful and stiff. "And we'll repeat the operation several times for three or four weeks until the owners get the message. Several times a week if necessary."

Smelzkoff consulted his notes again: Element of surprise; catch them off guard. By the time summer came and the tourists were in force the message would have been sent.

"General," said Gloria Deacon. "You're beautiful."

She took her case and started for the door. "What about Animal Control?"

"Oh, yes. They'll be stationed in the parking lots at the end of Venice and Washington to remove the unlicensed dogs," said Smelzkoff.

⇛•⇚

Smelzkoff finally found a spot on the fifth floor of the parking garage and pulled in. He took another large swallow of water from his bottle and got out of the car. He had already finished two bottles at home, before he left, and the urge to urinate was strong. He walked in short, unnatural strides to the parking garage elevator. The doors opened and he moved to the back and leaned against the wall. The number four lit up and the car lurched to a stop. Smelzkoff waited while a woman and two small children got on. At three, an old man in a walker got on and tried to turn around but he couldn't pull the walker out of the way of the doors and it obstructed the path of the doors and prevented them from closing. On two, the doors opened again and two women entered the car and Smelzkoff said, only slightly under his breath, "Right, let's stop on every floor. I'm in no hurry." His full bladder made it difficult for him to make sudden movements and the walk to Dr. Zieman's office a block away, took him longer than usual. On the way he thought about Ed.

Ed had been the primary reason Smelzkoff had scheduled the first appointment with Dr. Zieman. Ed and his plump wife lived next door. After a routine physical examination revealed a problem with his prostate, Ed had undergone surgery and was now incontinent and impotent.

When Zieman left the message on his voice mail ("Your PSA was normal but I want to repeat one of the other tests") Smelzkoff didn't understand. He called the doctor to set up the necessary appointment, but the man didn't really give him a chance to ask: If the PSA was normal what did the other test mean? Dr. Zieman told him to drink three bottles of water before he came in, but again didn't elaborate. Ed from next door said the doctor was probably going to measure his flow rate.

The lobby and corridor of the medical office building were being remodeled and construction materials and laborers competed for space. The smell of paint and drywall compound filled his nostrils. Inside the waiting room Smelzkoff sat on the flower-print sofa and picked up a magazine, but he barely had time to open it before the door leading to the examination rooms opened and Dr. Zieman stuck his skinny neck and head in through the opening.

"Did you drink the water?" said the doctor. Smelzkoff held the bottle up. "Good. I'll be with you in five seconds."

The frosted glass window slid open and the receptionist stood up. "Mr. Smelzkoff, did you bring your insurance card?"

Smelzkoff thought her accent was Russian, but he couldn't tell for sure. The woman in the lab downstairs was Russian, or so she told him when he had given her a sample of his blood, a week earlier; she had smiled and fussed so much that Smelzkoff was fairly certain that she was flirting, but she was way too fleshy for him and he pretended not to notice.

Smelzkoff gave her the card. "I make copy," she said. Smelzkoff's bladder was so full that he didn't bother to tell her that the doctor made a copy last week. Where did all these Russians come from? Was there something in particular that attracted them to urology?

The door opened again, and Dr. Zieman ushered an old man out, then pointed to Smelzkoff. The doctor led him to a room down the hall where a man in a lab coat stood in front of a monitor, set up next to an examination table. "Igor is going to do an ultrasound of your bladder then he'll do another after you urinate," said the doctor.

Igor instructed Smelzkoff to lie flat on the table and unzip his pants. "Pull your shirt up and put your pants down to here. He indicated on his own body to the spot just above his crotch.

"How long is this going to take?" said Smelzkoff, his discomfort quickly approaching the level of pain.

"Five minutes," said the technician.

"Five minutes?" said Smelzkoff.

"Two minutes," said Igor.

He moved a sensor over the surface of Smelzkoff's groin and punched in numbers on a keyboard then moved the sensor and punched in more numbers. This process of moving the sensor and punching in data continued for long enough for Smelzkoff to take a deep breath. "Be still, please," said Igor. "Almost finished." When he did finally finish he stepped into the hall and called for Dr. Zieman.

Zieman led Smelzkoff into the small lavatory. He looked at his watch and said, "I'm going to time you while you urinate. Signal me when you're ready to start." The doctor, chewing on his upper lip, stared down at Smelzkoff's crotch.

"You're going to stand there and time me?" Smelzkoff tried to decide if this was the way that the test should be done. He remembered Ed saying something about pissing into a funnel-like device that was attached to a computer.

"I want to evaluate your stream," said the doctor.

Smelzkoff unzipped his pants and pulled out his penis, which had shrunk to miniscule proportions. He pushed for a minute but there was no response. Finally the urine came: first a dribble, then two tentative rivulets, and finally a waterfall that foamed the water's surface in the toilet. When Smelzkoff was done, he shook it and quickly put it back. The doctor made a notation on a scrap of paper and said, "Now if you'll go back to Igor and when he's done come in the examination room next door. There." He pointed.

Igor repeated the procedure he had done before and punched in data, gave Smelzkoff a Let's-have-some-vodka! smile, and called again to Dr. Zieman.

Inside the examination room Zieman told Smelzkoff to undress and lie on the table. "I'm just going to catheterize you to verify that your bladder has been completely voided," said Zieman

"You're going to what?"

And before Smelzkoff could protest, or decide whether or not he should protest, he felt a stinging sensation at the tip of his penis that grew in intensity as it moved up the hollow toward his bladder. Smelzkoff felt a strong sensation to urinate, as if the tube had pushed open a trap door and entered the bladder. "Hmm," said Dr. Zieman He withdrew the tube rapidly in the manner of someone fishing an entangled extension cord from behind a piece of furniture.

Perspiration beaded on Smelzkoff's forehead. "Get dressed and come back into my office," said the doctor, now chewing on his lower lip.

&•⊰

Smelzkoff headed north in his converted golf cart toward the parking lot at Venice Boulevard. At Twenty-fifth Avenue he looked up to the second floor balcony when he heard the shouts.

"Officer, excuse me, officer," said the man, waving both arms. Smelzkoff took his foot off of the accelerator pedal and pushed on the brake. "Someone broke into my house last night," said the man. "I need to file a report."

Smelzkoff turned off the key. "Did you call it in?"

"I was about to, when I saw you."

Smelzkoff got out of the cart and walked over closer to the deck, but it was difficult for him to hear from down below, with the bulldozers pushing the sand around on the beach behind him. Most days there were tractors too, grooming the sand; sometimes there was so much equipment at work that it sounded like the country rather than the city. The man began to describe what had happened, but Smelzkoff could only piece together a few words.

"Where's your door?"

The man pointed to the back.

The apartment was homey inside. This ocean-facing area between Washington and Venice boulevards was an interesting mix of million-dollar houses and poorly constructed apartment buildings with four to six units. This particular building, dingy brown with rusted metal railings along the outside stairs and walkways, was an awkward square box, that looked like one of those fake, paddle-wheel steamers that had plied Lake Geneva in Wisconsin, where Smelzkoff had gone with his grandmother as a boy.

Smelzkoff stood just inside the doorway and glanced surreptitiously around the front room. The man looked to be about his age (his blond hair was silver at the temples) but on the wall of bookshelves there were pictures of him posed with other men, who looked decidedly younger.

"My dog scared them away," said the man. "I've had a cold and I took some flu medicine and went to bed early last night. Sometime in the middle of the night Fred started barking—he sleeps on the floor next to my bed—and I got up and opened the bedroom door and he ran down the hall. I didn't think much of it; I figured he heard the boy delivering the morning paper or something. But when I got up this morning I noticed that the window in my kitchen had been removed. That's how the guy got in."

The dog was sniffing at Smelzkoff's crotch and wagging his tail. "He don't look vicious."

"He sounded vicious last night. I don't know if he'd do anything if he actually caught someone. Labs are gregarious, but it just goes to show how important it is to have a dog in Venice with all our crime. The man must have gone out through the front door; I always lock it and it was unlocked this morning."

The hair on the back of Smelzkoff's neck bristled. Was this an attack? "Look, I don't enjoy chasing people with dogs, but if everyone kept their dogs on leashes it wouldn't be a problem. I've seen you out here without a leash and I let it go. In the future I won't."

The man looked at Smelzkoff's uniform shirt and sleeve stripes for a moment and then at him. "Look, Sergeant Smelz-koff? it seems like such a waste of your time to worry about dogs. I mean it's not like illegal parking and having dogs off-leash are the most serious crimes we have."

"Do you know what we spend most of our time on?" The man started to speak, but Smelzkoff cut him off. "Drugs," he said.

"Well, I don't agree with that either," said the man. "Prohibition didn't work. Whoever broke into my house probably wanted money for drugs. I need a dog to protect me and dogs need exercise. We need a nearby dog park, or at least a place where dogs can run on the beach. In France they allow them in restaurants."

Obviously this man knew the gay couple that owned *Playa de Jaime*. "Did you ever look where your dog puts his mouth? I don't reckon I'd want to eat in that restaurant. Do you live here alone?"

"What? Yes."

"What do you do for a living?"

"I'm a writer."

"You must do pretty well to afford to live here."

"If I wrote for movies, I'd live in Malibu. Not Venice. But let's talk about my break in."

"This is a mighty nice place," said Smelzkoff. "Great view."

"They took my cell phone and a five dollar bill. Luckily that's all the money I had in the house."

"The waves are huge today. Did you see the whales on Sunday?"

"Can I file a report with you? I'll need a report."

"What did they get?"

"Five dollars, and my cell phone. That's all I had in the open. Oh, and a pair of expensive sunglasses. Like I said my dog scared them away. I've lived here seven years and this is the first time a burglar has come into my house. I've had three bicycles stolen from my garage, though."

"This time?" said Smelzkoff.

"No, in the past." The man eyed him up and down for a minute. "Do you work out at Gold's? You look familiar?"

Smelzkoff remembered the man now, always with a young, attractive boy. Still, you couldn't tell by looking. Maybe he should introduce him to his son; maybe he could butch Bobby up a bit. The women cops he worked with were more masculine than his own son. Smelzkoff glanced at the shelves again and focused on one of the pictures. The man had his arm around a dark boy with curly hair and a Vandyke moustache. The boy looked sneaky. Probably hung around with this old guy for the money and to hang out at the beach. Then Smelzkoff thought about Violet.

"Could this break-in have been anyone you know?" he said.

ಬಿಬಿಬಿ Seven: To the Rescue 911

THE *CALL FOR FEMALE IMPERSONATORS* ("Must Be Able to Sing") in the *Advocate*, *Frontiers*, and *Edge*, as well as a host of more mainstream publications, brought four talented ingénues to Bobby's dressing room in the Olympic, but after two more weeks of ads, still no Salome. That's when Bobby decided to travel to New York for a weekend talent search and proposed the idea to Flo. "Do what you have to do, just don't stay at The Four Seasons," said Flo.

"I have a friend in Newark with an immense house. May I take Violet?"

The role of Salome needed not only a powerful stage presence, but also a fertile, rich voice. And in a remote part of Chelsea characterized by warehouses, which looked abandoned even if they weren't, Bobby and Violet found their chanteuse. Brandon had advised Bobby that he would be in Washington on a sexual discrimination suit until Friday night and had left the key to his house with the neighbor. When he called on Thursday to confirm that they'd gotten in all right, he told Bobby about the newly opened drag bar near Ninth Avenue.

Bobby and Violet took the bus into the city and jumped on the subway to get to Chelsea. He stopped in a favorite restaurant and went to the bar to talk to the bartender, who happened to be someone he'd known casually for several years. Bobby and the boy had flirted for a year, and nothing had ever happened, but they kept the banter lively and full of double entendres, as if even now under the right circumstances they could fall to the floor and wallow in reckless sex. Bobby ordered two glasses of wine and spent a few minutes telling the man how he was living in LA, how he had broken up with his boyfriend, how he was here for a short visit. No, he hadn't developed a taste for fish, he said, when Violet came up to stand at Bobby's side and claim her glass of wine.

The bartenders directions (he'd already been to the club and said it was not your conventional drag show) were precise: down poorly-lit, paper-strewn streets, past boarded and barred storefronts, left and right and left again, and they could barely read the address numbers, which had been painted over and matched the grimy dark brown of the wooden trim on the brick building. There were no signs on the outside of the building, nothing to suggest that such a noisy, smoky and crowded establishment existed inside. They went through the front room, past the drinking crowd listening to what sounded like alternative jazz-rap, and arrived at the back where a second door had been curtained off. The show had already begun, according to the tall hostess at the reservation stand just inside the curtain, and she pored over her reservation list, flipping back and forth between the pages, sighing and clearing her throat so frequently that Bobby began to think she had a rather advanced case of asthma. "You really must phone ahead in order to get a table. I only have that tiny one," she pointed with her pencil, "behind that load-bearing column," she said, and Bobby suspected that her description served to preempt suggestions from customers that the impediment be moved. Bobby nodded and she led them to it, weaving their way through the tables at the back of the room.

Initially, Bobby felt that he and Violet had chased a false lead, for there was nothing unusual about the drag show; it included the usual lineup of grotesque, carnival-like impersonators, parading through their routines of what had become standard repertoire for drag queens. One impersonator roller-skated on stage, twirled a flaming baton, and lip-synched to two early Barbra Streisand hits. The second rode onto the stage on a pony and sang "Happy Trails to You," in Dale Evans, suede-fringed drag. The third came out dressed as Hillary Clinton and lip-synched "He's Just My Bill." Of course the lyrics had been changed to make the song more blasphemous. Then, the fourth act of the evening and headliner: Dame Ethyl Chloride. A seasoned performer from Liverpool, England, who sang in her own voice and played the trombone; at six-foot-something, Dame Ethyl weighed nearly three hundred pounds. She strutted, or rather plodded, around the small stage, alternately singing and playing her horn.

Dame Ethyl Chloride would be perfect to originate the role of Salami. Never mind that Salome was a fetching young girl. When Bobby had seen the opera, the part had been sung by a sixty-something coloratura. The sight of her aging body, rolling on the floor in front of Herod, had brought most of the audience to snickering and some to outright laughter. Well, he was all for suspending disbelief; opera required that (consider Beethoven's *Fidelio:* could a girl disguised as a man really fool hardened prisoners? and he'd seen some pretty hefty Mimis in *La Boheme*) but a portly, aging Salome had gone too far. Though not too far for *Salami.* For Salami, such largeness would be perfect. Perfect.

"You Got to Have a Gimmick," Dame Ethyl sang, his long red curls flying, and then he leaned over the stage and aimed the slide of the trombone at the head of a front-row hunk. "If you want to get some head." She, who now seemed thoroughly female, finished with, "There is Nothing Like The Dame."

఼•ఌ

All evening, after Bobby and Violet had gone backstage to meet The Dame and give her the pitch while she took off her red wig and make-up, Bobby sang, danced and whistled his way around the city.

He hadn't been able to promise The Dame much in the way of salary, but he had been able to offer him a place to stay; since The Dame really wanted to see Los Angeles after New York, they were able to work things out quickly. "Can't you picture him singing opera?" said Bobby.

Violet had been quiet to the point where Bobby had to ask if she was having a good time. She assured him that she was simply taking it all in and having an amazing experience; it was just that she was in his world now and it was most definitely a new world for her.

Friday morning they went back into Manhattan, but this time with no specific purpose other than to give Violet a walking tour of the city in the daylight. "The people are so thick you could stir them with a stick," said Violet.

"May is my favorite time in New York," said Bobby. "I'm surprised you've never been here before."

They climbed the stairs of the subway exit and emerged on Broadway in brilliant sunshine. It was early in the month, the air cool enough for jackets and sweaters, which almost everyone in the streets seemed to be wearing.

When they arrived at Columbus Circle, Violet said, "I didn't know you went to college."

"I don't think there's a college in town I haven't gone to. Tisch School of the Arts—that's part of NYU—Fashion Institute, Parsons, you name it." Bobby classified Violet as inquisitive and understood that when she failed to ask questions it was because she didn't want to be perceived as stupid.

"Poppy never told me you went to college," said Violet.

"I'm not sure he knows. Mom and Tom came to visit, but Poppy was apparently too busy."

"Poppy's so smart; I wonder why he didn't go to college," said Violet.

Bobby considered the remark before responding, and had to admit that his father possessed a certain native intelligence; he understood machines and kept up on world events. "College, I think, would have taught him to be more tolerant of people who are different. He doesn't really understand why people don't all have the same view of the world. Personally I think we learn more from those who disagree; it forces us to examine the other side of things. Poppy doesn't like people who challenge him—and he takes it personally. After you've been in college classes and seen people arguing about how to interpret *Paradise Lost* and getting all heated over whether Monet had more of an impact on Impressionism than Manet, you come to understand that nothing is simple. The hardest thing for most humans is seeing that others often have an entirely different and unique way of looking at issues and situations."

"Poppy suggested that I take some courses at Santa Monica College," said Violet.

"You're kidding," said Bobby. They turned the corner and the arch on Washington Square came into view. "That's it," said Bobby, pointing ahead. "It's too bad it's not Sunday. The place rocks on Sunday."

"It scares me a little," said Violet.

"No way. It's safe here. I mean there's crime and drugs and all but I wouldn't characterize this as a bad neighborhood. Look at the houses." He slipped his arm around her waist. "You're with me, Sweetie. Who's going to bother you when you're with such an intimidating dude."

Violet smiled. They dodged between taxis going in opposite directions to cross the street, then slowed down, and walked under the arch. Bobby checked out the food vendors and was about to suggest that they get a drink and sit at the edge of the fountain to watch people for a while, when Violet said, "Going to Santa Monica College scares me. I'm too much of a fool to go to school."

Bobby stopped and faced her. "Honey, I understand being afraid of things, believe me. I could tell you, sure you're smart enough, more than smart enough in fact, but until we try things for ourselves there's always that fear that we'll fail. Be bold. Take a chance. Hey, it takes a lot more courage to face those boneheads at Fantasy everyday. *Carpe diem*. Now there's an overworked slogan for you." Bobby bought two cherry-flavored Popsicles from the vendor and handed one to Violet.

On the path in front of them a girl had coaxed a squirrel to take a peanut from her hand. "See, take a chance. You might like the peanuts."

"I wouldn't know what courses to take," said Violet.

"Try something that capitalizes on your strengths. You have people skills. You know how to communicate. You have a great sense of fashion and style." Bobby's hunger increased. "Let's get some lunch; I have to take my meds."

"Meds?" said Violet. "Are you sick or something?"

"How did you start dancing anyhow? I've always been curious as to how girls make that plunge."

"After high school I started hanging out at the beach and I met some older girls and we all started playing volleyball together. I found out later they were dancers, and they convinced me to go with them to Fantasy one night—because I always complained about not having any money. They laughed, said all the cheapskates came on amateur night because the lap dances were only a dollar and they served shrimp cocktails for ninety-nine cents. After we got to the club they convinced me to go on stage. I won three hundred dollars."

"First prize?"

"Nothing but."

"I love this city," said Bobby.

"So why did you move back to LA?"

"Several reasons. A failed marriage for one."

"I'm sorry. I didn't know. So when did you, how long ago did you divorce?"

"Just before I moved back. It had been brewing for a while though."

Bobby hadn't discussed Jason with anyone back in Los Angeles and he hadn't come to New York to see him either, but since Brandon was due back tonight and (since they were staying at his house in Newark) Bobby knew that Jason's name would come up. Brandon and

Jason were still friends and saw each other occasionally, though to be sure Brandon tried not to gossip with Bobby about what he knew. He'd make a joke or critical remark about Jason (he recognized the man's selfish qualities) but until Jason's behavior affected him personally Brandon refused to make moral judgments. The advice he gave Bobby was: move on.

Bobby didn't like being a visitor here. The fact that he couldn't at any moment get into a cab or on a subway and head for his apartment distressed him. Suspended between two worlds, he didn't feel at home yet in Los Angeles and he no longer belonged in New York. He looked down at his thawing Popsicle and then up ahead on the path to the nearest trash barrel. New York had always made him feel that he was a part of something important. No one cared about being part of LA.

At the edge of the park on the opposing street they came to a store with outdoor, color-arranged displays of fruits and vegetables. "Let's pick up some groceries and fix dinner for Brandon tonight," said Bobby. "Shall we have *boeuf* as in Bobby or *vitello* as in Violet?"

Violet shrugged and smiled. "Let's have brandied peaches as in Brandon."

"An excellent suggestion. And lamb for the main course. Lamb as in Violet, my little lamb."

"I hope he likes me," she said.

&•&

Brandon's house, a three-story frame in an historic residential area of Newark, was a hundred and ten years old. The kitchen had over-sized, commercial-grade appliances, an island in the center of the room for food preparation, and every style and design of cooking utensils. Brandon's German shepherd sat close to the action and surveyed the floor for morsels. When Bobby dropped a slice of onion, Duke immediately took it in his mouth and bit into it once or twice before dropping it back onto the floor. "Duke is always on vittles patrol," said Bobby. "I miss Ginger. You would love Ginger," said Bobby.

"Was Ginger your dog?" said Violet.

"Ginger thought she was a person," said Bobby.

The kitchen door opened and Brandon entered from the back driveway, his smile immediate and large. He had often expressed his pleasure in having houseguests and his appreciation for the simple things that made a house a home. That's why Bobby had candles burning in the kitchen, fresh flowers in the bathrooms, and meat roasting in the oven. Duke lost interest in the kitchen floor for a time and greeted his master with enthusiasm. Seeing Brandon's grateful reaction made a difference for Bobby too; for the first time since he had arrived back in the New York area he felt connected. Brandon set down his suitcase and garment bag and moved to embrace his friend. Violet edged backwards, closer to the dining room.

Bobby turned and reached out to her. "Come here. Since when did you get so shy?" He introduced the two and gave Brandon a seductive look.

"Guess what?" he said, but he didn't wait for Brandon to guess. "We found Salami at the club you suggested." Brandon wanted details and fired off a series of questions while Bobby continued preparing the salad. After he had apparently satisfied his immediate curiosity, Brandon took off his jacket and tie and announced his intention to go upstairs to shower and change. "Take this with you," he said, handing him a glass of red wine.

Now that she had actually met Brandon, Violet had questions too. She wanted to know about his age, his profession, how he and Bobby had met, and yes the inevitable one: Had they ever had sex? Bobby told her that Brandon, at thirty-seven, was considered one of the country's leading experts in civil law; he recounted how they had met in a popular Village bar and become immediate friends. "Our relationship wasn't complicated by sex. I like him too much." There was energy between them, he knew, but something had kept them from acting on it. Brandon had never had a relationship and seldom spoke about his sex life. Bobby heard Brandon's footsteps in the dining room and looked up as he came into the kitchen.

"Duke looks like he's gained weight," said Bobby.

"If you keep giving him table food, he's not going get any smaller," said Brandon.

"I miss Ginger," said Bobby. He tested a paring knife for sharpness against his thumb, picked up a cherry tomato, and began to peel it. He had already carved two dozen radishes to make decorative florets.

"Go Martha," said Brandon.

"Have you seen her?" said Bobby.

"No," said Brandon. He had been standing across from Bobby at the island and he turned now and looked around the kitchen. "Where did you put the wine?" he said. Bobby pointed to the countertop under the window that framed the view of the carriage house out back. Brandon went over to refill his glass, and then he opened the cabinet next to the window and took out a pack of cigarettes. He lit one, pulled up a stool, and sat down next to Violet.

"Violet, would you get the cilantro for me? In the crisper drawer of the fridge," said Bobby. Something had happened that Brandon didn't wish to discuss. For a second, Bobby almost accepted his answer, but the way his friend changed the subject alerted him to the possibility of latent gossip. Then Bobby's pride prevailed. Rather than ask about Jason, he wished to affect an air of detachment, though he insisted to others when dispensing advice that revealing one's injuries was a sign of strength. One should put ones ego out of the way, he always said; if you're hurting, say you're hurting. After all, it felt good to talk. "Ginger's okay, right?" said Bobby.

"She's fine. Jason is looking for someone to take her. He's going away," said Brandon, as he exhaled.

Bobby fanned at the smoke with his hand, and said, "What about Caroline next door?" Distracted entirely from his preparation, he said, "How long is he going away for?"

"Six months," said Brandon.

"Six months." Bobby wiped his hands on his apron. "Then I'll take Ginger back with me. Mom won't care. The backyard is fenced in and when I get my own place I'll make sure they allow pets."

Brandon swirled the wine in his glass, then stuck his nose below the rim and sniffed. "This is great wine," he said, stubbing out his cigarette.

"Ginger never meant as much to him," said Bobby. "The poor thing; she must think no one loves her. I have to call the airlines and book space for her. Will you call Jason? I have half a notion to call 911 and tell them to go to 60 Gramercy Park and pick her up."

"Sure, I'll call. Tomorrow," said Brandon.

"Where's he going?" said Bobby, unable to stay silent about Jason.

"None of us have seen much of him. Apparently he's going on some kind of trek through the Himalayas, to Tibet."

"So he's still doing the Buddhist thing," said Bobby. "Have you talked to him?" Brandon had stood up and gone to the cupboard to get down a box of crackers. "Oh, I bought peppercorn pate and Brie. Would you put it out, Violet?"

The flow of conversation was interrupted but not in Bobby's head. His blood pressure had risen he knew, though he tried to remain focused on the preparation of dinner. Something was up; he could feel it. His first thought had been about Ginger, but the sudden revelation that he hadn't known Jason as well as he thought he had, disturbed him.

"He met someone, didn't he?" said Bobby.

"You might as well hear it from me. You'll hear soon enough," said Brandon.

"So much for the karmic cycle of things. What's he like?"

"He's into Buddhism too, he's young, about your age, maybe two or three years younger "

"So they're going on this trek together. What's the new Mrs. Mercer look like?"

"Marty saw them at the gym. He's total attitude. He's got brown hair, he's about five-ten, and steroided out "

"A bodybuilder? Jason is dating a Buddhist bodybuilder? Has he shaved his head yet?" Brandon smiled.

"As a matter of fact—"

"I'm going to be ill," said Bobby. "Violet, open another bottle. What was he going to do? Take Ginger back to the pound?"

Bobby awoke early on Saturday, due in part to the fact that he was still on Los Angeles time, and also because he hadn't slept well after the disheartening news about Jason. Bobby had brewed coffee and taken Duke for a walk and was peering inside the refrigerator when Brandon came downstairs in his robe. They exchanged greetings and Bobby said, "Will you call Jason now?"

"I already did. Last night, after dinner. He's going to leave the key with the doorman. You can pick Ginger up after two."

Violet came into the kitchen wearing a chemise, and smiled at Bobby and Brandon. "I slept like a mouse," she said. "I love this house."

"I take a lot of grief for living in Newark, but this is a smashing neighborhood," said Brandon, looking at her more closely than he had the night before. "I grew up in Morristown. You know you have a preposterous body. I'm not one to notice a woman's anatomy as a rule, but I mean really. Turn around." He made a twirling gesture with his index finger.

"I saw her first," said Bobby.

"You're a bottom," said Brandon. He looked at Violet. "A big old bottom."

"That's good. I'm a top," said Violet.

"Let's have breakfast," said Bobby. "Eggs and waffles?"

He took out the things he needed for the breakfast. He diced onion, green pepper, and mushroom; he shredded cheese and filled the skillet with sausage. Brandon excused himself to shower and change again, and Violet poured herself a cup of coffee and sat on a stool.

"Ready to hit a couple more clubs tonight?" said Bobby.

"Is it all right if I meet you later? I'm invited to have dinner with some friends and I thought if you didn't mind "

"I didn't know you knew anyone here," said Bobby.

"Two girlfriends, that's all. We used to dance together and I called them last night. Is that cool?"

"Sure. I'll hang out with Brandon. You can catch up with us later; Brandon always takes his cell with him. Bring your friends if you like."

❧•❦

Brandon wanted to take Bobby to a new Icelandic restaurant in Alphabet City. He said it was nearly impossible to get reservations, but he had managed to secure a table from a business associate who was a partner in an investment-banking firm. Bobby entered the restaurant and blinked till his eyes adjusted to the darkness. The sound of hissing steam and purling water surrounded him; fog swirled in blue light; the air was chilly, perhaps too chilly for comfortable dining. Brandon nudged Bobby and indicated a blond waiter attending a nearby table.

"Gorgeous," said Brandon.

The hostess, a detached girl with model posture, led them to a booth. Everyone working in the restaurant was tall, fair-skinned, and blond: the women wore native costumes, long-sleeved, ankle-length dresses covered with bright-colored aprons and the boys all wore bib overalls with suspenders. "It's like something out of a Nazi propaganda film," said Bobby.

The hostess waited while they slid into the booth, then handed them menus. A panoramic picture of an erupting volcano hung just above the tabletop. The booth was warmer; Bobby felt heat rising up from a vent in the floor. "I didn't think you liked blonds," he said.

"A recent phenomenon. I decided not to fight it," said Brandon.

"I can't believe there are enough people in Iceland to have developed a national cuisine," said Bobby.

"I'm told all the seafood dishes are fabulous, but the real ticket is the free-range reindeer steak with turnips," said Brandon. "You have to be in a group of four or more to order the Sheep's Head."

The busboy, a short dark man, not an Icelander apparently, delivered bread, and hurried away. Bobby decided on *Saithe, in Cream and Butter Crustaceans Sauce.*

"Save room for desert," said Brandon. "The Crowberry pie is to die for. Violet seems nice. How did you meet?"

"She's dating my father," said Bobby.

"So, Daddy's a swinger," said Brandon.

"I don't know what's going on with him—mid-life crisis or something. I don't know what motivates anyone anymore."

When Bobby had gone to the apartment in Gramercy Park to rescue Ginger, for the second time, he'd been surprised to find a cleaning lady. He thought that Jason might be there to hand their pet over, despite the fact that he'd told Brandon he'd be gone, but instead he had simply left instructions with the woman that someone would be coming to pick up the dog. The woman didn't speak much English. She nodded and smiled whenever Bobby spoke, but when he couldn't find the dog's leash and asked her if she had put it away somewhere, she simply smiled again and kept on moving the dust around with a pink feather thing. As for Ginger, Bobby had never seen her quite so excited; she kept her head and rear end down and wagged her tail so hard when he came in through the front door that she banged the leg of the table in the entryway and knocked over the framed picture of Jason with his mother in front of a grand piano. Bobby, who had previously dismissed the photograph as pretentious and clichéd, found that he detested it more than ever now.

He stooped to pet Ginger. She licked his face, and when he stood to go into the living room she followed. He had to gather her toys, her stainless steel food and water bowls, her food (Jason had switched to a poor-quality brand available at a nearby market), her brush, and her leash, which he located behind the couch in the living room.

So what had the three years with Jason meant? Apparently for him, the breakup had been a minor setback and things had been made right as quickly as the time it took to hire a cleaning woman. Ginger was shedding; it was obvious that Jason hadn't taken time to brush her.

"Where do you want to go after we eat?" said Brandon.

"Do you think Jason ever had any feelings for me?" said Bobby.

"So that's why you're not talking," said Brandon. "Is he the real reason you came back?"

"Am I supposed to apologize for having cared about him?"

"Look, don't start getting pissed off at me," said Brandon.

The food came and awkwardness lingered at the table until the server left. The break came at a good time; it allowed Bobby to calm down a little.

"I'm sorry. I feel like there was this conspiracy and I was the only one not in on it."

"Jason makes a fine friend, as long as you don't expect too much. I wouldn't want him for a lover. I know I introduced you two, but what did you get out of the relationship? You got very little and yet you stayed for over three years."

"Two years and ten months," said Bobby.

"I don't care how long. At some point you're responsible for staying in the relationship."

"I wanted a partner," said Bobby.

Suddenly the lights went down and a grumbling roar filled the room: the sound of steel and iron, twisting and warping, emanated from the sound system; heavy bolts and screws squeaking and torquing in stereophonic intensity; fatiguing metal in counterpoint with splintering wood; metal ricocheting off metal. Several people in the restaurant screamed and got up from their tables. Then a shaking in the booth. The whole room it seemed suddenly in motion. At first, Bobby thought that a gas main had ruptured below them in the city and then he tried to figure out which subway line lay buried far below them. Glasses on the tables trembled, silverware clanged together, and then steam from the ceiling filled the room, shrouding them in a musty, lime-smelling haze. Brandon sat across from him grinning while Bobby gripped the edge of the table. Suddenly as quickly as it had begun, the constancy of the motion and noise was interrupted by three successive jolts, as if a giant hand had picked up the room and slammed it down, picked it up again and slammed it down, picked it up, slammed it down, and then there was stillness. No one in the restaurant moved or spoke or breathed, and then screams of relief, shouts for joy, laughter, and applause. Standing ovations by some and then the music came. Bobby saw some of the speakers in the light as the fog dispersed from the room. An anthem of some sort. Yes, the national anthem of Iceland. The waiters and waitresses all stopped and stood respectively, most of them sang along, and at the end, a pseudo-military flourish that characterized anthems all over the world, cheers all round and they got back to the business of feeding the patrons.

"Wow," said Brandon. "Pretty wild, eh? This is an old theater; they used to show 3-D movies here in the sixties," he said. "The booths are on tracks and wired to vibrate."

"Great special effects. I've read that Iceland has more tremblors than California and Italy combined," said Bobby. "Is this a Spielberg restaurant? I'm sorry Violet missed it." He tasted his fish and made an umm sound. "The waiters should be nude though," he said. "And we need folk-dancing."

ಐಐಐ Eight: Chemistry

VIOLET HADN'T PLANNED on missing her flight; she hadn't planned on having anything other than dinner with two crazy friends; and she hadn't deliberately lied to Bobby when she said she would call him on Brandon's cell phone after dinner. Michelle, if anyone, deserved the blame for manipulating and tricking her, and Jenny too had been in on it. She admitted as much just before Violet climbed into the cab and left for the airport. "We wanted you to meet Freddy, Sweetie, and you should thank us. It's about time you had some fun cause that asshole cop of yours is a loser. You're a beautiful girl and you deserve a beautiful man."

Michelle pleaded and coaxed. "Billionaires is way cooler than Fantasy Mansion," she said. "All the girls are winners, and the clients have class." There was a dress code (coats and ties were required; jeans were prohibited) and the club featured elegant chandeliers and extra-plush wall-to-wall carpeting.

Michelle and Jenny called him Freddy, but he told Violet, in his sexy accent, to call him Frederick. He had moved to New York from Austria to study acting and seemed to be thriving, judging from the way he threw his money around and from the rings he wore and the size of the gold chain around his neck. Come to think of it, Frederick had worn black, kid-leather pants and a silk shirt; with cheekbones like his, management apparently didn't care whether he wore a coat and tie or not.

How did it all start? How does it ever start, with these things? Violet liked his confidence; she liked the way he strutted and flaunted his physique. Up in the VIP room, he had taken off his shirt and that impressed her. Why not? This was a club where women took off their clothes, pretty much, except for the G-strings they wore, and Frederick was saying, My body is as magnificent as any woman's. Most of the girls stayed close around him, and some of the men glared at him, but no one said anything—and Frederick made it clear that he wanted her. He pulled Violet against him with his athletic arms and he laughed at her jokes and, after she had had a couple of lines, she squeezed his pecs and pinched his nipples with her fingernails. She couldn't remember now who first offered the cocaine, but it mixed well with the Special K and GHB and made her feel so good.

By the time she thought to call Bobby, the opportunity had vanished. It was Saturday night, or Sunday morning to be exact, and they weren't leaving until Monday at noon, and she reasoned that he would understand. But then she thought, Understand what? She couldn't talk about Frederick to Bobby, since she was supposed to be dating his father.

Michelle and Jenny met two men who had a suite at the Plaza, and they wanted to leave Billionaires and go back to party. They didn't ask Violet and Frederick to come; they told the men they wouldn't depart unless Violet and Freddy came along too. After that the two businessmen, executives, what ever they were (who cared at this point what the heck they did?) put pressure on them to shove off.

Violet hadn't done any Special K for a while, and the cocaine kept her pretty alert so that she wasn't staggering in the hotel lobby like Michelle and Jenny, but she was relieved when the six of them got into an empty elevator to go up to the suite. Michelle and Jenny got loud when they partied and swore worse than Uncle Collie. That time in Malibu, Michelle almost toppled off the balcony into the ocean and Jenny almost fell backwards through their host's glass coffee table. The man told his young friend to get their jackets, and Michelle had slurred, "Are we eighty-sixed?"

Frederick encircled her waist with both arms when the doors opened on their floor and he helped her out of the elevator—one of the few moments clearly etched in the chronology of events that occurred that night. All other moments of affection blurred together: his full, wet lips on her cheeks, his straight black hair rhythmically tickling her forehead and eyelashes, his huge hands on her neck, shoulders, and, yes, her breasts. On his lap in the swivel chair by the window, she felt his arousal and, not being in her shy mode, she squirmed to arrange herself. She buried her head in the curvature of his neck, kissed him, tasted him; she tongued the smooth skin of his chest and blew her hot breath on his nipple; she savored him, and his passion grew. She nuzzled him too, pressed her lips against his navel and blew noisily, like a horse fluttering its lips, and Frederick laughed like a boy being tickled.

Michelle and Jenny kept the other men at a safe distance from themselves, and Violet remembered little about them. The more aggressive one, kept trying to touch her and even pressed his hand against her chest until Frederick told him to back off; after that the man just put the spoon under her nose from time to time so that she could do more. Late in the morning she had had difficulty focusing on Frederick's blue eyes.

So she rode to LaGuardia with a headache, neck ache, backache, and enough guilt to satisfy a convent of nuns. When she called Bobby back in Los Angeles, he freaked her out big-time. "It's pretty inconsiderate to worry everyone the way you did," he said. "I'm sure you have a good explanation for not letting me know what's going on and I can't wait to hear it. I didn't know whether to fly home or stay to turn you in as a missing person. You're damn right I'm pissed." And then for the first time he revealed his prejudice about her profession. "How was I to know what might have happened. The perverts that you—" And then he had cut himself off.

"How did Ginger do on the trip?" said Violet.

"I finally decided you were a big girl and could take care of yourself," said Bobby, his tone not as harsh now. "Great. She loves Mom's backyard."

€•

Violet slept on the flight to Los Angeles, she slept on the cab ride into Venice, and she went to bed almost as soon as she had closed her front door behind her. First she had to feed Whiskey. He had eaten all the food she left and meowed frantically until she refilled his bowl. Violet slept so long and so soundly the rest of Tuesday afternoon that she missed work that evening and had to say she was sick when Kent called her at home. That wasn't a lie. Her head ached dully and her feverish body felt like it had been beaten with a plank.

Nestled under her down-filled comforter with all four pillows gathered around her, she concentrated to conjure up the features of Frederick's face. Ecstasy they said didn't completely leave ones system for several days and that no doubt accounted for the fact that she felt sexually aroused again and without, however temporary, guilt.

Unfortunately when Violet awoke to answer the phone some of her memories were of the unsavory sort and after she told Kent she couldn't come in to work she immediately called Dr. Young to see if she could squeeze in an evening appointment. Dust balls swirled in her apartment like tumbleweed and, despite the claims of the manufacturer, Whiskey's litter box had begun to smell like a fertilizer plant. Cleaning would have to wait. Seeing Dr. Young took precedence, and she couldn't afford to take any more time off from work. Kent hadn't really threatened her. He usually relied on tone of voice more than words to bring errant girls into line. Kent had been a Mr. Universe contender in the sixties, though it was impossible now for Violet to imagine him without a beer gut. To be frank, Kent's appearance alone was enough to scare her, and it wasn't simply the scars that marked his complexion.

Dr. Harvey Young greeted her in the reception room and ushered her into his office, his previous patient having just departed through a different door. Violet could smell traces of perfume. Traces? The woman must have sloshed it on with a mop if Violet could detect it with her clogged sinuses. People weren't supposed to be ashamed of their emotional problems. So why were patients encouraged to sneak out the back way like criminals?

Dr. Young gestured toward the couch, proposed coffee, which Violet refused, and asked her how she was doing.

"I messed up," she said.

"Tell me about it," said Dr. Young.

"I went to New York with Bobby and—"

"And?"

"I went out with girlfriends from LA and I met someone and we got to partying and had such a good time that I changed my flight home and now Bobby's pissed at me," said Violet.

"Slow down a minute, Violet. Is Bobby upset because you missed your flight or because you went out with friends?"

"I think because I met my friends he might be jealous," said Violet.

"And what makes you think Bobby is envious. It seemed like he was very fond of you," said Dr. Young.

"He started yelling at me and observed about my friends being perverts," said Violet. Dr. Young nodded and waited. "My friends aren't any weirder than his drag queen friends."

"Exactly when did Bobby yell at you?" said Dr. Young.

"On the phone," said Violet.

"He telephoned you, or you telephoned him? Tell me the circumstances, the events that led up to his getting upset, so I can understand."

"I called him to tell him that I wouldn't be able to make my flight and he lost it," said Violet.

"Well, I think Bobby was wrong to yell at you; there certainly are better ways he could have handled the situation." And here Dr. Young started to drum his fingers on the armrest. Cheryl said all shrinks were nuts and that was why they were so good at analyzing everyone else; Violet didn't know if Dr. Young was nuts or not, but he sure was nervous. "Is Bobby the only reason you're distressed? I'm more concerned about you. You sounded pretty frenzied on the telephone. You said earlier that you met someone and you partied. Did you mean you met your girlfriends or did you meet someone else?"

"Someone else," said Violet. She averted her eyes, filled her lungs with air, and resolve, and then exhaled. "A guy from Europe. He's living in New York. Studying to be an actor."

"Tell me about him," said Dr. Young.

Violet hesitated and tried to understand why she suddenly resented Dr. Young's intrusion. She had to stifle the urge to say something real catty, like: Well to start with he's got a real big dick which I'm sure you'd have fun with. "He's my age," she said. "I like that."

"Where did you meet him?"

"At this club. He already knew my friends and they wanted me to meet him," said Violet. "We hit it off right away."

"Tell me about him," said Dr. Young. "How did you hit it off?"

"He liked me. And I could tell he wanted to be with me. Michelle and Jenny met these other guys and we went back to their hotel and the one kept trying to touch me and grope me and Frederick told him to cool it. Without him there it would have been the same old thing of trying to be nice and polite and still make the nerd understand that he couldn't just paw all over me."

"So this Frederick protected you and that felt good?"

"Frederick's buff. That loser wasn't going to mess with him," said Violet.

"What else did you like about Frederick, Violet?"

"The chemistry. We had chemistry."

"Were you and Frederick intimate?"

Violet nodded.

"And you're okay with that?"

She nodded again.

"Violet, I don't want you to talk about anything you're not ready to talk about, but you seemed very disturbed when you called and said you had to see me," said Dr. Young. "I moved my schedule around and I'd hate to see us lose an opportunity to make progress. Are you following me?"

She had no one to blame for this one but herself. She should have ridden out her drug-induced guilt alone, let the crisis pass, as she had the sense and history to know that it would, but instead she had called Dr. Young and insisted on an appointment. Now, she had a dilemma. Violet remembered the flashes of light when the assholes had taken pictures. She blamed Michelle and Jenny for that. If she had known they were all going to stand around and watch she wouldn't have gone into the bedroom with him in the first place. He apologized later. It was the drugs. Frederick agreed that it was the drugs. So what. It wasn't the first time she'd given a couple of nerds a cheap thrill. Next time would be different. Next time would be romantic.

"I did a lot of blow," said Violet, "and got real low."

Dr. Young picked up his pen and made some notes. "And how does that make you feel?" he said.

Violet stared at him for a minute. He wore his short, brown hair combed down over his forehead in bangs. His head reminded her of an acorn. What part of the word *low* didn't he understand?

☙•❧

Later that night after her appointment with Dr. Young, Violet found Bobby in the dressing room at the Olympic, surrounded by books and papers, and listening to opera. "It's beautiful, isn't it?" he said. "Strauss. I'm trying to work on the libretto for *Salami*."

"Are you still mad at me?" said Violet.

"Dogs get mad," said Bobby. He tapped the front of his teeth with his pen and gazed down at his notebook. Then he hummed and waved the pen in the air like a baton. "Yes," he said. "That would work." Violet couldn't tell if he was really concentrating that hard or if this was the silent treatment, like Cheryl employed. Bobby looked up at her. "You said you'd never been to New York before and to disappear without a word. Hey, I had every right to be worried. I was responsible for you. What kind of friend would I be if I didn't give a shit? Is that what you want?" Bobby didn't give her a chance to answer. Now he shifted into one of his chatty moods.

"And it's my fault too, honey, because I'm having more trouble with the show than I thought. I started getting stressed in New York and by the time I landed in LA I was a total wreck. I convinced Dame Ethyl to move out here to be in the show and I've hired four other boys besides him and I don't have a decent libretto yet, no sets, and no music

"I need time, Violet. I'm in trouble. I probably took out my frustrations a little on you and I apologize."

"What's a libretto?" said Violet.

"Drag queens are funny. Especially, big ones. But they have to do funny things, say funny things. You know?"

"Bobby, what's a—"

"The story," said Bobby. "The libretto is the story.

"See I don't know if I should keep the story the same and simply make it a satire or if I should employ poetic conceits and make it an allegory with a sense of timeliness.

"Flo has agreed to give me a couple more weeks; I convinced her to let the guys do their best numbers in the meantime, sort of a musical revue. Dame Ethyl was hilarious wasn't she? That ought to bring the crowds in and after we're established, then we can do *Salami*."

"In that case, is it okay with you if I postpone coming to work for a while?" said Violet. Bobby stared at her without speaking. "Kent is already pissed at me because I've missed work."

"I thought you had it settled and that Kent was okay with you missing the weekend," said Bobby.

"I missed Monday—and I'm missing tonight too," said Violet.

"Well what does that matter if you're quitting? You know you look really tired. Where were you?" said Bobby. "You never did say."

"I'll tell you, but please don't tell Poppy. Let me tell him. Promise?"

"Sounds serious. Since when do I confide in Poppy?"

Should she tell Bobby? Poppy always said he was too old for her, and now she had met someone younger. So what was the problem? Things were working out. Right?

"I met a hunk," said Violet. "I mean, he's not just a hunk. He's gorgeous, but he's also considerate and smart and funny. He's from Europe, he's an actor, he's my age, and I am so hot for him, Bobby."

"You just met him? Honey, you're worse than Rosina in *The Barber of Seville*. In love after one serenade."

Violet wanted to tell Bobby all about Frederick. Well, not *all* about Frederick. Some things she couldn't tell. She certainly couldn't tell him about the details of the night in the hotel suite.

But she did tell him that in addition to acting, Frederick was a male dancer. And she told him that she had invited him to visit her in California. She decided to leave out the fact that she had already mailed Frederick an airline ticket.

৪৩৪৩৪৩ Nine: An Impressive Armada

WHEN DR. ZIEMAN COMPLETED the so-called uro-flowmetry (or piss test as Smelzkoff called it) he had made an appointment for yet a third test: an ultrasound of Smelzkoff's prostate. Smelzkoff sat across from him, listening while he spoke to the radiology unit on the telephone. The man used words like *nodule* and *abnormal* and then, *possible biopsy*. He also prescribed an antibiotic for Smelzkoff to prevent infection and told him he couldn't eat after four and couldn't drink any liquids after midnight. Then there was the prospect of the enema.

There had never been any prostate cancer in Smelzkoff's family, as far as he knew, but then he didn't know a whole lot about his family. After his mother died, his dad had left him and his half-brother in the care of their grandmother, which hadn't bothered Smelzkoff as much as it did his brother, who got into fights almost daily and then decided to capitalize on the rage and become a boxer. He had enjoyed a modicum of success for a few years after turning pro but at $500 a fight there was no way to make a decent living, considering the punishment one took, even in victory. Smelzkoff chased the thoughts of family from his head and returned to the more immediate situation: that of his health. Dr. Zieman also told him that African-Americans were particularly prone to prostate cancer. So what was the deal here? Family heredity not a problem and the last time he checked he was white. It seemed inconceivable that he might have it, but Dr. Zieman, a specialist after all, seemed to have charted an irreversible course.

The girl met Smelzkoff when he entered the hallway just off the waiting room lounge. "You are here for ultrasound and biopsy?" she said. Another accent. Had he become the target of some KGB plot? She smiled, with great enthusiasm it seemed to Smelzkoff, and he wondered if this was because it was Friday, or merely a strategy to settle him.

"*If* the biopsy is necessary," said Smelzkoff "Doesn't it depend on what you see?"

The girl, who wore glossy lipstick the color of plums, smiled again and nodded, but said nothing. No one, of all the other patients in the waiting room, was as young as he—or so it appeared. The girl led him down the corridor and pointed to a dressing room. "Remove all your clothing and put on the gown," she said, smiling as cordially as if he were only here to try on some new slacks and a shirt. "Then you will please come in this room." She pointed again.

Smelzkoff had followed the preparatory instructions about not eating or drinking and was surprised that he wasn't hungry since his body was devoid of food and waste. He fumbled with the gown, too small and oddly cut; he put his right arm in the sleeve opening and the left in the other side and realized there was yet a third hole. The front of his body was still exposed and he looked down at his crotch and noticed that the left side had more than a few gray hairs. That was a rather specific sign of the aging process—not that having ones prostate photographed wasn't dramatic enough evidence. The remaining hole in the gown was too small for his head and then it dawned on Smelzkoff that he could hold this whole ridiculous piece of cloth together if he inserted his right arm in the third hole. When he felt that the gown was secure he left the dressing cubicle and walked across the hall, where the girl waited in front of a computer monitor. She instructed him to lie on the examination table, and he watched as she loaded a syringe with fluid.

"What's that?"

"An antibiotic," said the girl. "For after the procedure."

"I've been taking pills, " said Smelzkoff.

"This is stronger," said the girl.

She told him to turn onto his left side, facing away, and he took a deep breath when he felt the probe being inserted. No physical discomfort, but his heart raced. She moved the probe around on his prostate, and he could hear a clicking sound from time to time as if she were taking snapshots and planning an album. Smelzkoff hadn't let himself think about what might happen to him if he had to have surgery; if the cancer was well established he supposed he would be impotent. He pictured himself on his back and Violet straddling him and staring down at his face and he felt like crying. What if he couldn't control himself and had to wear plastic underwear? As Smelzkoff's stomach groaned, he wildly considered expelling the probe and running from the examination room. His life was over.

"You have a very healthy prostate," said the girl, moving the probe again to a new position.

Smelzkoff had his back to her and tried to look over his shoulder at her but he couldn't get his face in the right position and beside the lights in the room were turned off. He tried to reconcile this information with his situation. What was it that had prompted Dr. Zieman to schedule the test? And exactly what had been abnormal?

"A very healthy prostate," she said. "It's not even enlarged."

Smelzkoff lay still in the darkness while the girl continued moving the probe inside him. "How much does this test cost?" said Smelzkoff "I have a thousand-dollar deductible."

"With the biopsy, it's about $800," she said. "You can sit up now. Your doctor will be here soon." She took a stack of negative-like photos, which the machine had produced, smiled at him once more, and left the room. Smelzkoff looked at the monitor: a view of his prostate was frozen on the screen. For all he could tell it might as well be a picture of an asteroid.

Smelzkoff was straightening his gown when Dr. Zieman shot into the room, with the girl and another man in tow. The doctor held the photos in his hand and wore a grim expression; his hair, an unruly mane, stuck out in all directions. He didn't acknowledge Smelzkoff; he put the photos down next to the computer and pulled on a latex glove. "Turn over on your side," he said to Smelzkoff, without looking at him.

Smelzkoff turned over obediently and Dr. Zieman plunged in with his finger and began to rake it back and forth over the surface of Smelzkoff's prostate. "It doesn't feel as firm on the right quadrant," he said, as if to the others in the room. And then under his breath, "That could be the architecture of his prostate." He continued his digital examination in an aggressive manner, as if mining for ore.

Smelzkoff placed the recent events relating to his prostate in chronological order and established that Dr. Zieman had scheduled this test even before receiving the results of the blood tests. "How did my blood work turn out?" he said.

"Your PSA was normal," said the doctor, and then after a pause, "but fifty percent of all prostate cancer is detected digitally."

"You said there was a nodule," said Smelzkoff "I heard you say nodule on the phone when you scheduled this test. Now you say 'it doesn't feel as firm.' How were my other results? When you stuck the tube up my—" Smelzkoff looked at the girl; she had her back to them and was studying the photos. The other man looked on silently.

"You retain a lot of urine in your bladder," said Doctor Zieman

"I was nervous with you watching. I could have forced it out."

"I don't want you to force it out."

"How much did I retain?"

The doctor sat in the chair and looked at Smelzkoff's file. "Eighty c.c.'s," he said.

"What's normal?"

"Anything under a hundred and fifty."

With his eyes locked on the doctor's, Smelzkoff sat for a moment, silently reviewing and assessing his situation.

"So my blood tests are normal, the pictures of my prostate look good, the extra tests came out okay, and you want to do this biopsy, which costs $800. How uncomfortable is this biopsy?"

"There will be some blood in your urine." Smelzkoff saw the girl look at the doctor and frown. "But I'd feel a lot better telling you that you had a negative biopsy." He looked over at the man who leaned against the wall at the doorway.

"You don't have to convince me," said the man.

Smelzkoff got off the examination table, stood up straight, and looked at the third man. "Who the hell are you?" said Smelzkoff.

The man first looked to his left and to his right as if to move to a new position and said, "I'm the director of Summit Medical Imaging."

"And you are here because?"

"I have to protect myself legally," said Dr. Zieman. "If you were to have—"

"If I refuse a test how does that make you liable?"

Dr. Zieman had shrunk down in his chair, and Smelzkoff took another step toward him. "I do this for a living," said the doctor, and Smelzkoff thought he saw the doctor flinch.

"Well it's my body and I say *No*," said Smelzkoff. He hadn't imagined it. Dr. Zieman flinched again.

"Very well," said Dr. Zieman, suddenly in the mood to accommodate. "I'll just put a note in your file that you refused the biopsy and—"

"Put whatever the hell you like in my file," said Smelzkoff, and to himself thought, I won't be back.

The doctor and the director left the room without a parting comment, and no sooner had the door closed behind them than the girl gave Smelzkoff her most exuberant smile yet. And a thumbs up too. "The test is very invasive," she said, shaking her head. "You can haf blood in urine for veeks. And no exercise for veeks. These doctors, sometimes vhen you haf good insurance—" She leaned back against the table and her uniform stretched tightly across her breasts. "No sex for two veeks, either," she said.

❧ • ❦

What a fool he'd been. The stores on Wilshire Boulevard gave him the idea of buying a gift for Violet. Even better: something from one of the ritzy stores on Rodeo Drive. But what? A sweater or a purse or a belt? Or lingerie. Or a dress? Yes. A dress that clung to her hips and revealed her nipples and breasts, a chocolate-brown dress with spaghetti straps that slipped off her shoulders. He got excited at the thought of her changing into or out of such a dress.

He had always been hopeless at women's gifts. He had gotten Carol a food processor for one of their anniversaries and had heard about his thoughtlessness every anniversary thereafter. Women's clothes, especially figuring out what size they wore, had always been a riddle. Then there was the nightmare of jewelry. Some necklaces were too old, some too young, and as far as bracelets went, girls only seemed to wear them on their ankles these days.

How many men his age would give up a testicle to sleep with someone like Violet? Plenty. What had he been thinking? It was about time he started treating her right. Sure, he'd been worried about his prostate. That idiot of a doctor had had him going. What was his agenda? What had he, Stanley Smelzkoff, expected? The man had chosen urology as a profession. Now really. What kind of a man decided, *Hey, I like putting my finger up a guy's butt hole? I'm going to be a urologist when I grow up*. The lunatic had him going for a while. But no longer.

Things were progressing on the job too; as much as he hated to admit it, he and the Deaconess were seeing eye-to-eye. She talked too much and didn't understand her place in the world, but at least he had to hand it to the old wench: she recognized that he'd done one Hell of a job on the strategy and wasn't afraid to say so. Smelzkoff could hardly wait until evening. After tonight no one would take his police skills and knowledge lightly.

He drove down Lincoln, turned west onto Washington, and accelerated. He didn't have to go on duty for another two hours. Violet hadn't called him; she and Bobby should have gotten back from New York late yesterday. He turned on Dell and drove to Linnie Canal and pulled into the graveled parking area behind Violet's house. Her car wasn't there, but it was too early for her to have gone to work and he thought that perhaps she had already started with school and was at class. Smelzkoff imagined her in a school uniform and smiled, and then he pictured her in a cheerleader skirt with no underpants. Inadvertently he put his hand down to his crotch and squeezed.

Up on the small porch he tried the door. Locked. He peeked in the window next to the door and he heard her cat meowing. Disappointment washed over him. He had hoped to find her in one of her little short slip things, and barefoot, so he could hold her pretty little feet and kiss her painted toenails. He imagined her lying back on the bed and extending her feet, one at a time, so he could massage her insteps and squeeze her ankles and rub her well-shaped calves. The table lamp glowed in the corner of the living room. The way she had left it when she went to New York. He heard the radio, too. He'd taught her these tricks to make people think someone was at home.

He got into the car and drove back toward Lincoln. Maybe Bobby knew where she was, assuming they weren't together. Come to think of it Bobby would be the perfect one to help him pick out something sexy for Violet; Bobby certainly knew more than enough about women's clothing to insure a good selection.

He parked at the curb and peered across the lawn and though he didn't see Bobby, he got out of the truck and walked up the driveway at the side of the house. He glanced in the living room window. The home entertainment center that Tom bought for Carol on her birthday covered the entire wall. What an egomaniac.

Smelzkoff started to push open the gate, but stopped when he heard a growl. He stood up on his toes and looked over the fence at the ridiculous-looking animal. The pooch barked and growled more energetically, and tried to jump too, but could only get its front paws an inch or two off the ground.

And then Bobby appeared at the back corner of the house. He hurried to the gate, took the mutt by the collar, pulled open the gate, and said, "Poppy, meet my Ginger. I brought her back from New York. She's a great watch dog."

"He looks fierce all right," said Smelzkoff.

"*She*, Poppy."

"I thought you didn't like labels," said Smelzkoff.

Smelzkoff followed his son around the side of the house to the backyard pool. The dog wasn't rushing him or anything, but it had fitful seizures of growling and barking. It lay down some distance away and when Smelzkoff sat in the deck chair next to Bobby, the dog quieted and then limped over to him to sniff at his shoes. Smelzkoff couldn't resist making an abrupt growl-like noise and snapping his jaws at her. This prompted an outburst of renewed barking. "Poppy, do you always have to intimidate everyone with your power?" said Bobby.

"It's a little joke. Okay? How can you stand yappy dogs? What are you doing anyway? Don't you have nothing better to do than sit around listen to that opera shit?"

"It's not opera. It's Mahler. *Das Lied von der Erde.* For your information I'm working night and day on my show to get it done. Is that why you came? To give me hard time?"

"I came to ask a favor. I need some help picking a gift for Violet."

"What's the occasion?"

"No occasion. I been neglecting her that's all. Do you know where she is?"

"Not right now. She stopped by the theater when she got home."

"Home from where?"

"New York."

"I thought you guys went together."

"We got separated and she took a later flight."

"A later flight?"

"Poppy, don't worry. She's a grown up. What kind of gift?"

"Clothes. A dress or something sexy. Separated?"

"When do you want to go? Now? I've got some time now."

"I can't go now. I'm going on duty. What's that mean? Separated. How in the Hell do you get separated? You were staying together, weren't you?"

"Please stop interrogating me. She went out with a couple of girl-friends. We made arrangements to fly home separately."

When they first started seeing each other Violet had disappeared for two or three days at a time. Smelzkoff had suspected that another man or drugs might be involved, but he had never pressed her for information. What he didn't know couldn't hurt him after all.

"What's your mother going to say about having a dog here to shit all over the place? Is it trained?"

The dog sat next to Bobby's chair, and he put out his hand to her. "Paw, Ginger," he said. The dog stuck out its paw and ducked its head slightly.

"She's probably got *roll-over* down from watching you," said Smelzkoff, with a smile.

Bobby looked at him and feigned a smile. "We really must continue these little father and son chats. They do so brighten my days," he said. He paused. "I still plan on getting my own place."

"Keep Nutmeg away from Ocean Front Walk tonight," said Poppy.

"*Ginger,*" said Bobby. "That's so funny, Poppy."

So Violet had disappeared in New York. A spice of a different sort, and Smelzkoff didn't like the smell of it.

•

The drivers of the animal control truck pulled into the Venice Boulevard parking lot and took the spot behind the beach maintenance shed, which Smelzkoff had marked off. Another truck, this one a smaller backup van, was already in place in the parking lot at the end of Washington. From his command post in the hexagon-shaped lifeguard tower, Smelzkoff alerted the rest of the team by radio that everything was *Go*. One didn't have to memorize the battle plans of Geronimo or Napoleon or Rommel to know that numbers (and the element of surprise) were essential. So he had read a West Point textbook or two about famous battle strategies. So what. Common sense, a strong sense of purpose, the desire to do what was right would be sufficient for them to prevail—with proper preparation.

Smelzkoff consulted his synchronized military wristwatch. "Minus two minutes and counting," he announced into the walkie-talkie. "Prepare to advance at eighteen hundred hours."

Secrecy too. Secrecy counted. He probably shouldn't have said anything to Bobby. He shouldn't have warned him. In the future he wouldn't be able too.

Cavalrymen on horseback were posted under the fishing pier at Washington, out of sight. He could barely see them even through binoculars, though it was still an hour until the sun set. The force of ten would move north along the water's edge in synch with the ten officers paired in five Sport Utility Vehicles on the beach and the ten cavalry cops on bicycle, who would advance on the boardwalk. The police car units were ready on Speedway Avenue as well. A force of twenty men was stationed on foot at the Venice Boulevard parking lot too.

The strategy, simply, involved sweeping the dogs and owners north to Venice Boulevard into the hands of the waiting foot patrolmen. The routes of escape would be cut off as they tightened the noose.

Two helicopters flew past, one at a slightly higher altitude, rattling the windows of the observation tower. It had rained earlier in the day and the skies hadn't cleared until three. Smelzkoff had worried that there would be a light turnout, but the owners and dogs were out in force, the more arrogant of them allowing their dogs to romp across the sand, and in and out of the surf. He moved the binoculars to the grassy area east of the bike path. A quick estimate told him there were at least forty dogs and owners, and he didn't see a single leash in use. All his efforts had led to this. No one listened. No one cared. They would reap what they had sowed.

Smelzkoff gripped the walkie-talkie. "Attention all units. Attention all units. Minus twenty and counting." He watched as the second hand swept forward. "Minus ten, nine, eight, seven, six," he said. Every hair on his neck, on his arms, on his body for that matter, stood at the ready. His skin prickled with excitement. Finally the moment he had waited for. "Attack," he yelled into the transmitter. And then thinking that attack might be a bit too aggressive, he said, "Proceed. All units proceed north to the target area." He saw the horses first, as they galloped out from under the pier, and then the Sport Utility Vehicles sped onto the sand from the Washington parking lot. He saw the bicycles on the boardwalk last and he radioed the helicopters to confirm that the officers on Speedway Avenue were in motion; after the confirmation came back, he focused on the dogs and their owners. The gangly, freckled woman who owned the freckled pointer named Cinnamon turned and stared in the direction of the advancing troops. Smelzkoff saw her mouth open as she yelled at the others and he watched as she excitedly began waving her arms. The word spread faster than a brush fire in Topanga Canyon, confirming to Smelzkoff the importance of surprise and speed. On signal the helicopters had begun flying in concentric circles over the area. "Do not attempt to leave the area," Smelzkoff said over the public address speaker mounted on the lifeguard tower. "Do not attempt to leave the area."

The force Smelzkoff had assembled moved north with great speed. The horses galloped in the surf, as the swell of the sea broke upon shore, further agitating the water and creating a hurricane of spray. The Sport Utility Vehicles left a storm of swirling sand and dust in their wake; the bicycle cops pumped the pedals of their bikes furiously, and sirens blared from the cruisers advancing on Speedway

Avenue. The owners scrambled for their leashes and tried in vain to fasten them on their dogs' collars before the force reached them, but they were no match for the battalion of trained soldiers, which Smelzkoff had assembled. He thought about the homo who had been robbed, and scanned the ground in an effort to spot him. "Dogs are our protection," the man had said. But they can't protect you from yourselves, thought Smelzkoff.

For the next few minutes so much happened so fast that Smelzkoff would have trouble later putting events in proper sequence for his written report. Several offenders jumped walls and took refuge in some of the ocean facing houses and apartments; about a half dozen were fast enough to bolt across Speedway before the units could intercept them and Smelzkoff assumed that they had crossed Pacific Avenue and disappeared among the canals. But all the others, thirty-one dog lovers, to be specific, were captured and taken to the animal control van in the Venice lot for processing. Ten or so stood defiantly and refused to run, refused even to budge and they ultimately had to be handcuffed and led with force to the truck.

Tickets were issued for all sorts of violations. *Dogs on sand, dogs on bike path, dogs without city licenses, dogs without proof of vaccination.* A couple of owners attempted to supply false information, claiming they were new to the area, but Smelzkoff, who had come down from the tower to supervise the citation process identified each and every one, shuffling through his stack of manila file folders until he located the proper one.

"According to my records Mr. Kaufman, you've lived here for seven years; your dog, Kimba, a Bull Mastiff is five years old and you've already been cited three times in the last year for having your animal on the beach." A pause, three beats to allow the man to reflect on things, and Smelzkoff said, "Any questions? Supplying false information to a police officer is grounds for arrest. You're going to need a lawyer."

"Where did you get my picture?" said the thin man, his jaw set in anger.

People were coming to the parking area in large numbers now to see what the commotion was all about. Seeing the horses and bikes and jeeps and cruisers all gathered together in the parking lot, Smelzkoff had to admit that he had marshaled one impressive armada. All they lacked were tanks. The invasion at Normandy hadn't been any better planned. It wasn't necessary to take most of the owners to the station; they were angry and in shock but too traumatized to protest to any great extent.

Smelzkoff wasn't sure, but he suspected that Gloria Deacon was who had leaked plans of their operation to the media. Almost every station sent a reporter and camera crew.

ഔഔഔ Ten: The Men Who Came To Dinner

T HE COMBINATION OF SAQUINIVAR with the other drugs, especially with the d4T, didn't sit well this night. He worked in his dressing room for a full hour after the others left and would have stayed later if it hadn't been for his stomach doing the fandango. He started to perspire too, on his way home at two in the morning; driving took concentration and perseverance, because his discomfort persisted. His New York doctor, Simon, had referred him to a friend from medical school, now practicing in LA, and had advised him not to delay getting in touch. Simon had scratched the name and number on the top sheet of a prescription pad, torn it off, and handed it to Bobby. "Dr. Phillip Manna," said Simon, "in North Hollywood. He's conducting several clinical trials that might enable you to reduce the cost of your medication. Phil is wonderfully wry. You two will hit it off."

Though Bobby had called Dr. Manna a few weeks earlier, to introduce himself, he hadn't as yet made an appointment to go in and actually meet with the man, and for that reason—and in view of the lateness of the hour he didn't consider calling him tonight, though he did for a moment think about going to the emergency room at Pacific Oaks Hospital. But then about halfway to the hospital, with all the windows of his mother's car open to keep the air circulating, he began to feel better and decided to continue on toward home and just get into bed as soon as possible.

He slept till ten-thirty on Wednesday morning, and felt well enough to go through his usual routine after he awoke, but he made a mental note to call Dr. Phil Manna later in the day—since his supply of prescribed medication was running low.

After he put on the coffee, he went into the front house to feed his mother's cockatiel, then came back to the guest house and got a plastic bag to take a by-now-frenzied Ginger out in front of the house to do her business. He picked up the morning newspaper from the middle of the driveway on his way back, then put on a recording of Wagner's *Parsifal*, poured himself a cup of coffee, and sat down in the sun to brush Ginger, who had started shedding again, to such an extent that he feared she might have the mange. It wasn't till after he had finished her grooming that he removed the rubber band and unfolded the morning edition of *The Los Angeles Times*. And it wasn't until after he read the article on the AIDS vaccine being approved for human testing (the article said that when the virus circulated through the blood it was protected by a shield similar to the retractable roof on a domed stadium, and how on earth did they find out such things?) that he turned to the *Metro* section and saw the picture of Poppy.

Seeing his father's glowering face surprised Bobby, to say the least, but the headline astonished him even more. *LAPD Veteran Responsible For Arrest of Thirty-one in Venice Canine Sweep*. The details horrified him. He had no idea his father disliked dogs so fervently. Surely even he must realize that there were more important issues for the police to be involved in. Next they'd be dragging jaywalkers into jail. Bobby would talk to his father about this, though he knew it wouldn't make a difference: nothing he'd ever said had made a difference with Poppy.

The phone rang; Bobby put down the newspaper and went to answer it. He hadn't been responding to the telephone; he simply waited till it stopped ringing and then checked for messages. But since Dame Ethyl was due to arrive by train at Union Station today he wanted to be sure that there weren't any last minute changes in plan. As it turned out it was Flo who wished to change things, and not Dame Ethyl. "My mother's coming in for a visit," said Flo, "and I don't have any room; just for a week, The Dame will have to stay with you."

Bobby stripped the bed in his mother's and Tom's bedroom. They weren't due back for months so playing host to The Dame shouldn't be a problem. Bobby didn't really want to call Greece, though he had a number in case of an emergency, because telephoning involved too many numbers and a muffled connection—and who knew if they were at home or not. And then there was the difference in time. After he hung up with Flo, he called Amtrak (not his mother in Greece) to verify that the California Zephyr would arrive on schedule.

At Union Station, Bobby found Dame Ethyl standing at the curb in front of the entrance, as instructed, surrounded by suitcases, trunks, and a dog kennel carrier. In his hand the transvestite held a leash, and sitting on the pavement beside him was the apparent, former-occupant of the kennel. Since the dog wore a red, plaid sweater, Bobby could not be certain of the animal's heritage, but a quick appraisal told him that the dog was more or less equal parts of Pomeranian, Chihuahua, and French Bulldog.

He had seen The Dame without makeup backstage, but this was the first time he'd see her dressed in men's clothing, and he looked less formidable as a man (Was it the width of the shoulders or his pear-shaped derriere?) though to be sure, Dame Ethyl was a large creature. And then there was the matter of the small passive dog.

Bobby got out of the car and walked around the back to greet Dame Ethyl. Then he looked down at the dog, which raised its eyes for a second to consider him then averted them again to watch a nearby group of Japanese tourists as they loaded their luggage onto a bus. The dog didn't stand, or bark, or wag its tail. There was no jumping, scratching, sniffing, licking, or humping. The dog, through its lack of animation, conveyed disinterest and boredom, perhaps even contempt.

The Dame peered down at his pet, then up at Bobby and said, "'I think Crab my dog be the sourest-natur'd dog that lives. My mother weeping, my father wailing, my sister crying, our maid howling, our cat wringing its hands, and all our house in a great perplexity, yet did not this cruel-hearted cur shed one tear. He is a stone, a very pebble stone, and has no more pity in him than a dog.'"

Bobby clapped his hands, bent at the waist to pet the dog once more, and laughed. "I adore him. Is his name really Crab?"

"When you get to know him, you'll see. I had no choice. It's the perfect name," said The Dame.

After Bobby had folded down the rear seat in his mother's station wagon to accommodate the luggage and they had packed up the car, The Dame wedged himself with Crab into the front seat, and Bobby got in behind the wheel. As they drove through downtown Los Angeles to the Santa Monica Freeway, everyone kept silent. When Bobby glanced over, The Dame was smiling but Crab, who sat on his master's lap, looked as bemused as ever.

"I met a simply tragic, fat, prepubescent boy in the dining car. He slipped away from his mum to have a second breakfast of Coco Puffs and waffles with chocolate chips; he was forever turning around and craning his neck to make sure she hadn't followed him; he fidgeted and picked at his arse between bites during the entire meal. He certainly was interested in me. Mark my word that kid will turn out to be a trannie."

On the freeway Bobby worried about how to explain The Dame if his father stopped by the house. He could almost hear him. Who in blazes is this? Then Bobby chastised himself for caring. After all, he wasn't a child any longer.

∾•∿

As it turned out Poppy didn't come to the house until two days later, and Bobby had already taken The Dame to his voice lesson in Culver City. He thought it would be a good thing to arrange for coaching, after having struck up a conversation with a man at Abbot's Habit coffee shop, who as it turned out had graduated from the Indiana University School of Music and taught voice in his spare time.

"What's in blazes is this?" said Poppy.

"Poppy, meet Crab," said Bobby. "He belongs to a friend. I'm dog-sitting."

The dog had curled up on the chaise lounge that Poppy usually sat in when he visited and didn't stir despite the fact that the tall man loomed over him.

"Where's the cripple?"

"If you mean Ginger, she's on my bed. Sleeping."

"Ugh," said Poppy. "It makes my skin crawl."

Bobby sat at the glass cabana table poring over sheet music and jotting down lyrics. He ignored the cheeky comments and had decided that this wouldn't be a good time to bring up his father's newfound notoriety when Poppy said, "Did you see my picture in the paper?"

"Did you know that when Oscar Wilde first wrote *Salome* it was considered too vile to be performed in London? It was actually first produced in Paris," said Bobby.

Bobby felt his father's eyes on him, but didn't look up. Instead he hummed a few bars of the music, erased a word or two, and scratched his head as if deep in thought.

"Salome of the Bible?" said Poppy. "The dance of the seven veils? That Oscar Wilde?" said Poppy, his voice tinged with irritation.

Bobby looked up. "Very good. Salome was just a girl, dancing a striptease for a man old enough to be her father. Well in this case he even was her stepfather. Almost sounds like you and Violet, doesn't it?" Bobby smiled broadly and stuck out his chin.

"No it does not. Violet is thirty. She's old enough to know what she wants. And every one says I can pass for forty. Let's change the subject."

"You may have to accept it, Poppy. Violet is a bit of a grisette."

"Did you see my picture in the *Times* or not?"

Bobby nodded.

"I thought you might want to share in my victory," said Poppy. "Come out front I want to show you something."

Poppy smiled, and Bobby stacked the sheets of music, pushed them to the center of the table, and placed a rock on top to keep them from blowing away, then stood and followed his father, who had turned to make sure that he was coming. Ginger suddenly emerged from the bedroom, which prompted Crab to jump down from the chaise and shake himself. Single file the two men and two dogs walked alongside the house, through the gate, and across the driveway to the street. In a flourish of theatricality, Poppy made a sweeping gesture toward the giant Jeep-like vehicle parked at the curb.

"My new Hummer," said Poppy. "For a job well done. Just wait till your mother and that asshole husband of hers sees it."

Bobby stared without comment at the black and white behemoth: the thing was wide enough to span two lanes of traffic and the tires could support a bulldozer in a swamp. The Los Angeles city seal was emblazoned on the front door and just above it in two lines, one above the other, the caption: *General Smelzkoff. I Serve and Protect.* Bobby had seen a few of these military trucks on the highway before and was aware of their growing popularity among civilians, especially civilians who wished to make a statement about wealth and virility, but was this leviathan really necessary to control the city's population of dogs?

"I'm speechless," said Bobby.

Ginger sat next to Bobby smelling the air in the direction of Poppy, who had gone to the truck to wipe a smudge of dirt off the front fender with his handkerchief. Crab approached the truck, stood next to Poppy, and sniffed the tire; then raised his leg and pissed a stream so high and so strong that it not only doused the surface of the huge tire but it also splattered both of Poppy's boots.

≈•≪

Bobby and Dame Ethyl stood over the table in the center of the stage; Bobby unrolled the sketches of the set and spread them out on the surface. "These aren't final, but they capture the feeling I want to evoke. Sort of an industrial plant feeling, like our hero John the Baptist has been sentenced to work in a sewage treatment plant for his crimes."

"What are his crimes?" said The Dame.

"I don't know yet," said Bobby, with a frown. "Preaching against the government, protesting something, I think. We'll have smoke stacks and metal catwalks in the rear. Turbines and generators here." He indicated on the drawings with his index finger. "A crow's nest where Herod oversees things will be up here. He'll come down the stairway to watch the dance. We'll have a circular pool stage right, with a giant stirring mechanism and a bridge that spans it. In the final scene the soldiers, or sewage plant workers, will shove you into the sewage to your death, you know, instead of crushing you under their shields. We'll have a cloud of steam and fog and the opera will end."

"Sweet thing, you've got a lot of work to do," said The Dame.

"Don't I know it," said Bobby. "Flo has been very generous with allowing me more time and since his mother is visiting he's busy entertaining "

"And in the meantime Flo's not losing money. We had at least three hundred last night for the revue. They really seemed to like me."

"Are you kidding, they loved you. And they're going to go crazy for *Salami*. But it's important to make this production contemporary. That's what's holding me up. Like setting *Richard III* in the 1930's. Instead of simply being a history lesson, the universal themes resonate more powerfully. It forces people to see the morality of the play. We need an issue that is current. Like abortion versus right to life, or gays in the military—or police brutality. I wonder…"

"Excuse me," said Dame Ethyl, "I think your fragile flower friend is trying to get your attention." He indicated with a nod of the head to the wings at stage left, where Violet stood.

"So why are you standing over there like some backstage groupie?" said Bobby. And then he saw the beefy boy with her.

"You look busy—but I want you to meet my friend, Frederick," said Violet. She took hold of the boy's arm, led him from the wings on stage and to the table, and attempted to make introductions. But Frederick didn't suffer from shyness; he broke from her grasp, ducked his head to give Bobby a playful, one-two jab in the gut with his fists, and said, "Violet has told me much about you. She has told me that you are producing a show. I myself am an actor. I have been living in New York, studying the Stanislavsky method at the present. Perhaps you have a good part for me?" He lurched forward suddenly and bear-hugged Bobby and gave him a loud, smacking kiss on the neck. Then he pushed back, but now gripping Bobby's thin, upper arms with his large hands. "I am very happy indeed to make your acquaintance," said Frederick, his smile wider than ever.

For his part Bobby didn't know whether to laugh or run to his dressing room to masturbate. Frederick, dressed in body-hugging spandex from his neck to his feet, had the most amazing build he had seen on a man (though Bobby wasn't ordinarily into physiques) and his face framed with that thick black hair and sharp blue eyes was handsome and chiseled enough to grace a billboard on Times Square. But the personality and his manner of dress. And what was the deal with the steel-tipped cowboy boots?

"Hello," said The Dame. "I don't believe we've met. I'm Chopped Liver." He offered his hand and stood. The Dame and Frederick were the same height, but that was where the resemblance stopped; Frederick was all shoulders and chest and arms and legs, and The Dame carried the bulk of her weight in her mid-section.

Violet stood silently watching while The Dame teased Frederick (about his biceps, his blue eyes, his accent) and Frederick pretended to be embarrassed at the flattery. Violet's friend had let go of Bobby and, after shaking hands with The Dame, had slapped him on the shoulder and said "You're are a very big guy," he said. Dame Ethyl in return had smacked him back harder and then squeezed both of Frederick pectorals in his hands and said, "So are you, I'll wager. So are you."

Bobby looked Frederick up and down and decided that, in spite of the boy's obviousness, there was an air of sincerity and grace about him. The boy liked people—and certainly didn't appear to be prejudiced.

"Violet says you are a dancer, too," said Bobby.

Frederick stopped speaking in mid-sentence and turned once more to Bobby. "I can dance any way you like. He pulled his clinging shirt out of his tights and started to peel it off. "Naked. I can dance for you naked."

"That's all right. I'm not sure about your costume yet. But you won't be wearing much. Violet, Dame Ethyl, I think we have our John the Baptist. I want you and The Dame to start rehearsing together right away. How soon can you start?"

"Now. I start now," said Frederick. He let out a series of whoops and warlike screams and began to jump in the air and spin around, choreography of jerks, twists, lunges, gyrations, and pelvis thrusts. He stopped, faced the theater seating, and began to snap his fingers and slink forward. "Vhen you are jet, you are jet all the vay, from your first cee-garette," he sang. Then as abruptly as he had started, he stopped, took Violet in his arms and said, "Thanks, Baby. Tell Booby. He von't regret using me in show. I vill make zee people come."

"Bobby, please. Not Booby. And that won't be necessary," said Bobby, "but sexy is good."

"Can I talk to you?" said Violet to Bobby.

What was it about this girl? Bobby suddenly felt like taking her in his arms to reassure her. To reassure her about what? He knew next to nothing about her, only the superficial: she of course looked beautiful and as strange it sounded in a profession where people were unlikely to say, *She's got class*, Violet did have class. But the only thing aggressive about her was her dancing; none of that audaciousness or boldness carried over to her behavior off-stage, and she seemed bent on surrounding herself with strong, if not overbearing, people.

He put his arm around her. "Where have you been? I've missed you," he said.

Violet blushed. "Oh, here and there," she said.

"Let's go in my dressing room," said Bobby.

The dressing room had become more a storage room than a place where someone could apply make-up or change clothes. Books on opera, old record albums, CD's, drawings, fabric swatches, make-up kits, wigs, dresses, portable drink coolers, old tires, pieces of broken furniture, and even an old commode had been dragged into the room and referenced for possible use in the production now in the making.

"Pull up a toilet and have a seat," said Bobby.

"Why do men always leave the lid up?" said Violet.

"Now, what's the crisis? I can tell. You're quieter than usual."

"I haven't seen Poppy in a week. He keeps coming over at my house and leaving me notes but I'm working all the time and missing him."

"So you haven't told him about Frederick?"

Violet frowned for half a second, then quickly smiled. "Hunk or punk?" "What do you think?"

"Hunk, I think. But I always have my guard up around his kind."

"I don't understand."

"The provocative flirt type," said Bobby. "I keep my distance."

"How much distance? Cause I need a favor," said Violet.

"Shoot."

"Until I talk to Poppy, could Frederick stay with you? It could be like part of the payment for him being in the opera."

"Does he have a dog?" said Bobby.

ಐಐಐ Eleven: Command Performance

FTER VIOLET LEFT FREDERICK behind at Flo's Olympic Theater, with Bobby and The Dame, she drove west to Santa Monica. Initially she planned to stop at the Third Street Promenade to buy one pair of shoes, but as so often happened she went home loaded with boxes and shopping bags. It all started innocently enough. The first pair of shoes, squared heels and squared toes, made her salivate and then her eyes grew larger when she saw the Latex dress in the window of the store next door. When she wore the dress and the shoes together, Frederick would be the one drooling. A few doors down was a second dress and a second pair of shoes (Italian designers of course) and she couldn't resist a silk shirt and slacks and a linen jacket for Frederick. Bobby was right, when he said, "The boy is a stud, but the clothes say dud." Those were her words, not Bobby's, but that's what he had meant. After four dresses, six pairs of shoes, six tee shirts, two pairs of shorts, a few more outfits for Frederick, and some new makeup, she had just enough time to get home and change for work, and then she drove past the thrift shop on Pacific Avenue. She only had to circle the block once to find an open meter and she just happened to have a quarter.

Capri pants, open-toed high heels, and a polyester blouse with raglan sleeves and then she saw the rack of bowling shirts and picked one out for Bobby.

She trusted Bobby with Frederick, but The Dame had been bold enough to actually say, "I'm going to be all over you Freddie, like a cheap suit." Not that The Dame's loudmouthed infatuation would lead to anything, but certain gays made Violet nervous. Not the virtuous types like Bobby, but those desperate drag queens, who were so taste-less and aggressive. Their motto: *Try, try again if at first you don't succeed.*

Once parked in her gravel-covered space, it took three trips for her to get all the boxes and shopping bags in the house leaving no time to put things away. She lined the booty up against the bedroom wall. Poppy hadn't been by, or at least he hadn't left a note, for two days now. For a week she had come home to find a message taped against the front door and there were a few phone messages too, but she'd been so busy that she hadn't been able to get back to him. Well it was more than just being busy, wasn't it?

She turned the television on and stepped into her shower and when she finished and stepped back out to dry she heard Poppy's voice. At first she imagined that he was inside her house and then she realized his voice was coming from the television. A local talk show: "Make Way For L.A."

"The majority of the people in our fair city are sick and tired of tramping in dog crap everytime they try to take a walk," said Poppy.

The interviewer and host, a woman with short, auburn hair and a radical nose job, leaned back. "But critics say the effort is overblown and too costly," she said.

"Then how much should we spend to keep a vicious Pit Bull from tearing an arm off a small child?" The lights in the television studio glinted off Poppy's sunglasses.

"Has that happened?" said the hostess, aghast.

"You betcha. And one ripped into one of our police horses too," said Poppy.

"How long do you anticipate that such strict enforcement efforts will be necessary?" said the hostess.

"Until each and every dog owner in the city gets the message and starts to respect the rights of all citizens," said Poppy.

"Ladies, our guest today has been Officer Stanley Smelzkoff, General Smelzkoff as he's known in the department, and I just have one request before we go to a commercial break." She leaned forward. "Could you take off those sunglasses so we can see your eyes? I'm told you have the most gorgeous blue eyes." The audience applauded, and Poppy removed the mirrored lens, looked directly into the camera, and smiled as if he'd just won at keno during breakfast at Denny's in Stateline, Nevada.

☙•❧

Violet swerved into a parking spot, jumped from her car, and ran to the back door of Fantasy. No sooner had she pulled open the door and crossed the threshold when she heard Kent's voice. "We ain't running no fucking sorority here," he said. "This is a business establishment and we need the fucking employees to get here on fucking time"

"Sorry, Kent, but traffic was a bitch," said Violet.

"Think how fortunate you are to have two strong legs," he said. "Girls in China go to bed with broken legs and can't dance."

Backstage no less than three girls mentioned Kent to Violet. "If you ask me he's nothing but trouble," said the first. "He's a freak," said the second. "You need to be careful." "If I were you I'd get that cop boyfriend to stop by on a regular basis again. Honey, you need to send a message. Remember what happened to Tess."

The crowd, a typical early-afternoon bunch of layovers from LAX, out of work losers, and nightshift laborers, sat scattered through out the club nursing non-alcoholic beverages. Often when Violet danced she was aware of Kent lurking in the murky shadows at the edge of the room. After talking to the other girls backstage today she had chosen a costume of roman sandals and feathered angel wings, because she knew that the outfit was a favorite of his. At first, after she came on stage, she saw him standing by the horseshoe-shaped bar at the rear, then in the balcony looking down, and finally settled in a spot right at the edge of the stage. Violet turned her back on him and grabbed the brass pole with both hands and stuck her ass out in the direction of his face. She flipped back her head and began sliding her hands up and down the pole in a pumping motion and resolved, during this command per-formance, that she needed to talk to Poppy as soon as possible. But not about Frederick. Not just yet.

❧•❧

As soon as her shift ended and Violet had changed she hurried to the back exit of the club. Kent stood waiting at the door; his reddened face contorted and his pupils were dilated. Most everyone at Fantasy did cocaine and Ecstasy, but Kent was the one who others pointed to as having a problem. He took hold of her arm and said something about her being in an awful hurry but she twisted loose and replied, "I'm late, Kent. See you tomorrow."

She saw his headlights in her rear view mirror; he made no at-tempt to disguise the fact that he was following her. Kent was aggressive enough, but under the influence of uppers he was like Alice on poison mushrooms. Violet turned left on Motor, and Kent turned left. She turned right on Venice, and he turned right. He knew her address so even if she did manage to lose him, he might show up at her door. She continued north on Dell, exited the canals, took a roundabout route to Poppy's house, and parked in back. She watched to make sure that Kent's headlights were no longer visible before she got out of her car.

The lights were off in the back bedroom so she walked around to the front and went up onto the porch. She really didn't know what to expect; Poppy's moods were unpredictable to say the least. The living room was dark as well, but she saw the flicker of his television and the back of his head at the end of the sofa.

She tapped on the window. "I was beginning to think I'd seen the last of you," said Poppy, when he opened the door.

Violet said she'd been working extra long hours and shifts because she'd overspent in New York, though of course she hadn't spent any more than she did during any other similar period.

He motioned to the chair and sat back down on his sofa, but she chose to sit next to him. She scratched the nape of his neck with her fingernails and asked him if he'd missed her. "I came looking for you, didn't I?" he said.

"You could have come to Fantasy," said Violet.

"I been busy. Ain't you seen? I been in the papers and on TV."

"I saw you with that funny looking woman with the red hat," said Violet.

"I'm keeping clippings. Want to see?"

"Why should I want to see clippings when the real thing is sitting next to me?" Violet put her hand in Poppy's crotch and found his penis and pressed and rubbed until it began to stiffen. Then she put her leg across and straddled him and stuck her tongue in his mouth.

Poppy held her head and caressed her hair. He seemed more intent on kissing her than hurrying things along. Something was different. The tenderness that had been lacking of late consumed her with feeling—feeling that she had believed no longer possible with Poppy. She could tell from his breath that he hadn't been drinking beer, and she had refused drugs at the club. She was enjoying what Dr. Young referred to as sober sex.

A sliver of sunlight came through the east-facing window of Poppy's bedroom. Poppy had already gone to work, and Violet stretched out her arm and placed the palm of her hand on the sheets where he had slept. His body left an indentation, not quite in the middle of the bed, but somewhat closer to the side that afforded him quick and easy access to the bathroom.

She stretched and yawned, feeling a little like Scarlet O'Hara on the morning after Rhett had carried her up the flight of stairs to the mansion bedroom—although in this case she'd been the one to do the carrying, not literally of course, but practically speaking she had as usual been the aggressor. Not that it mattered. Last night had been a shock. Tenderness and affection marked their lovemaking in a way that she had experienced too seldom in her life.

In the kitchen she found the coffee on and a note from Poppy: *Help yourself to orange juice and mocha java. I bought cereal for you. In the cabinet above the fridge. I'll try to stop by the club tonight. Love, Poppy.*

Love. Poppy had never said or written such a thing. And then she thought about Frederick. She looked up at the clock above the window of the kitchen; almost ten and she hadn't checked her messages.

❧•❧

No one was in Bobby's backyard, except for Ginger and Crab. Both dogs came out of his room to greet her when they heard her open the side gate. Violet peered into his room in the guesthouse. Bobby's bed had been made; there was a round dent in the center of the spread and an accumulation of reddish brown and yellow dog hair where the dogs had made their nest. She went to check the master bedroom, where The Dame slept, but she couldn't see through the French doors because the drapes were closed. Frederick had probably slept in the front main house too.

He had left a message on her voice mail at midnight, saying they were still at Flo's working and that he'd call her when they got back to Venice but he had never called a second time. Violet left the shirt she had bought for Bobby and the clothes for Frederick in Bobby's room at the foot of the bed and went to her Mustang to make the journey into Hollywood. The morning fog gradually disappeared as she drove east and the temperature climbed as well. Violet kept the radio turned off and contemplated her new predicament, trying hard to come up with a solution.

The amount of activity at the theater surprised her. No less than four carpenters (Violet recognized one of them: a drag queen named Sally Monella, hired early on by Bobby for the show) were involved in building the set. The sound of table saws and drills screamed through wood, hammers beat out a steady percussive rhythm, and soaring occasionally above the din, the music and voices rehearsing the opera.

"Violet," said Bobby. "We've got our Herod. A friend of Frederick's. He's been living in West Hollywood. They danced together in New York. Just wait till you see him. He's a competition bodybuilder and wants to be a professional wrestler." Bobby laughed and whispered in Violet's ear. "Two hundred eighty pounds and only five foot nine. His thighs rub together when he walks and he's the color of a tangerine."

"Where is he?" said Violet.

"He and Freddie went to pick up lunch."

"How come a bodybuilder?" said Violet.

"Cause they're funny," said Bobby. "And, it just feels right. He says he studied medicine at Harvard."

"Can he sing?"

"Men's chorus at Harvard. Am I lucky, or what?"

Well, yes, thought Violet. Bobby was lucky. And like Cheryl used to say: "Sometimes it's better to be lucky than good."

"Are you ready to start work yet?" said Bobby.

"I have to ask you something before Frederick gets back," said Violet.

Bobby looked at her now, his thumbs hooked in his front pockets. "Shoot," he said.

"I haven't had a chance to see Poppy yet. Can Frederick stay with you a while longer?"

Bobby grimaced, took out his Chap Stick, and coated his lips. "Maybe he can stay with his friend Rex." Violet shrugged. "Our Herod," said Bobby.

ဆဝဆဝဆဝ Twelve: A Little Night Music

D URING THE LAST TWO WEEKS, Smelzkoff had planned and executed six canine sweeps along the Venice beachfront. Hundreds of arrests had been made; dozens of citations had been issued. Real results had been achieved. In some cases, where dog owners had been particularly negligent, (no license, no distemper or rabies shots, no leash in possession) their animals had been confiscated and taken to the pound.

All of the individual battles had involved cavalry (on horseback and on bicycle), foot soldiers, troops in cruisers, in sport utility vehicles, using helicopter backup, and in an ironic twist, with the use of a K-9 unit. This, in one instance, had led to a ferocious dogfight when the attending officer unleashed his German shepherd and allowed it to attack a mouthy woman's fox terrier. By the time Smelzkoff could jump from his Hummer and assist in pulling apart the two snarling animals there was a great deal of blood and enough fur in the air to make a rug.

Gloria Deacon continued to arrange for media coverage: Smelzkoff had appeared on half a dozen television talk shows already and details were being finalized for a five-minute slot on "Regis and Kelly". The Deaconess had appeared with him on a few of the early shows, but she had unfailingly allowed him to have most of the credit and hadn't hogged the spotlight. When one hostess brought up Deacon's choice of a career over family and pointedly asked if she had ever regretted not having raised children, Gloria Deacon seemed at a momentary loss for words, but she recovered quickly and said, "Who knows, if The General had been around when I was a girl, I might not have chosen to study law and then go into politics." While the audience whistled and applauded her response, he blushed.

But really, he did appreciate her low profile. Even strangers in Gold's recognized him now, and people approached him on the street daily to tell him that they had seen him, or at least his picture, on television, and only once or twice did they ask about the woman with him, in the red hat. Of course with some he wasn't famous, but infamous. One lady, her face a tangle of wiry, gray hair and moles, had approached him and said, "Are you that General fellah, that's locking up the dogs?" And when he replied, "Yes, I'm The General," she had spit on his badge, turned, and walked away. Still, except for dog owners who lived in Venice, people often approved of the pilot program, "The War on Dogs", as they now referred to it in the media. The local stations devoted ten minutes each evening to a summary of events, with theme music from *The Planets* by Gustaf Holst, and there was even talk in city council of extending dog control efforts to greater Los Angeles. Like Gloria Deacon said, "Don't think that city officials have overlooked the fact that some dog owners, in places like Griffith Park and Bronson Canyon, have had the audacity to let their pets roam off lead because of the lack of visible law enforcement officials."

In Santa Monica they were considering launching their own version of The War. Statistics pointed to a downturn in serious crime, and as a result, there were enough idle police in the force to concentrate on the so-called lesser or victimless crimes. In Santa Monica, the self-proclaimed jewel on the ocean, jaywalking had been moved to a higher priority and it wasn't uncommon for the police to issue citations and, in some cases, to take people to jail. A friend on that force (Smelzkoff knew him from the gym) told him that city officials were so hard on jaywalkers they had taken a woman's baby, put it in the custody of a matron, then handcuffed the woman and taken her to jail.

The last evening sweep in Venice had nabbed three additional owners and their dogs; for two days now General Smelzkoff hadn't seen a single animal off leash, but that didn't mean that it was time to relax efforts. One didn't win the war by celebrating a few battles. Relax and one might allow the enemy to form a resistance movement. Relax and they might cut telephone lines or barricade the beaches. Relax and they might bring in reinforcements. Relax and they might start to publish underground newspapers. No, General Stanley Smelzkoff would not relax. It was time to attack on a different front.

After Violet disappeared, and before she reappeared, he hadn't slept well. One night at three A.M. he took a walk on the beach, and that was how he knew that some dog lovers allowed their pets to swim in the ocean under the camouflage of darkness. Being off-duty, he hadn't made any arrests (he hadn't been in uniform), but he had decided then and there that the time for a night raid would come. Gloria Deacon told the media that Venice was the number-two tourist attraction in Southern California and that it was her mission to see that it became number-one. "I'm for family values, and families value a safe environment. There is no room for free-ranging dogs, day or night."

In addition to searchlights, the helicopter had been outfitted with an infrared photography system; thus, even on a moonless and starless night, it would be possible to pinpoint the exact location of dogs and owners on the beachfront.

With Violet back, and things on the job going so well, with his prostate firm and healthy, he had only one regret: that the news of his heroics most probably hadn't reached Greece. Carol and Tom weren't due back, and Smelzkoff didn't miss them, but even though he knew they'd learn eventually of his successes, it wasn't the same after the fact.

Oh, and then there was the matter of his own son: the breach between them was wider than ever. Bobby had practically laughed at his Hummer. What kind of a man would laugh at a Hummer? The answer was all too obvious. And after the way he had reached out to his son. As far as he was concerned, if Bobby had any feelings for his old man he would just have to make an effort from now on, because Smelzkoff resolved not to stop by Carol's house to visit Bobby again.

⇛•⇜

Two A.M. No moon. The air warm and still. Smelzkoff sat in the cockpit of the Hummer, engine idling, parked in the beach maintenance lot. He leaned back against the headrest and listened to the crackling police radio. It had taken a great deal of restraint not to tell Violet. He left Fantasy Mansion at eleven-thirty, after she danced, and after they sipped a ginger ale together, without being specific, saying only that he had to go by precinct headquarters to clean up some paper work. "I may not be home until late," he said. "Go on home and I'll come to your place after I get off. The change of scenery will do us good. And don't let me find you in bed with anyone—except for your teddy bear," he said, and laughed.

"You're my teddy bear," Violet had said, and leaned into him, giving him an instant erection.

He took a deep breath, and tried to respond with a witty remark, but the best he could manage was, "That's all I am to you? A toy?"

"You better not be too tired to play when you get home," said Violet.

The air on the beach was still, and the surf had died down. Sometimes when the waves hit the shore they could be heard for blocks, but tonight they merely lapped, sluggishly, at the sand. Smelzkoff bit the inside of his cheek. Sometimes he fantasized about leaving on his uniform and boots and pulling back the covers to expose Violet while she slept. He often masturbated while imagining her stirring, waking, and then crawling, naked, over to the side of the bed, where he stood with his hands on his hips. In his daydream she unzipped his fly and took him in her mouth.

"General," the radio sputtered and Smelzkoff sat forward with a start. "Two pedestrians approaching the beach at Twenty-fifth Avenue, with canines. Stand by."

"I read you," said Smelzkoff. "Signal the chopper. All units in place."

There was no margin for error with a smaller force, even though for this particular operation they were using several unmarked cars. Smelzkoff drove across the parking lot to the edge of the sand with his headlights off.

"This is unit 6701. They're crossing the grass and the bike path. They're on the sand. No more light. We're losing them."

"Attention all units," said Smelzkoff. "Take up your positions on Speedway Avenue and in the parking lots. Let's give them five minutes. Get the chopper down here now!"

Immediately Smelzkoff heard the thwok-thwok-thwok-thwok of the helicopter approaching from the north, and he drove onto the sand and inched forward until he was parallel with Twenty-first Avenue. It was eerily dark and instinctively he wished to see further ahead, but at the same time he realized that the blackness was what had lured the culprits onto the beach in the first place. He saw the lights of the Venice fishing pier in the distance, but in the area between him and the pier nothing was revealed.

"Units at Washington, stand by," said Smelzkoff. The helicopter was directly overhead now and the roar of the engine made it necessary to yell his commands. "Chopper, give me floods." For a minute he almost said something about seeing Charlie, but that would have been really stupid since he'd never even been to Vietnam. He'd been given a deferment at the police academy

The helicopter came down low; the beam of its searchlight darted in circular sweeps of the sand. "We've got them on the infra red," said the officer in the chopper. "They've seen us, but I don't think they realize we're after them. Wait a minute. They're onto us. They're trying to get the dogs out of the water."

Smelzkoff turned on his own lights and his siren now and sped across the sand. He remembered the television coverage of the attack on Iraq; the way tanks catapulted over dunes and flew through the air, and he wished it were winter on the beach, when they piled the sand high in one continuous berm, to protect the houses onshore. As it was he made one small, diving plunge, where the sand crested about twenty yards from the surf, and raced along at the water's edge. His headlights and running lights and floodlights, combined with those of the heli-copter, so low it had created a sandstorm, lit the beach like Las Vegas. "We've got them on infra red," said the chopper officer, adjusting the beam of his searchlight to expose them. "They've got the dogs back on leash and they're running east toward the grass." And then Smelzkoff saw them too. One man and one woman and two dogs—a very large woman in an ankle-length dress. Her size and her clothing slowed her flight, and the man had run a considerable distance out in front of her. Smelzkoff took up his microphone and announced on his loud speaker, "This is the police. Do not try to run. Stay where you are."

The helicopter hovered low overhead: its inverted funnel of light shined with intensity down onto the lawbreakers; its rotor churned the air and swirled the sand. In seconds the entire police force, except for the eight officers in the four unmarked cars which could not drive on the sand without getting stuck, arrived on the scene as well, and com-ing as they had from three directions the ten police cruisers now completed the circle around the man and the woman. (Smelzkoff had sped south and turned east, so that he faced them from the water.) So much light was directed on to the two captives from above and below, that every inch of them, save the soles of their bare feet, was exposed.

Smelzkoff jumped from his vehicle, his heart pounding, and stood next to his Hummer, taking it all in. What a magnificent sight; that's all there was to it. The beach was lit better than the Hollywood Bowl, and with the roar of the helicopter, police car doors slamming, men crouched, pistols drawn and yelling, the screams of the woman, and her pathetic efforts to hold her dress down in the hurricane of wind, the dogs' mouths opening and closing in inaudible barks, straining at their leashes (as if two such comical looking animals could actually defend themselves or anybody else), the man shaking his fist in the air, well it was music to his ears, worthy of an episode of *COPS*, and he of all the people involved was the one who had made it happen. He was just about to move forward and confront the two when he realized that he had an erection so swollen, so solid and blood engorged that he dare not get into the stadium of light lest it be revealed to everyone.

⇛•⇚

It should've been a simple collar. Two citations to write and then everyone, all twenty-two police officers, the two civilians, and the two dogs could go home and go to bed. Most of the other cops did leave. Just Officers Johnson and Perez stayed behind with Smelzkoff. They put the dogs in the back of the Cherokee and waited for The General to finish with his interrogation of the captives. If Smelzkoff had known he would have told Johnson and Perez to take off as well. "I'll handle things from here on," he could have said. Should have, could have, would have. Smelzkoff sat in his Hummer, parked behind his house, with his forehead resting on the steering wheel.

It was messy from the moment the two were led off the sand to the street and put in the back of his vehicle. During the questioning, the woman, if that's what she really was, refused to show any identification, saying only that she was a singer from New York and that her name was Dame Ethyl Chloride. "Certainly, my dog's not licensed in California," she said. "I just recently arrived in your enchanting city." Well, maybe General Stanley Smelzkoff wasn't the best-traveled man in the world, but he sure as Hell knew an English accent when he heard one. "New York, eh?" said Smelzkoff. The buff man with her, dressed only in one of those skimpy European-style swimsuits, claimed also to be from New York, but his accent sounded just like Arnold's and if

Smelzkoff remembered correctly he was from Germany or Serbia or someplace like that.

"Frederick Lieder. My name ist Frederick Lieder. It's not my dog," he said. "Zee dog belongs to *fruende*."

"So where are you two staying while you're here in our," Smelzkoff paused, "enchanting city?"

And at the exact same moment the two said: "2240 Superior Court in Venice." Smelzkoff's head snapped around to peer at them in the back of his truck. He squinted, searched their faces for a moment as if to convince himself this wasn't a bad dream, and though his mouth hung open in readiness to speak he never had the chance because Officer Perez pulled open the front door of the Hummer and got inside and said, "General, you're not going to believe this but the I.D. tag on the gimpy dog says 'This dog belongs to Bobby Smelzkoff.' What are the odds of this guy having the same name as you?" He laughed. "Specially a name like Smelzkoff. What is that anyway? German?"

After driving the two foreigners (the big goof of a woman and her gigolo friend) to his own ex-wife's house, after he had to confront his own flesh and blood, he had driven straight home, no way would he be able to get it up for Violet after this. What if word got out that this Smelzkoff was his son? His own son allowing his dog to romp on the beach. What a slap in the face. Smelzkoff could only hope no one looked too deeply into things. He felt like crying. And then he smelled something. He got out of the Hummer, opened the door to the back seat, and spotted the source of the odor on the floor mat.

ಬಬಬ Thirteen: D.O.G.S.

THE LONGING WAS EVER PRESENT, sometimes closer to the surface, and at other times held in check by a busy (one might say uncompromising) schedule of work. Bobby had never been able to contain his desire. All he knew was that he had been willing to endure a flawed relationship with Jason in an attempt to suppress the emptiness he felt, all he knew was that in the end only one thing had saved, could continue to save him. Art.

He had painted and sculpted. He had tried to write. He had acted: bit parts here and there. But he wasn't an actor. And he couldn't sing or dance that well.

His shoulders relaxed when he took a seat on the aisle to see a movie; his fingers stopped fluttering when he sat in the fifth row to see a play; his face stopped twitching when he stood in the rear balcony to hear a concert or opera. And working on *Salami* had consumed him, made it possible to cope with the loss of Jason (a fantasy) and the uncertainty of his health (a reality).

And now the betrayal from his own father. He couldn't comprehend such pathological behavior. How far would his father go to exercise control and experience a sense of power? What kind of a man would throw innocent people and dogs in jail? His own son's dog?

Flo loaned him the $250 to pay for Ginger's California license—and the citation for being on the beach. He parked at the curb, put four quarters in the meter (the maximum allowed), and went inside the Animal Regulation building. All drab beige and gray, chipped paint, acoustical ceiling, steel doors, chicken wire glass, bureaucratic employees, stacked notebooks of procedural instructions, chattering people, bawling dogs, and yowling cats. But then you could tell what you were going to find inside by the very name the city had chosen for the building: Animal Regulation. Not Animal Shelter, but Animal Regulation.

Bobby could not forgive his father for traumatizing Ginger. There was no reason for him to lock the poor girl up in some cruel metal cage. With her arthritis it must have been agony, and God only knows what she thought was happening. She must have thought that it was the end, that she'd be gassed at daybreak. After waiting for two hours a clerk finally led, or rather dragged, Ginger from the holding pens and into the reception area. With her ears flat against her head, her tail between her legs, she braced her crippled legs and tried to stand her ground, but the clerk (who either didn't like animals or perhaps was simply not fond of unattractive animals) snarled like a dog himself, showing his three remaining yellow incisors and both of his blackened canines, jerked at the leash and said, "You want the boot?" When he saw Bobby he said, "You should put this thing out of its misery."

When Ginger saw Bobby she perked up a bit and allowed herself to be led to him, but she would not look at him. Outside on the sidewalk he held her and stroked her and talked in a soothing voice. And then he saw the yellow notice on his windshield. His quarters had run out. He removed the ticket, turned it over, and read. There was something wrong with a system that levied a fine of forty dollars for an expired meter when the fee charged for parking was in increments of twenty-five cents.

❧•❧

Bobby left Ginger in the dressing room with fresh food and water, took his copy of the libretto, and went to find Georgia Bush. "Got your sketch pad handy?" said Bobby, when he spotted the boy at one of the improvised work areas at the rear of the theater.

Georgia, a tall black boy with rust-colored, almond-shaped eyes, who had seen Bobby's original ad and come all the way from Atlanta, had been hired as costumer. "Two seconds, till my nails dry," he said. He held his fingers splayed upright in the air; his toenails were separated by cotton.

"I have ideas for Herod's costume," said Bobby. He began to draw the stylized figure of a bodybuilder in LAPD uniform. He talked while his pencil scratched on the paper in heavy, circular strokes. "I want the regulation issue, knee-high boots, pistol and holster, ammo belt, and a prosthetic erection, a foot in diameter and two feet long," he said. "You know the basic idea. *Tom of Finland.*"

Georgia Bush blew on her fingernails. "Honey, I am pregnant with possibility. Billy club with spikes and nipple rings?"

"You got it." Bobby made as if to leave. "And I'm changing the character's name in our production from King Herod to General Herodkoff," he said.

❧•❧

In addition to the sixteen members of the cast, there were now forty-six others involved in Bobby's production of *Salami.* The theater seated eight hundred, but the work force had quickly outgrown the available space in the other parts of the theater, so when the antique lighting store next door had gone out of business a couple of weeks ago, Bobby had immediately inquired about leasing it. The owner of the building agreed to make it available, at a reduced rate for a month or two, until he could find a suitable and permanent tenant, and once Flo agreed on Bobby's promise that he'd make his money back tenfold after the opera opened, the set designers and carpenters and painters began to spill over in to that area.

The increased elbowroom facilitated the progress of work on the set, now nearly complete. With its overhead catwalks, pipes, and aeration pools, the stage looked like a combination refinery, steel smelting plant, and sewage treatment plant. At dinner one night with the cast, one of the waiters, a tow-headed blond, reminded Bobby of the Icelandic restaurant in New York and he had immediately instructed the set designers to give him more special effects: steam, belching smoke, and fire.

He went to the dressing room for Ginger. If necessary he'd stay up day and night to finish the libretto, but he needed the quiet atmosphere of home to concentrate. Now that he knew what his production had been missing, he felt things would progress rapidly. Ginger had gotten over her anger. When Bobby entered the room, she stood, stretched, and wagged her tail with so much spirit that it thumped against the chair and dressing table.

In Venice, Bobby turned right onto Abbot Kinney Boulevard, drove north, and parked in front of Abbot's Habit. He opened the door and picked up Ginger, set her down on the sidewalk, clipped on her leash, then tethered her to the fire hydrant and went in to get coffee. When he emerged a tall man with a chocolate Labrador had stooped to pet her. The man looked up and smiled, then stretched upright, and said, "She's a sweetie. How old is she?"

"She's a rescue; so I'm not really sure," said Bobby. He couldn't tell how old the man's Lab was either (his muzzle was completely gray) nor for that matter could he determine the man's age. Perhaps forty or forty-five, though he had a youthful manner and a thick head of hair, blond on top and silver at the temples.

The man's dog and Ginger were taking turns smelling each other, front and back, and Bobby started to ask the dog's name when the man handed Bobby a sheet of paper from the stack rolled up under his arm. "Have you heard about dogs?" he said. Then he spelled it. "D-O-G-S." Bobby accepted the leaflet, glanced at it, and waited for the man to continue.

"I'm sure you're aware of police harassment of dogs here in the city; we've got over two hundred members now." He paused and looked up at the sky for a moment. "I think the cops are jealous, because dogs do a better job of protecting the public than they do. My apartment was robbed and eight police came in and made this big deal of writing up a long report and taking fingerprints and I never heard a word back. It was my dog that scared the intruder off in the first place. The same thing happened when my garage was broken into and two bikes were stolen. I think they file their reports in the garbage." The man's voice, choked with emotion, trailed off.

"Are you going to be at the meeting?" said Bobby.

"If you could see what they were doing in front of where I live! You better believe I'll be there."

"May I buy you an espresso?" said Bobby.

The man glanced at his watch. "Yes, I have time for a coffee. Thank you. Coffee would be nice." He seemed pleased.

Bobby went in to get the drinks and when he came back outside, the man had taken one of the chairs that lined the sidewalk in front of the brick building. Bobby sat next to him and handed him the cardboard cup. "My name is Bobby Smelzkoff," he said.

The man's eyes, blue-green with flecks of gold, narrowed, and he leaned back in his chair. "Daniel Denison," he said. "Any relation to General Smelzkoff, the cop?"

"I'm afraid he's my father," said Bobby. "But we don't have much in common. Certainly not our views on dogs." And then he recounted the story of his argument with his father on the night previous. He explained how, when he refused to promise to not take Ginger onto the beach again, Poppy had driven away with Ginger and taken her to spend a night in the pound to teach him a lesson.

"I assume you know then what the DOGS acronym stands for," said Denison.

"Not really," said Bobby.

"Look on the bottom of the flyer I gave you."

Bobby set his coffee cup down on the sidewalk next to his chair and picked up the sheet of paper that Denison had given him. At the bottom in small print, flagged by an asterisk, he read: *Dog-owners Outsmarting General Smelzkoff.

∾•∿

The Copland Third Symphony played on the radio, the coffee maker sputtered with yet another pot, and through the opened French doors Bobby could see the first pale light of dawn. Some of the lyrics in Salome had been funny as originally written, and it hadn't been necessary to recast them. When Narraboth, the Syrian Captain of the Guard (now General Herodkoff's personal assistant and bodyguard) sings rapturously about Salami at the beginning of the opera, describing her as a "princess who has little white doves for feet" and then imagines her dancing, Bobby slumped over the table in a prolonged fit of uninhibited laughter. The thought of the giant Dame Ethyl stomping around the stage, her flat, calloused feet encased in size fifteen sandals, surely would make the dourest of individuals smile. And The Dame had such a great sense of comic timing that he knew how to get a laugh with the thrust of a hip, a flick of the wrist, a toss of his red ringlets.

Bobby only had a few pages to go to finish the libretto. He had arrived home from Abbot's Habit a little after six, showered, and immediately sat down to work. Glancing at the clock on the nightstand he realized that he had worked uninterrupted for almost twelve straight hours. The birds had been making a ruckus for a couple of hours, but before that, save for the noise that The Dame and Frederick and Rex made when they came home from rehearsal (or drinks after rehearsal) there had been nothing but an occasional siren to disturb him.

His concentration had wavered from time to time, as he thought about his encounter with the writer, Daniel Denison. On one hand he was pleased to find the man so interesting and, well, sexy. It had been a long time since he'd been willing to think of someone in sexual terms, (the waiter in New York, the pool man he had seen next door, and the lithe skate boarder on the bike path were exceptions) and he found himself unexpectedly wondering how it would feel to put his arms around Daniel Denison and kiss him. He even tried to picture what they might do in bed; Denison was well built after all and had large feet and beautiful hands. But on the other hand he didn't need any distractions to the work that lay before him; time and again he chased the image of the handsome Daniel Dension and continued to work. But thoughts of the man resurfaced again and again and it was only after Bobby reminded himself of his promise to attend the DOGS meeting on Thursday night that he was able to finally and completely put the writer out of his immediate thoughts.

At seven-thirty in the morning he wrote the final line of text for the opera and closed his notebook. ("Kill that woman" became "Kill that thing.") Time to take his medicine, snatch an hour or three of sleep, and then head back into Hollywood to Flo's. As he swallowed his pills, one at a time, he thought about Denison again, and this time the thought provoked an empty feeling in his stomach (an emptiness not attributed to hunger) and a sense of dread that made him wish to sleep forever.

&°•◅

The crowd at the meeting of DOGS jumped up from their chairs and roared their approval each time a suggestion for dealing with The General came forth. The atmosphere in the room resembled a political convention (though the group of two hundred or so hadn't sung "Happy Days Are Here Again") and the one thing Bobby could positively conclude was that The General, Poppy, his very own father, had certainly unified the community.

Daniel Denison, who chaired the meeting, ran to the back of the room when he saw Bobby arrive. The writer smiled and patted Bobby on the back. Though Bobby had thought of Denison many times since their meeting, it had been increasingly difficult for him, as time passed, to recall the features of the writer's face. Seeing him again brightened Bobby's mood: Daniel Denison was still a fox. "Don't leave before I get a chance to talk to you," said the writer. Bobby smiled, nodded, and took a seat in the last row.

One of the plans to outsmart General Smelzkoff involved a strategy employed before the Invasion of Normandy, when The Allies had amassed decoy plywood airplanes on the coast of England. The assumption was that German surveillance would believe they were real planes and decide that they had identified the launching point for the invasion. With that as inspiration, each and every member of DOGS had been instructed to bring a stuffed dog toy (some were so lifelike one almost expected them to bark) so that the stuffed decoys could be scattered on the beach, from Venice Boulevard all the way to Washington Boulevard, just after sundown the following night. With the decoys in place, dog owners could take their real pets swimming south of Washington and north of Venice.

Another plan called for owners to collect all their dog droppings and bring them in plastic garbage bags to one central location. A designated team would then drive to Smelzkoff's house and spread the dog shit all around the front and rear entrances of his house.

In addition there were plans for a candlelight march, with dogs, down the Venice Boardwalk on the upcoming Saturday night. One bleary-eyed woman (Was she drunk?) said she and "Lulu" would even sit in the road in front of an Animal Control truck if necessary and predicted that such a photograph would be as famous as the one of the student in front of the tank in Tienman Square.

Bobby watched Denison: the way he walked out from behind the lectern to answer a question from the audience, the way he gestured and emphasized with his hands, the way he smiled and laughed at a humorous remark, then nodded with compassion when the speaker turned serious. The man had an infectious smile with dimples that made him irresistible. But what sense was there in getting all excited? Bobby didn't know for sure if the man was gay—and if he were, there was no assurance that he would be interested in someone so much younger. Someone younger and HIV positive. Still there was a connection. He hadn't imagined it.

"Ladies and Gentlemen," said Denison, "I have a special surprise for you." Bobby felt his heart beat loudly and irregularly when he realized that Daniel was looking at him. "Bobby, come up and tell everyone about *Salami*."

ಬಂಬಂಬಂ Fourteen: Collision Course

WHEN POPPY DIDN'T SHOW UP at her house, Violet succumbed to paranoia. Had Bobby mentioned Frederick? If he had, she would have some explaining to do. Why couldn't she just go to sleep? Rolling from one side of the bed to the other and struggling with the pillows solved nothing. Six times she started to telephone Poppy's house to see if he had returned, but each time she decided it would be better not to speak with him right now.

At six-thirty she slipped her feet out from under the blankets, disturbing Whiskey who had settled comfortably across her ankles, then got out of bed, put on her robe, and went to the kitchen to pour herself a tumbler of juice. The sky was light but saturated in fog, and Venice was so quiet she could hear the foghorn beyond the shore. She turned on the kitchen radio, to that morning talk show, and then took the coffee out of the refrigerator.

She considered calling Poppy again. No, she would wait till nine and call Dr. Young. She should call Bobby though, to see if he had said anything. She checked her work schedule, secured by magnet to the refrigerator door, and tried to arrange her day.

"We'll have the weather and traffic report in a minute, but first here are today's headlines," said the radio host. "General Smelzkoff, the dog czar, has struck again. In a carefully planned operation involving more than sixty police officers, thirty squad cars, and a helicopter, this time at three o'clock this morning, dog owners were dealt yet another blow. The surprise operation caught two dog owners, apparently trying to take their pets for a late night swim, and two citations were issued. One dog was taken into custody," the announcer paused, "for questioning." He let out a groan, then a belly laugh, accompanied by the sound of cymbals crashing. "Let's hear it for the General," he said. Canned boos, laughter, and catcalls followed.

"I'm sorry," said the announcer, "but am I the only one who thinks this dog shit, pardon the pun, is a little out of hand? Call us at 555-1234 and give us your opinion. Here's Lane Switcher with the traffic report."

Violet filled a glass and watered the African violets on the window ledge. That could explain why Poppy never came over. He was fanatical about getting eight hours of sleep each night, and had often told her there was no point in working out hard with weights if you didn't give your muscles a chance to recover. He said he did best when he got nine hours and wasn't opposed to ten during the flu season. Violet sighed involuntarily. Still, talking to Bobby to make sure he hadn't gossiped about Frederick would be a good thing. That gay guys were sensitive was true enough, but everyone knew that they couldn't keep a secret.

❧•❧

The trunk of Violet's Mustang was crammed with packages. She placed the ornate wooden and wire birdhouse from Thailand, which to her resembled a domed capitol building, on top of the new sheets, towels and blankets in the back seat. This obstruction, more than her distraction over personal matters, caused her to collide with the blue Bentley as she backed out of her spot in the Beverly Hills parking structure. The sustained blast of the horn from behind preceded by a split-second the musical shatter of glass and the groan of bending metal. She rested the nape of her neck against the head rest for a moment to collect herself, though she hadn't sustained any injury, then put the gear lever in drive and pulled back into the parking spot. By the time she opened her door, swung her legs out from under the steering wheel, and stood to face the other driver, he was already approaching from his car. His face was flushed, his jaw muscles tensing. Rich assholes were usually difficult to contend with—even when they hadn't had one of their playthings damaged.

"Look at this," he said, pointing back at his car. Violet did look, and was surprised to see no damage. Then she checked the rear of her own car and saw a crunched bumper and broken taillight.

"I'm so sorry. But it's not bad, is it?"

The man had black hair, shaped into a round bushy mass, and he wore blue slacks and an orange shirt. Were it not for the TAG watch (and diamond ring that he sported on his left pinkie) she would have put him in an older and cheaper car.

"What do you call this?" He put his hand on the front bumper and Violet moved forward to examine it. "That's red paint from your fender," he said. "Do you have any idea what it costs for body work on a Bentley?"

Violet shook her head, aware now that he was checking out her bodywork. "We can exchange names and numbers," she said. "Naturally I'll compensate you for your repairs. It's a gorgeous car. But it really doesn't look too bad, does it?" She rested her left hand on her hip and offered her right. She stood very straight and threw back her shoulders ever so slightly, in a move calculated to accentuate her breasts. "My name's Violet," she said.

"Well—" Bentley man was about to take her hand, presumably to introduce himself, when a driver pulled up directly behind the stopped automobile and began to honk his horn, though there was plenty of room left to pass and move on up the garage ramp.

"Why don't we go someplace to exchange information," said Violet, before Bentley had a chance to address honking man or wave him past. "You could park and we could go for an iced coffee. How does that sound? Do you have time?"

The blocked driver honked again, and that seemed to help Bentley make up his mind. "I'm Brad Zieman," he said. "My next appointment isn't till two. Let's go."

He opened the passenger door, and Violet ducked in, onto the leather upholstery, and fastened her seat belt. The spacious interior of the car allowed her room enough to cross her legs.

The man, Brad Zieman, only had to drive up one more level before finding a spot to pull into, and Violet saw him glance at her legs as he shifted into park and shut off the engine. "Either your car is new or you take really good care of it," said Violet, unfastening her seat belt.

"It's new. That's why I got so annoyed. Your car seems to have taken the worst of it, though. But I'll still have to have the dealer check mine out, to make sure the chassis didn't get tweaked—although I don't really anticipate any damage. These beasts are built to take collisions like tanks. I apologize for being boorish." He turned away, stared at the instrument panel for a second, and then faced Violet again. "If you have the time I'll buy you lunch. I know a great Ukrainian restaurant a block from here." He behaved in a more courteous manner, now that he'd apparently gotten over his concern about his car.

They made their way to the elevator and entered it when the doors opened. It stopped at the next floor and a mother and two small boys got on, and Violet inched back, closer to but not quite touching Brad Zieman The two children poked and stabbed at each other with toy missiles and when the mother tried to intercede, each of them blamed the other for having started the quarrel. Notwithstanding the boys' noisiness, Violet heard Zieman's nervous breathing, and they both remained silent until the doors opened again on the street level. "This way," said Zieman, motioning right.

"What line of work are you in, may I ask?" said Violet.

"I'm a doctor. Here in Beverly Hills," he said. "And you?"

"I'm an actress, and choreographer," said Violet.

"Really?" said Zieman "Have I seen you in anything?"

"Do you go to plays?" said Violet.

"No, I'm mostly a movie guy," said Zieman

"I was in a production of *Salome* in Hollywood," said Violet.

"A play?" Violet nodded. "Comedy?" She nodded again.

"So you're a doctor," said Violet. "Do you have a specialty?"

"Urology," said Zieman.

⁊•⅋

At home Violet dropped the last of her shopping bags on the bed and tried to decide where to put the birdcage. She had wanted parakeets as a little girl, but Cheryl had never allowed her to have them. Violet went to the front room and studied the possibilities. In the corner by the window, next to the empty aquarium, on a table so they could see outside, appeared best for the birds, so she went to the bedroom to get the cage and found Whiskey lying on top of it, his tail draped over the side and twitching, as if he knew for whom, or for what, the enclosure was intended.

"Sink one claw into my birds and I'm getting a dog," said Violet, and then she thought it might be better to wait till Whiskey got used to the cage before she actually bought the parakeets.

The doctor had an interesting face, with a long forehead and heavy brows that hooded his wide-set eyes, and a lean physique. She couldn't help but picture him with a more stylish haircut (a Mohawk would be an improvement) and decent clothes. She disliked shaved heads and Vandyke beards but, with such wiry hair, baldness might be

Dr. Brad Zieman's only option. After lunch, after they had exchanged addresses and telephone numbers, after they had walked back to the parking structure, he had asked her out—sort of. And she had agreed to meet him at the Beverly Hills Hotel for cocktails Friday afternoon, after he had an estimate from his dealer. Violet was almost positive that he wasn't interested in collecting any money from her. What he wanted was what she had implied he could have, if he played his cards right, so to speak.

∂•∾

It wasn't until after Violet danced her last turn that she saw Kent. She had expected him to be waiting at the door when she showed up for work and when he wasn't, relief had washed over her. She didn't need Dr. Young to tell her that she was trapped. She had no skills that could enable her to make the kind of money she did at Fantasy Mansion, and since she had become so accustomed to spending money, she needed to continue making plenty more.

A pounding at the dressing room door and then it opened without invitation. "I need you in my office," said Kent, closing the door before she could reply.

Violet finished dressing, went upstairs, and tapped on the door. "It's open," he called from inside.

Violet stepped in as Kent closed his desk drawer and snuffed his nose. He had the air conditioning cranked high, making it at least fifteen degrees cooler in this space than in the rest the club. He sat forward over the desk, eyes watering, to stub out a cigarette in a platter-sized, ceramic ashtray that brimmed with butts. "What's up with you lately?" he said, without any air of formality. He reached for the pack of Kent cigarettes, pulled out another, and lit it. Violet watched his chest and stomach rise as he inhaled.

"I don't know what you mean," she said, enveloped in the smoke he exhaled.

"You know fine. Time off, showing up late, dancing like you got the sleeping sickness, and giving people here the high hat. What's up with that?"

"I was late twice, three times at the most because I have friends visiting from New York," said Violet. "I don't see what the fuss is. It's not like I'm a nurse and some old lady doesn't get her medication if I'm late."

"That's what I'm talking about. Your uppity attitude. I'm running a business here and you make good money, and I figure you'd like to keep on making good money. Am I right?" Kent had raised his voice higher with each succeeding word and he stared at her now, eyes narrow and close, nostrils flaring.

Violet took a chance. She leaned forward and placed both her hands on his left hand, stretched in her direction and resting on his desk mat. "I appreciate you taking me on here, Kent. I do. But it's just that I don't want to dance for the rest of my life. You know?"

For a second perhaps, Kent appeared to settle down a bit. His face relaxed, and there was a softening around the eyes. But then he pulled his hand out from under hers, leaned back in his chair, took two consecutive puffs on what remained of this cigarette, and put it out. "No one said you have to dance for the rest of your life. There are career advancement opportunities." He stared at her, and Violet watched as his eyes left her face and stared at her breasts.

He pulled open the top left desk drawer. "Want to do a line?" he said.

Violet looked over at the drawer. "I'm supposed to meet a friend, after I get off, but I got a little time," she said. This was dangerous ground, she knew. If she could do just a little blow, to appear sociable, enough to get Kent off her back, and then leave, then things would be fine. But she didn't want to set a precedent and make him think she was going to get intimate.

"Make sure the door is locked," said Kent.

Violet went to check it, and when she returned he had taken a vial of cocaine from the drawer. He unscrewed the cap, which had a tiny chain and spoon attached to it, then inserted the spoon in the bottle and took out a dose. After he had done two blasts in each nostril, he handed the bottle to Violet.

"The door's locked, right?" he said. And even though she nodded, with the spoon poised below her nostril, Kent stood and walked over to check for himself. As Violet inhaled the first spoonful of cocaine she heard him try the knob, and then as she inhaled in the other nostril she felt his hands on her shoulders. The hands were strong and the cocaine was pure and had it been anyone else massaging her she most probably would have relaxed and enjoyed it, but as it was she sat silent and tense until he finally withdrew from behind and returned to his chair.

"There's someone you should meet," said Kent. Violet had set the vial down on the desk pad and Kent took it now and returned it to the drawer. He picked up a paper from a tray at the corner and looked at it for a minute. "You're on days again next week. Why don't we make a date for dinner one night and I'll introduce you."

"Who is it?" said Violet.

"One of our investors," he said.

"Why do you want me to meet him?" said Violet.

"He makes movies. He has a project that might be right for you," said Kent.

߭•m

About halfway home the cocaine began to wear off. Violet hadn't done much, maybe ten lines total, but it had been good stuff and with its positive effects now easing, the reality of Kent's proposition hit her like a headline in three-inch-high block letters: VIOLET FACES DESTRUCTION AND RUIN.

Lucky for her that Kent's phone had rung; lucky for her that a matter needed his urgent attention and that she'd been able to excuse herself without a commitment to anything (other than dinner the following week) which gave her seven days to formulate a course of action.

Violet turned around and headed back in the other direction. Often, when she drove on Los Angeles streets and freeways, she tried to imagine what she would do in case of an earthquake. She monitored the side of the road and breathed easier when she left a suspended overpass and crossed over onto a section anchored to solid ground. She remembered television pictures of the last quake, when whole sections of an overpass crashed to the ground, arbitrarily killing some motorists and leaving others on a freestanding, isolated section of highway. She wanted to be one of those who crossed the bridge before it plummeted to the ground. Well, who wouldn't? In her imagination it was like a ride at Universal Studios: she stayed seconds and inches ahead of the destruction, trailing in her wake. Columns toppled, bridge spans fell, chunks of concrete rained down from above and were she to slow for one second the devastation could claim her as a victim. She felt like that now. She would have to move fast to avoid injury and possible death. But there was no outrunning such danger. If disaster wanted to claim her, it would. And she knew that.

In Hollywood, Violet parked, got out of the car, and walked up the street to Flo's theater.

Two people she'd never seen before were having an animated conversation at the box office, so she didn't interrupt. She waited at the entrance while three of the set design workers struggled to squeeze a tall section of painted backdrop in through the right-side double doors. And when finally she decided to enter through the left-side double doors, The Dame (practically naked) and Georgia Bush came bursting out with armloads of sheer organdy fabric. "We must trust the man," said The Dame. "He has a vision." "But we're running out of time," said the other transvestite. Both towered over Violet, and if they noticed her at all as she ducked out of their way and fell into the flanking potted shrub, they didn't let on.

In the lobby people dashed to and fro, left and right, as if in a maze. One boy, headed on a collision course with Violet, suddenly reversed himself and darted off in the opposite direction. People clogged the aisles of the theater and, on the stage itself, many of the performers appeared to be involved in rehearsal. Violet spotted Frederick at the rear of the stage, wrestling playfully with a bodybuilder, so short and over-developed that he made Frederick look like a Milan fashion model. Frederick had the beefy boy in a headlock; the writhing boy in turn had his arms around Frederick's waist. Violet was considering going up the right aisle to get Frederick's attention, when Bobby ran on stage from the wings and yelled at the two.

"Hey, guys. Check into a motel, later. We don't have time for that now."

He clapped his hands twice. "Everyone. We open tomorrow night. We're down to the wire. Frederick, go try on your costume and come back in so I can see how it looks. Rex, come center stage. I want to go over the part where Salami is insisting on John's head."

Then Bobby addressed the sound technician in the orchestra pit. The man, in sunglasses and wearing his long purple hair in a ponytail, stood at the ready in front of a giant computerized control board. "Mark, cue the music at the bottom of page ninety, where Salami " Bobby consulted the libretto for a moment and continued, "demands John's head for the seventh time, and Herodkoff tries to dissuade her with jewels." Bobby sang the lines: "I have jewels hidden in this place, jewels your mother has never even seen

"Cue there, Mark. Rex, I want you—Rex, watch me," snapped Bobby, and then he tramped, in a perfect imitation of Rex's walk, to the edge of the sewage treatment pond. "Here," he finished.

"Sally, I want you over here." He hurried to his right and stood in front of a huge horizontal pipeline, with control valve, that cut diagonally across the stage, and then went up into the rafters. "Herodias is opening this valve and when she overhears Herodkoff singing to Salami about the jewels she turns and does a wicked double take. You know, arched eyebrows, head back, curled fingernails up to the face. Okay?" Bobby went to center stage again. "Let's run through that once, just make sure we've all got it."

And then he spotted her. "Violet, honey. Good to see you, Sweetie. Everything all right?"

Violet nodded.

"Don't forget, tomorrow night. I'm leaving two comp tickets for you at the box office. Sorry I don't have time to chat," he said. He turned and spoke to Rex again.

In Venice, Violet stopped at Poppy's house, but he wasn't home. Then she went home and telephoned Dr. Young's office. His message said he was on vacation until the thirtieth, and even though he had left a number in case of emergency, Violet decided that she needed to talk to someone face-to-face.

She stooped to pet Whiskey for a while, and then went into her bedroom to check her closet. In less than twenty-four hours she would be meeting Doctor Bradley Zieman, at the Beverly Hills Hotel. Though he would probably show up, dressed like a jester, the occasion definitely called for her to wear red.

ཨོ࿐ Fifteen: Sleeper

BOUT FORTY TICKETS HAD BEEN SOLD in advance, and perhaps another fifteen patrons paid for admission at the door. Bobby looked out from behind the curtains to the main floor. A sprinkle of people, back to about Row M, and five or ten more in the balcony looked lonely in a theater that held so many. Bobby scanned the faces to see if Daniel Denison's was among them.

In the pit, Mark was doing a sound check at the computer control board, prompting Bobby to remember the malfunctioning computer at the opera in Royce Hall. No question, there was plenty to worry about tonight, but he told himself that he'd done all he could to insure that things ran smoothly. Nothing to do now but pray.

He dodged stagehands and extras, smiled, patted backs, and wished everyone good luck as he made his way among them to his dressing room office. Appearances were important and he was determined to put up a good front, though in his entire life he'd never been so disheartened.

❧•❧

Brandon, unable to make the trip out from New York, had sent flowers and Bobby smiled as he read the note: *I am unable to attend the opening night, but I'd be glad to come the second night—if there is one.* (Bobby had sent two tickets and a note that said: *Enclosed are two tickets to the opening of Salami. Bring a friend if you have one.*) Noel Coward and Winston Churchill aside, any optimism about the future of his play would be hard to sustain given tonight's turnout. There were flowers from Daniel Denison too, with a warm note, but Bobby didn't have the time or energy to think about the significance of that.

He heard the stage manager, down the hall, knocking on doors. "Five minutes, everyone," he said. Bobby took a breath, reached for the tube in his pocket, and applied a coat of balm to his lips.

❧•❧

As the curtain went up, revealing the green-lit set and swirling, smoggy mist, Bobby could hardly believe they'd come so far in such a short time. And though it was far too early to be self-congratulatory he had to admit the surreal, industrial set (with its standpipes and catwalks and smokestacks and storage tanks) looked every bit as smashing as a stage on Broadway. Too bad there were so few on hand to appreciate it.

The stereophonic sound of dogs and cats, howling and yowling, emanated from the giant theater speakers and then the music of Strauss's opera began without overture. As Narraboth, in standard LAPD uniform, sang the opening line, "How beautiful is the Princess

Salami tonight," the orangey-red spotlight snapped on Dame Ethyl at the opposite side of the stage. Ripples of laughter trickled through the audience as they took her in, standing on a forklift in front of the backdrop and lit windows of the control room where Herodkoff's banquet was taking place. Bobby had doubts that Salami's costume was absurd enough (she wore an oversized, silver-metallic brassiere with foot-long, pointed nipples and a G-string) but it triggered the first laugh of the evening, and a pretty decent one at that.

"Who are those wild beasts howling?" sang the first policeman. "The cat people, disputing about whether cats are better than dogs," sang the second policeman. A rumbling of laughter, but no hysteria, and Bobby was suddenly fearful that the audience might be laughing at and not with them.

Still the laughs, though not raucous, continued while Narraboth and the policeman sang about Salami's beauty, thanks mainly to her camping and vamping in the spotlight. The biggest outburst came when she blew her steamy breath on the metal cups of her brassiere and then pulled a rag from inside her G-string to buff the tips in the manner of someone hunched over a pair of wing-tip shoes.

When Frederick finally made his appearance as John the Baptist, the mood of the spectators changed. First, his strong, rich voice echoed from the darkened cell at the opposite side of the stage: "After me shall come another mightier. The eyes of the blind shall see the day and the ears of the deaf shall be opened." And then the prison was bathed in a second spotlight, this one a golden yellow, but still not revealing John the Baptist, locked inside.

Salami jumped off the forklift and pranced down the stairs of the platform, her hands fluttering the air like wings. This time the laughter from the seats was louder and sustained. "Who was that who cried out?" she sang.

"The dog offender," sang the first soldier. "Herodkoff has forbidden any one to speak to him."

Frederick sang again from The Baptist's cell, but he still couldn't be seen. Even more intrigued, Salami sang, "He says terrible things about my mother. I desire to speak to him."

Bobby had wanted to build excitement in the theater, the way the opera did when performed successfully, in concert halls. He wanted to replicate the curiosity that Salome felt about The Baptist's face, and it did seem that those in the audience were practically breathless with anticipation, for they had grown eerily quiet. When at last, in compliance with Salami's demands, John the Baptist was released from his cell and he stepped out into the now-intensified golden light of the spot, the audience began first to whistle, then to cheer, and finally to stomp their feet. Dressed in construction boots, an athletic supporter, and a baseball cap, his brown hair bouncing in loose curls on his shoulders, and leading a tall, massive, black and white, harlequin Great Dane, Frederick looked spectacular, and erotic, as John the Baptist. Body paint had been used to highlight the definition of his muscles, and his physique (so athletic, so long, so lean, so perfectly proportioned, so devoid of fat) could reasonably be compared to that of Adonis.

"Where is she who plots to rid our city and beaches of dogs?" sang Frederick, John the Baptist, and on cue the Great Dane, heeling at his side, barked nine times (in staccato clusters of three) into the small microphone fastened round his neck, a deep basso profundo rumbling bark, so magnificent and resonant that it reverberated in the theater and raised the hair on Bobby's arms. The audience burst into sustained applause and whistles and didn't stop until The Dame ran in a full gallop across the stage to get a closer look at The Baptist.

She sang, "It is of my mother, the Deaconess, that he speaks. He is terrible, he is terrible!" Apparently it took a moment for the audience to realize whom the Deaconess was, but once they did, they yelled their approval anew.

"What is this?" sang Frederick, pointing at The Dame, looking her up and down.

"I am Salami, daughter of The Deaconess, Princess of Venice," sang Dame Ethyl.

"Back, daughter of Babylon," sang Frederick.

"Thy voice is like sweet music. Speak to me again and tell me what I must do," sang Salami.

"Come not near me. But cover thy bulbous body with a blanket and get thee to the voting booth and drive your mother the Deaconess from office," sang The Baptist.

"Let me touch thy body," sang Salami, reaching out.

"By woman came evil into the world. Speak not to me," sang The Baptist.

And for a moment Bobby overcame his nervousness, bending over in laughter and wiping tears from his eyes when The Dame sang in tremulous exaggeration, "All right. Hate the body, love the hair."

"Back, daughter of Sodom! Touch me not!" sang Frederick.

"Thy hair is horrible. I love not thy hair," sang The Dame.

Later on Bobby would remember the following section as one of the funnier moments in the production. After The Baptist denied Salami the chance to touch his body or his hair, she began to beg pitifully, "I want thy mouth; I want thy mouth." She cavorted around the stage, lapping the air with her tongue, and finally threw herself at his feet, provoking the Great Dane to renewed barking. And when Narraboth, captain of Herodkoff's guard, could not stand Salami's begging and killed himself with his sword, The Dame rose from her prone position, looked down at the body for an extended period of time, then up at the audience, shrugged, vaulted nonchalantly over it, and dismissed the inert figure with a "whatever" wave of her bejeweled hand. It was a moment that required flawless timing and The Dame chewed the scenery with every ounce of her comic skills. The audience laughed so hard that Rex had to delay his entrance as Herodkoff.

When Herodkoff finally came down the industrial staircase to center stage for his first appearance, the people responded with laughter again, at the sight of his costume. Georgia Bush had devised a studded, leather harness to hold the giant penis, which jutted two feet out from his crotch, in place. Rex lumbered down the stairs in knee-high motorcycle cop boots, wearing a police hat with LAPD badge on front, his body oiled and glistening.

Behind him was Herodias, The Deaconess, in a red floor-length robe and red, silk, stovepipe hat, singing, "You must not look at her! You are always looking at her!"

Bobby had decided that Herodkoff shouldn't pose, once he arrived at center stage, but Rex had begged for permission to do a double biceps and most muscular, or crab as he called it, and Bobby had finally relented. There were apparently a few people in the audience who were attracted to body builders, for there arose a chorus of wolf whistles and cheers from the gallery as Rex went through his posing routine for Salami. As he turned to do a lat spread, he lost his balance and slipped in Narraboth's blood, but he ignored the implications of the blood just as Salami had done and began to sing. With his strong tenor voice and professional training he was by far the most talented singer in the cast. "Come drink wine with me," he sang. "Eat fruit. I like to see your teeth marks in the fruit."

During the ensuing argument between Herodias (the Deaconess) and Herodkoff (she wanted John the Baptist to be destroyed for allowing his Great Dane on the beach) he displayed a grudging respect for The Baptist and seemed to fear, if not him, the people's reaction were he to be put down the disagreement became physical. Herodias slapped at Herodkoff's giant penis, grabbed for the huge swaying balls and Herodkoff in turn ripped her red dress, revealing the fact that she too had a penis, though not as large as his. She quickly gathered her dress around her body again, covering her unappetizing secret, while in the background a chorus of singers, in costumes resembling those in the musical *CATS*, sang that the dog owner, and dog, should be turned over to them.

After Herodkoff begged Salami to dance for him, she at first refused but when she finally agreed, slaves (men dressed as female meter maids) danced on stage to perfume her, remove her sandals, and dress her in the seven veils.

The dance itself was well received. The Dame tromped and strutted, up and down stairs, rolled on the floor, did the twist, the jitterbug, and the tango, and got so carried away that she inadvertently pulled over a pipe railing at the edge of the sewage treatment pool. Since the railing looked like iron, this unplanned bit of shtick served to make the dance even more hilarious. During the dance, Herodkoff's giant penis gradually became fully erect and by the time Salami finished it pointed straight up to the ceiling.

Just as in the real opera, *Salome*, Bobby felt that his production bogged down a little after the dance. When Salami demanded the head of The Baptist and the head of his Great Dane, Herodkoff of course reacted with revulsion and pleaded for other alternatives. He promised jewels that Herodias didn't know about, which gave Sally Monella her moment in the spotlight.

But after that, after Herodkoff agreed to give Salami the head of The Baptist and his dog on a silver platter, after she camped around from one end of the stage to the other kissing the mouth, and petting the dead dog's head, it began to get a little tedious, despite The Dames' gift for milking a scene. Bobby resolved that some tightening should take place. At the very least another gag or two would be inserted. At one time he had considered putting The Baptist's penis on the silver tray along with the two heads, but he decided that there were already enough penises in the production. A giant, black cloud traveled across the moon and the stage got dark, and Herodkoff climbed the stairs, his head hanging, his penis deflated.

"I have kissed thy mouth," sang Salami.

"Kill that thing," sang Herodkoff, as he continued his climb. The slaves dragged Salami to the pool of seething sewage at center stage and threw her in. All the special effects (thunder, lightening, exploding volcanoes) were triggered here, and in a twist reminiscent of "scratch and sniff" in *Polyester*, sulfur was blown out over the audience by huge fans near the wings, and the curtain went down.

So what if there were only forty-nine people in the audience. The important thing was that they were enthusiastic about the opening night performance. That's what Daniel Denison said when he came backstage to Bobby's dressing room office.

"You don't owe anyone an apology," he said. "I had a thoroughly good time. *Salami* is hilarious, and quite inventive." He held on to Bobby's hand even after he had stopped shaking it. "I've been to poetry readings where the poet laureate was the guest of honor and only twenty people showed up," he said.

Well he might be right, but that would hardly satisfy Flo, who needed to get some of her investment back. "Do you have any suggestions? As a writer, I mean," said Bobby.

"A few minor ones. To be honest, I think the play's fine. What you need now is the audience you deserve. With the right kind of promotion, you've got a real sleeper here." Daniel sat in the ragged, overstuffed chair to face Bobby, who had pulled the room's only other chair (straight-backed and uncomfortable) out from under the dressing table and turned it around to sit with his back to the mirror. The upholstered chair, which had probably been in the theater since it first opened, had broken springs, and Daniel sat so low his movements were constrained. "If you're free tomorrow, we could have lunch," he said.

"It'll have to be early. We have another performance tomorrow night and a matinee on Sunday," said Bobby, "assuming Flo doesn't cancel us. But thanks. I'd love to. Maybe you'd like to join us all for a drink tonight? We're going to Musso and Frank's."

"I'd only be a distraction. I'm sure you have a lot to discuss. Besides, believe it or not, I still have some work to do. How's eleven for lunch tomorrow?" said Denison.

"Fine. Perfect in fact," said Bobby. Denison wore khakis and a long-sleeved, blue cotton shirt, which went well with his suntan and silvery blond hair. Bobby had a sudden urge to go over and sit in the writer's lap.

"Well then," said Denison. "I guess I should be going."

"Let me help you up," said Bobby, with a smile.

"I feel as if I've suddenly developed osteoporosis," said Denison, smiling too as he took Bobby's outstretched hand and stood. Instead of letting go he held tight, and said, "I meant what I said about your opera. It's good, Bobby. Really good." And then he put his free arm around him too, pulled him in close, and embraced him. When he pushed back, his face was flushed with color, and he let go of Bobby's hand and averted his eyes. "Tomorrow then," he said.

"Daniel," said Bobby.

At the door, Denison turned.

"A sleeper is something unnoticed that attains sudden prominence, isn't it?" Denison smiled, raised his eyebrows, and nodded. "How sudden, do you think?" said Bobby.

"Make sure you read the *LA Times* in the morning. *Calendar* section," said the writer.

ಬಬಬ Sixteen: Cold Cuts

THE FIRST HINT OF DISASTER came when The Deaconess called at five-thirty in the morning. "Put things on hold as of now," she said, "orders of the mayor." When Smelzkoff tried to question her, she said, "Just do it. I'll give you your precious explanation later."

He couldn't sleep after the call; he kept replaying the terse conversation over in his head, trying to figure out what had happened. Maybe it was a good thing; maybe they were ready to expand the operation to other areas of the city. He had the plans for that already drawn up. Still, Smelzkoff had a sour sense of foreboding.

He hadn't seen Violet for two days. And there was the matter of Bobby allowing those freaks to take his flea-infested dog onto the beach. When the others at the Pacific Division asked him about the Smelzkoff dog he had ignored them, but privately he wondered if they knew. Anyone bothering to check could confirm that Bobby was his son; it was all there in his personnel file.

He shut off the blender, poured a glass of wheat grass, drank it down without pausing, and went to the door to get the morning paper. Daybreak was still an hour away, but in the illumination provided by the streetlight, he saw the newspaper on the sidewalk, and he stepped barefoot onto his cold, damp porch to retrieve it. Unfortunately the light was not sufficient to reveal the numerous piles of dog excrement that virtually covered his front steps, and it wasn't until he placed his foot in a cold, creamy heap and felt the matter ooze between his toes that he got his first whiff of it. When he subsequently slipped and landed on his butt in the waste, he realized too late that his enemies had targeted him. Holding his breath, he stood, arms, elbows, and rump covered in the foul-smelling excretion, and hurried to wipe his feet on the door mat, then he walked carefully through his living room, his hands held out away from his body, to the bathroom to bathe. The hot water and steam magnified the odor in the shower enclosure, causing him to gag, shudder, and shake with revulsion as he rinsed off the clinging dung. Despite his anger, it took all of his resolve to keep from throwing up.

After standing in the scalding spray for more than half an hour, after depositing his soiled underpants in the washing machine, after hosing down his front porch and steps, he returned for the paper and glanced at the headlines on his way to the kitchen table. His outrage prompted such a desire for revenge that he considered calling The Deaconess to tell her what had happened and to beg for permission to hold just one more raid. But she had been adamant, and he knew he would have to find a different way to punish them.

He stood beside the table, his hands still quivering with agitation, and opened the newspaper to search for stories about him or the dog campaign. In the beginning, relevant articles had appeared in the *Metro* section, but after the so-called War on Dogs caught the public's attention the coverage had started appearing on the front page. He flipped through the other sections (on his way to the sports page) until a picture, caption, and review in *Calendar*, stretching across all six columns, stopped him.

The heading (*Salami*: Cold Cuts Indeed) and picture (a huge, naked woman with heaps of red hair, dancing in front of a professional wrestler-type with a yard-long penis) nauseated Smelzkoff even before he read the caption underneath: *Bobby Smelzkoff's inspired production is vicious and funny. Not to be missed. Salami is not only a hilarious satire of* Salome, *but also a masterful and provocative send-up of the overblown efforts of law enforcement officials in our densely populated, ever-changing society.*

Smelzkoff fell into the chair. His eyes flew over the text of the accompanying review. Salami *isn't pretty. It's awesome and awful—and hilarious. A reflection on our society—a society where restrictions on our personal freedom and the excesses of law enforcement officials swirl around us in a post-modern, Victor Hugo and George Orwell collaboration.*

Smelzkoff didn't have to read another word. He knew. Such bad publicity would most certainly spell the end of him. He would advance no further in the department and could never run for public office; he would never again appear on television; he could never again hold up his head in Gold's, and no woman, certainly not Violet, would ever be attracted to him again.

But he read on. *It's difficult to know where to start in talking about* Salami, *because almost everything about this production is wonderful and inspired. Let's start with the staging. It looks like an oil refinery or smelting operation of some sort, but with a decidedly ominous and threatening look. The moment the curtain rises on the surreal, green- and yellow-lit set, with the sounds of hissing steam and howling animals, this reviewer understood. There's evil here. The same kind of evil that inhabited Auschwitz and Dachau. Even those familiar with the Oscar Wilde play and Strauss operatic adaptation can't help wondering what sort of unsavory and ungodly madness is going to unfold.*

Start with The War On Dogs. Stanley Smelzkoff suddenly remembered that he had just wallowed in animal feces. The smell came back more putrid than ever. He took a series of deep breaths, rubbed his eyes and forehead and cheeks with his hands, and tried to enhance his circulation. When this new urge to vomit had passed, he read on. *Is there anyone who doesn't know about the excesses and heavy-handed treatment of dogs and their owners now going on in Venice by the Sea? If you don't then you probably just arrived from Pierre, South Dakota. And if you do, you're going to laugh till you burst when you see* Salami.

The music is all Richard Strauss with some of the libretto drawn from the original and some added or altered. This ensemble cast of beautiful male bodies and female impersonators is marvelous. No two-bit, limpwristed, lip-synching drag show here. These troopers do all their own singing and it's obvious that more than a few have studied voice professionally. Rex Wildman, in particular, terrific and pumped as the sexually-disturbed General Herodkoff, who can only get aroused by the female stripper, Salami, half his age and three times his size, is a tenor who could quite possibly hold his own with those other three, whose names escape me now. And there aren't words enough to praise the comic genius of the man who bills himself simply as Dame Ethyl Chloride who sings and dances like a dervish in the role of Salami. Frederick Lieder is simply sublime as John, The Baptist, and it doesn't hurt that he has the body of a male Barbie. Sally Monella is not to be overlooked either as the consort Deaconess Herodias in trademark red gown and hat. This deranged and emasculating woman has more than a touch of penis envy.

Deranged. Sexually-disturbed. Penis envy. Smelzkoff couldn't go on. The goddamned review covered most of the page. He skipped to the final paragraph. *I won't give the end away, but when Salami meets her demise it's clear. We haven't been in an innocuous and commonplace manufacturing facility. We've been in a death plant, where enemies of the regime are destroyed.*

Smelzkoff ran to the bathroom but didn't make it. Green, bilious liquid splattered the walls and floor of the hallway. He smelled like the bottom of a lawn mower. And he wasn't finished. He pushed open the door, took two steps, fell to his knees, draped his arms over the water closet, and surrendered to the throne. He vomited until there was no longer anything left to bring up, but the muscles in his stomach kept contracting in a desperate dry-heaving effort to purge all the liquid from his system.

ುುುುುు Seventeen: Ripe for Harvest

THINGS WENT SMOOTHLY at the Beverly Hills Hotel. Dr. Zieman wore an expensive suit, though brown definitely wasn't his color. Even before they sat down, Violet had mentally re-styled his hair. Not very nice hair, but at least he had hair. Wiry and black, dappled with gray. But it needed pruning. She wore a black slip dress and pearls and felt confident that she looked as respectable as any of the other women in the room, most of whom were older and many of whom had tried to remain youthful-looking by chopping off their noses, stretching their faces tight, and puffing up their lips with silicon.

Drinks turned into dinner, and no mention was made of the fender bender. If the doctor had gotten an estimate he didn't say so. "I grew up in Long Island, went to med school at Northwestern, and got married after graduation," said the doctor. This information didn't up-set Violet: Bradley Zieman didn't wear a wedding band. She liked hands. His were olive brown and smooth looking and the hair on them was light brown and inconspicuous. His fingers slender and well shaped. The nails kept short and even. "My marriage ended more than ten years ago," said Zieman "I enjoy being single." By focusing her attention on him, Violet managed to reveal little about herself. "Any children?" said Violet."

She had failed at many things in life. Some of it she knew was her fault and some of it, at least partly, the fault of others. (But this was no time to think about Uncle Collie.) Violet had a sense of style and the looks to showcase it—and she understood men. And was good at sex. Withholding it from Dr. Bradley Zieman, for a time, would be crucial. "You look very fit," she said. "What are you, about six-one?"

Dinner started with expensive caviar and champagne. "I prefer Crystal over Dom Perignon," said Violet. Proceeded with clams and oysters. "Oysters are my favorite aphrodisiac," she said. Continued with a main course of seared ahi. "Bobby says the last course should be light. The way they eat in northern Italy," said Violet. During dinner she knew. Zieman spared no expense and did not rush. In the time it took to eat (three hours) she knew. "No, Bobby is a friend. That's all. He's a director—and a producer," said Violet. She was going to see a lot of this man.

"I have two castings and a meeting with my agent tomorrow," said Violet. "I love to dance. Any other time I'd say, yes." She was in fact going to marry him and have a child. But not necessarily in that order. Already she had a blueprint. "I'm crazy for snorkeling too," she said, "and hiking. I love the outdoors." One more week at Fantasy. One week to find a new apartment and move. "I only eat desert on special occasions. I think this qualifies." Violet sat back, smiled at the doctor, and pushed her hair behind her ears with her fingers. "Crème brulee and decaf," she told the waiter.

One week.

The corny doctor was ripe for harvest. He would be her salvation. And she would be his.

๊๓๊๓๊๓ Eighteen: A Thin Man

LUNCH WITH DANIEL DENISON on the patio at *Playa de Jaime* passed so quickly that Bobby hated to get up and leave for the theater. There had been no shortage of topics to discuss over their meal: Denison marveled at the new James Buchanan biography by Judith Kranz (Wasn't it an exciting departure for the writer?); Bobby raved about the documentary on P. M. Roget that he'd seen on public television (What a stroke of caprice to use Ice Cube rap music for background!); the writer asked Bobby if he'd ever been to the drum circle, Sundays at sundown, on the beach (It's like the Massai Mara people of Kenya partying with the hippies of Venice, California.); Bobby announced his intention to attend a poetry reading at Beyond Baroque the following week (Angelica Huston reading the collected poems of Ian Randall Wilson); and Denison told a hilarious, Elizabeth Dole joke, with lots of profanity, in a perfect imitation of her genteel, Southern accent (The punch line: "Close, Bob, but no cigar!"). Then,

Bobby and Denison got so worked up over the fact that the developers were tearing down all the vintage beach houses in Venice and replacing them with monstrous, unimaginative, concrete chunks ("How about the one by the parking lot on Ocean Front," said Bobby. "It looks like county jail.") that Bobby almost forgot the time.

"I hate to say this," he said, "but I've got to go." Nonetheless, he looked forward with enthusiasm to the evening performance; Flo said the box office telephone starting ringing even before eight A.M. and that advance sales had surpassed two hundred by noon.

"Thanks to your review," said Bobby.

"A toast," said Denison. "To the play that will set new standards."

When Denison had blurted out, over his ostrich burger and fries, that he'd lost a lover to AIDS, almost four years earlier, Bobby simply nodded. Gradually, after a few deliberate bites of his Bikini Special (catfish sashimi), he regained the ability to speak, but alas didn't have the backbone to ask the questions for which he wished to have answers. Confirming that the writer was gay, simultaneously encouraged and unsettled Bobby. There was still no proof that Denison was attracted to him, and no indication that he'd be interested in dating someone younger. (Daniel Denison was at least fifteen years older by Bobby's estimation.) And if he were negative he might be reluctant to get involved with someone positive and have to face the awkward situation of sex.

When Denison motioned for the check, Bobby saw himself walking to the edge of a rocky cliff. He saw himself looking down into the cold, quarry water. And then he jumped: "I'm HIV positive," he said. "I've never been sick, really—" He hesitated. "Well, I was sick, fevers and—I got tired."

After a long silence, Denison said, "I'm really sorry. You're a thin man, but your color is so good."

"A year ago my viral load was high and they put me on a four-drug combination: two protease inhibitors, Saquinavir and Viracept, and two nucleoside analogues, d4T and Lamivudine. After a few weeks I felt better."

"I often wonder if Albert—Albert was my partner's name—had been able to go on the protease inhibitors, whether or not he'd still be here." Denison smiled. "Giving me shit."

"But in the meantime my lover had already bailed. You think I'm too thin?" said Bobby.

"You're beautiful," said Denison, "I'm a sucker for teal eyes. It would be healthier for you to carry a little extra, that's all."

Beautiful. He said *beautiful.* A sucker for teal eyes. Well. Guess this was a date after all.

"My tastes run to the Rubenesque. Speaking of Rubens, have you been to the Getty?" said Denison. He took a sip of iced tea and peered at Bobby over the rim of the glass.

"No. When should we go?"

"My schedule is flexible," said the writer.

"We're dark on Monday and Tuesday," said Bobby.

"The Getty is closed on Monday. How about Tuesday?

"Pick me up at ten?"

"Nine. We'll have breakfast first." Denison wiped his mouth with his napkin when the waiter delivered the check.

ଔଔଔ Nineteen: Cease Fire

A S IF DARK GLASSES could conceal his identity, Smelzkoff
kept them on when he stepped inside the Pacific Division
headquarters. He barreled through the reception area and into
the bullpen, bumping several desks on the way to his office at the back
of the building because his eyes hadn't been given time to adjust to the
interior darkness.

"Whoa, General," said Officer Perez, "where's the fire?"

"Yeah," said Detective Loman. "Too much coffee?"

"Something stronger than that I'd say," chimed Detective Dixon,
a fat man who enjoyed any chance to belittle Stanley Smelzkoff. "Must
be a stray back there," he sneered.

"Morning, Sam," yelled Smelzkoff, across the room. "Your truck-
load of donuts just pulled up in the parking lot."

In the hallway off the bullpen, Smelzkoff took momentary pleasure in the fact that his comment generated loud and sustained laughter, but his satisfaction evaporated when he opened his office door and saw The Deaconess sitting behind his desk.

She returned the documents to his top left drawer and closed it, without comment. Then she took some pages, stapled at the corner, from her valise and slid them across the surface of the desk to him. "*Venice Beach* magazine did a poll," she said," and the mayor got hold of it." Several of the poll results had been highlighted with a yellow marker. The statistic that first caught his attention had to do with the percentage of voters who thought that law enforcement efforts in the beach communities were being focused in the right direction. Eighty percent of those questioned said *No*. Only fifteen percent said *Yes,* and five percent said *Don't Know*.

The fact that there had been a poll, and that it was the reason for the councilwoman's visit took Smelzkoff by surprise. He feared that Gloria Deacon had learned about Bobby's pestilent dog being caught on the beach (though even she wouldn't be able to say that General Stanley Smelzkoff had given his son special treatment) or that she had seen the review of Bobby's play, *Salami*.

"This is bad," said Gloria Deacon. "Prop 1134 will never pass in November if people think we're wasting the resources we already have."

Proposition 1134 called for hiring 10,000 new police officers and was scheduled to appear on the ballot in November. "So we're talking about politics," said Smelzkoff. "What about making the city safe for tourists? What happened to making Venice the number one tourist attraction in Southern California?"

"September is a week away," said Gloria Deacon. "The tourists are packing up and heading home."

"Robberies and murders are down," said Smelzkoff, sitting in the chair normally reserved for his guests and facing Gloria Deacon. "People know we're serious about dogs, and they sure as Hell know we're serious about other crime, too," he said, slapping his hand on the desktop for emphasis.

"New stats are going to be in tomorrow morning's *Times*. They show increases in both categories over the summer. Homicides increased by more than ten percent. When that hits it'll only confirm the public's opinion."

"I don't see why—"

"Look, I don't have time to argue," said Gloria Deacon. "Even the courts have abandoned us on this. People aren't happily writing out checks to pay their fines; they're going to court—and the judges are agreeing with them; they're throwing out the dog cases."

"And that's my—"

"Look I didn't spend ten years as a city attorney and six as a councilwoman to see my career crash and burn. Listen to me. Every ticket written has been dismissed in court. Get it through your thick head: The war on dogs is over."

Beads of perspiration dotted Gloria Deacon's forehead and upper lip; she stood, took her briefcase, and came out from behind the desk. "The reason I came here is to tell you that you're to report to Lieutenant Portman again, effective immediately." She stooped to look in his aquarium. "You've got a dead loach in here. Your fish tank would be a great way to teach children about death."

She went to the door and opened it. Then she turned. "Oh, I need the keys to the Hummer. Our trial period is up—and we have to get it back to the dealer." She stuck out her hand and waited for him to fish them out of his pocket.

ಐಐಐ Twenty: Just When Things Were Looking Up

AFTER BREAKFAST (scrambled eggs, pancakes, bacon, grits, and collard greens; Denison came from Kentucky and knew of a restaurant that served soul food), he and Bobby drove to the entrance of the museum at the foot of the mountain, then five levels down into the underground parking structure. On the tram ride up to the museum complex, which sprawled atop the summit of the mountain like a modern Italian hill town, Bobby looked down upon the freeway that cut through the pass below, and then up at the surrounding cypress-covered mountains. "If they made this a roller coaster instead of a tram, they could combine the two best aspects of Southern California culture," he said. "Imagine, a day at a museum and an amusement park at the same time."

Daniel laughed. "The ride down would be wild. A vertical drop, a couple of loops out over the freeway, and a plunge into the darkness of the underground parking."

In a sense, to Bobby, it was like a vacation, or at least the kind of cultural day-trip that he had enjoyed when he lived in New York, and for some reason, perhaps the demands of putting *Salami* together, that he hadn't taken the time to make in Los Angeles. He and Denison sat next to each other on the train, close to the door. A young man sat across from them, listening silently while the old man beside him described in a monotone of detail the operation he had undergone. Bobby assumed the two were father and son. Denison leaned against Bobby as the tram rounded a bend, though they traveled at insufficient speed to actually cause him to pitch sideways.

Bobby felt good about *Salami* after a decent crowd on Saturday night and an even bigger one on Sunday afternoon, and he felt good about Denison too. It seemed more and more likely that at the very least he would have a good friend, but he couldn't allow himself to go beyond that concept at this time. It brought the entire specter of his health into the equation anew.

At the station on top they exited the train and looked around in the glare of sun that bounced off the white marble and granite of the complex of buildings. It was nearly impossible to keep ones eyes open without sunglasses. Bobby put his on. "Shall we see the Maplethorpe first, or the Grandma Moses?" he said.

Denison grinned. "I've been before. You decide." Then before Bobby could, he added, "I have a suggestion. There's an exhibit about the architect and the history of this commission. The whole concept of building this place is worthy of attention first."

As the one usually in charge of the itinerary, Bobby relaxed at the prospect of being swept along in this magnificent campus of culture. "And then the Impressionists. I get bored with the religious paintings," he said.

"We're off," said Denison, "like pants at a party."

"Sounds like my kind of party," said Bobby, though the comment seemed an unlikely one coming from the sophisticated Denison.

❦•❧

During the day, Bobby and Denison touched each other often. They leaned together at the shoulder while viewing Van Gogh's "Irises"; their hips and legs were in contact as they sat by the fountain sipping iced teas; Denison directed Bobby by the arm to a favorite work of Manet; Bobby nudged the writer and pulled him into the next gallery to view a drawing by Degas. And in one of the more solemn moments, Bobby surprised himself: as they stood on the plaza looking out over the city and mountains, Bobby removed his sunglasses, placed his hand on Denison's shoulder, and said, "The review saved our play. Thank you."

Denison took off his sunglasses too and hugged him. "A good review of a good play is nothing to thank me for. You're quite a special person, I think. I hope to get to know you better."

Bobby pushed back and looked at him. "Wow," he said. "Me too." His face felt hot and flushed from the sun.

"What next?" said Denison. "How about a tour of the central garden? An ever-changing work of art, according to the brochure."

"I need to call Flo to check on advance sales. Right after?" said Bobby.

Denison took a cellular phone from his pocket. "Be my guest," he said.

At first Bobby thought Flo was playing with him, but the fact that he talked so fast and was so short of breath, convinced Bobby take the big man seriously. "We're shut down. We're shut down. We're shut down," said Flo. He went on to relate how two goons from the city had come to inspect the theater, spending over an hour and a half, writing citations for dozens of violations. Electrical code irregularities, plumbing leaks in the public restrooms, flammable materials in the back hallways. "They haven't bothered me in five years," said Flo. "I would have offered them money if I thought it would have worked, but the assholes wouldn't even talk to me. They barged in and boy did they have a mission. They didn't really look at the wiring or in the fuse boxes. They were too busy poking in closets and opening up drawers. They were on a mission for sure. You better get in here. And just when things were looking up too."

Bobby hung up and stared down at his feet. "I smell The General," he said. Denison waited for him to elaborate. "Building inspectors. We're shut down. Flo said they came by and left a series of violations that have to be corrected before we can reopen. I've got to go." He wiped the sweat from his forehead. "Though I don't know what I can do."

"I'll go with you. Let's see if they're things we can correct. I'll call a friend at City Hall too and see what I can find out."

Bobby had always wanted to be one of those people who shrugged when adversity came. He saw others smile and whistle in trouble's face. But he couldn't. He had tried any number of remedies. He's had accepted, after an adjustment period, the prospect of his HIV infection; he had resolved to move on after Jason abandoned him; he was determined not to let his father's perverse persecution of him destroy his disposition. As if all that weren't enough, now his father's aggression threatened not only him, but also people who relied on him. If he had someone to count on (a partner or a parent would do) he might be able to withstand this onslaught of bad fortune. But face it, he had neither. Denison had been grand, as they said in the movies of the thirties, but Bobby wasn't about to drag him down too. Best to cut things off now, before he got too attached.

"I appreciate your support, Daniel. But I'd better handle this myself," said Bobby.

Denison persisted, "What if—"

"What if nothing," said Bobby. "This is my problem. Not yours."

The tram arrived at the terminal. Bobby and Denison both got on without comment and they continued down the mountain in silence too. Who needed a roller coaster? Life had enough ups and downs on its own.

On the way to the elevator, which would take them to the garage, Bobby considered saying something to soften his remarks, but his destructive streak prevented him from doing so. Denison was apparently wise enough and secure enough to let Bobby have his way on this and seemed content to make the trip down to the car, the drive up and out of the garage, down the freeway and into Venice without further discourse. At home in front of his house, Bobby opened the door and got out. "Thanks. I'm sorry how things worked out," he said, as if they'd had a lover's quarrel.

"Me too," said Denison. "Call me if you change your mind. I believe I can help."

Ginger waited behind the gate to greet him; Bobby crouched and let her lick his face. "Man's best friend, right?" he said. In the back yard, Frederick and Rex were sunning naked by the pool. The Dame, dressed in shorts and a bib apron emblazoned with the slogan *How do you like your meat?* was barbecuing on the grill. "Just in time for supper," he said to Bobby. "Shall I put on a Thuringer for you?"

A Roy Orbison CD emanated from the outdoor speakers. Such a scene might even give Bobby's mother a shock if she were to suddenly come home. This definitely wasn't the Disney Channel.

ॐ•ॐ

After Bobby explained the reason for his inability to smile, The Dame, Frederick, and Rex all chose to go with him to Hollywood.

When they arrived at the theater they found Flo in the middle of a row of seats about ten rows back from the stage. He sat slumped down, his head resting on the seat back, the violations clutched in his hand.

"May I?" said Bobby, reaching for the papers. He took them to the pit area of the stage and turned on the lamp on top of the computer equipment. He thumbed through the pages then tried to read the large, loopy scrawl of the forms, but interpreting data and translating legalese were not skills that Bobby possessed and (though he was determined not to allow the others to witness his helplessness) he felt instantly and hopelessly inept.

"What time does the curtain go up?" Bobby looked up to see Denison coming down the center aisle. "I reached my friend at City Hall just as he was leaving for home. He's already on the case," said

Denison, now a few feet away. Bobby smiled, too embarrassed to speak. And then Denison was at the railing of the pit. "I'd love to take a look when you're finished." The writer pointed to the paperwork in Bobby's hand.

"I was finished before I started," said Bobby, with another smile.

Denison didn't waste time. He methodically scanned each page for a moment, then returned to the first and began to study it carefully. For fifteen minutes he focused on the material, nodding, frowning, shaking his head, and sniffing. Once or twice he smiled.

During the whole time the writer read, Bobby waited with patience. Finally Denison looked up and clapped his hands together. "Any coffee around this place?" he said. Bobby nodded, and Denison began to roll up his sleeves.

"Should I boil water and tear sheets into bandage strips?" said Bobby.

"That's the spirit," said Denison. Then he glanced over at The Dame, Frederick, and Rex. They had been quiet, huddled close to Flo. Bobby was aware now that they had all been waiting and watching for Denison's reaction just as patiently. "Let's have a powwow," said Denison.

≈•≈

Some of the violations, said Denison, could be corrected with a little concerted and concentrated effort. As an example, he pointed out that the paint cans and rags and ladders and other equipment that cluttered the backstage areas of the theater could be removed. "We need manpower," said Denison. "We'll spend whatever time it takes tonight to take care of the minor stuff and—"

"And then what?" said Flo, sitting forward in his seat. "I can't afford to rewire the whole theater and make it earthquake proof. I've spent all my reserve just getting us to this point. There's nothing left."

"Leave the big ones to me for the time being. I have a friend who's going to help me interpret the sections of the code cited—and then maybe we'll get a second opinion if we have to. I'm no expert, but some of these seem a little trumped up. Torn and broken seats; snagged carpeting in the aisles; asbestos on heat ducts. Come on. Who are they kidding? The important thing is that if we can correct most of the things cited, and show good faith that we're working to comply "

"Dame, can you make some calls? See if you can get the others in here to help," said Bobby. He was plenty worried, but Denison's positive attitude and display of confidence bolstered his morale.

"Good point, Bobby. Spend five minutes with me and we'll make a list, then you and Flo can take over. I'm meeting my friend for supper at eight," said Denison. "The worst thing we can do is panic."

Bobby suspected that Denison was playing captain of a sinking ship, telling people to use spoons to bail water in an effort to distract them from the fact that they were about to drown.

ಸಿಸಿಸಿ Twenty-One: Death Valley

CLEARLY, HE WAS OUTSIDE the loop now. Gloria Deacon hadn't mentioned Bobby's production of *Salami* or shown that she had seen the review in the *Times*; Lieutenant Portman likewise hadn't made any reference to The War on Dogs or suggested that anything out of the ordinary had happened. Portman had looked at him without expression when he said, "Now's a good time for you to take a week or so of your accumulated vacation. Go fishing or hunting. Take a little trip. When you get back I'll have a better idea of what to do with you. Assignment-wise, that is." And then Dolores came to the doorway to tell the lieutenant that someone wanted to see him about the holdup at Alan's Liquor, and Smelzkoff's audience was over.

At least he hadn't been suspended. Though to be technical how could they suspend him? And why would they want to? He'd followed orders, gotten approval for everything he'd done. Had been praised for a time even. What a farce. A couple of weeks off. Indeed. He didn't fear them. If he had to, he'd get a lawyer and sue. Take the money and start a business. He'd set himself up as a private investigator. That's what dismissed, former cops became wasn't it?

As for The Deaconess, well, during his short-lived period of glory he'd forgotten what a royal bitch she was. He wanted to bring up the fact that Bobby was his son, that they were estranged, and that he hadn't had anything to do with the perverted play. But how could he? Gloria Deacon would either not believe him or conclude that he was too weak to control his own family. Surely she must know he hadn't been aware of the opera's theme. Besides, according to the review the Herodkoff character had been the center of ridicule; she'd barely been mentioned.

He cleaned off the top of his desk, put private papers in his brief-case, and dropped a two-week feeder pellet in the fish tank. He had to practically beg for the keys back to the Hummer to collect his personal belongings. This cramped office space didn't seem so bad now. At least it had four walls.

On his way through the bullpen, this time to leave, no one spoke. Perez and Dixon were both on the phone and the others appeared busy with paperwork. Maybe he should open a bar, he thought. No, the hours would kill him; a gym would fit his lifestyle better.

Smelzkoff drove to Violet's house and looked in through the living room window, but she wasn't home. Shopping bags and boxes littered the floor. Perhaps she missed him so much that she had gone shopping to avoid the boredom.

If he found her at work it would only compound his misery. There would be no time or proper place to talk and he was going to have a difficult enough time telling her that all fifteen minutes of his fame had been used. Best thing he could do would be to drive home, pack up some clothes and toiletries, get in his truck, and head north. Or south. Or east. There was no one else to tell. As far as he was concerned, he no longer had a son.

⊷•⊷

The sun had set by the time Smelzkoff reached the city limits, if one could even tell in a place like Los Angeles where the city limits really were. His Blazer felt small and impotent after the HMV, and he didn't sit up nearly as high behind the wheel, but he was determined to think positively.

He headed toward Las Vegas. Though he had never been an enthusiastic gambler, he thought he might play the slots. Someone at the gym told him that the machines near the elevator in the MGM had better odds in order to entice players as they went to and from their rooms. When he convinced himself that he'd have to win a half-million dollars to really change his life, less than an hour from Las Vegas, he decided not to bother. He pulled onto the exit ramp of the freeway; at the end of the ramp he turned into the service station and took out his map from the glove box. He considered his options and after a few minutes got out to fill the gas tank. Continue east then south into the Grand Canyon? Or north into Death Valley? No choice here, really.

Stanley Smelzkoff didn't believe in astrology and horoscopes, ESP or UFO's. He didn't hear voices and had never seen The Virgin Mary on the side of a barn, shedding tears for her dead son. For some reason, though, he knew he had to go to Death Valley, perhaps because of the name, perhaps because of the symbolism of what had happened to the wagon train of migrating souls so long ago, but metaphors aside, there was nothing grand about his past and nothing to look forward to in his life but death. So, he turned north.

Radio reception in the area, limited to Country and Western music, was full of static and Smelzkoff turned it off after listening to a woman sob her way through something called, "The Bed Sheets Don't Lie". He didn't have a tape deck let alone a CD player, so there was nothing to distract him from a summary of his life; not much to be proud of, he had to admit: he hadn't made a lot of money, though money hadn't ever really mattered to him, and his only marriage had ended in divorce because Carol said he was insensitive—but she hadn't leveled that criticism while the sex was good. Still he couldn't blame her because he stopped wanting her. Since then, many women (and most of them had been young) had excited him, but none stirred in him anything that he could label love. Violet came closest, but in between the end of his marriage and meeting her he had grown too old to want to start over. An attitude to be sure, but in all his life he'd never lived through a decade that had seen so much change. From twenty to thirty: who cared? From thirty to forty: nothing. Forty to fifty: so what? But fifty to sixty. He was young at fifty and old at sixty. How could one have covered so much ground in ten years? Most men had their children to keep them fresh. And then grandchildren. He had Bobby. Enough said.

In his twenties he could have driven through the night and never tired. But since he had no deadline, and with sleep tugging mightily at the muscles in his face, he decided to stop for the night. The sign said, *VACANCY*, which didn't surprise Smelzkoff, inasmuch as the Valley Winds Motel was obviously an independent operation and not affiliated with even one of the cheap chains. He drove in and stopped at the office, located in a small, separate front building. The owner or manager apparently lived in this building; the motel rooms, approximately a dozen or so, were side by side in a long building at the back. One high-mounted light and a full moon illuminated the area, revealing one car and a pickup truck. Smelzkoff approached the office, looked at his watch, and rang the night bell.

A table lamp had been left on, providing enough light for Smelzkoff to look through the window and see the reception desk, the lamp, and in the corner, a table with a coffee maker and packets of artificial creamer and sweeteners. He rang the bell again and this time the door before him shuddered, indicating that a second door had been opened creating a temporary vacuum in the room. A brighter, overhead light came on and a woman in a robe appeared in the room; she glanced at him through the glass, smoothed her hair with her hands, and walked toward him.

"Sorry to come so late," said Smelzkoff, raising his voice to be heard through the door. "I was trying to drive through "

The woman opened the door. "That's fine," she said. "When we don't want to get up we turn on the *No Vacancy* light." She smiled and looked out at his truck. "Just you?" He nodded. "Twenty-eight a night."

She stepped back from the door, went over behind the desk, and took out a registration card for him. Her robe didn't reveal much about her body, but Smelzkoff guessed her age at about forty and decided that she was in pretty good shape. He followed her inside, stood on the other side of the desk, and began to complete the card with the pencil she handed him. When he had filled in all the necessary blanks, she took a key down from the wooden rack and slid it across the glass surface to him. "Number one on the end," she said. "Should be nice and quiet tonight."

Smelzkoff took a twenty and a ten from his wallet and laid it on the counter. He tried a joke. "Did they ever catch that werewolf roaming these parts?" he said.

She smiled. "Tax brings it to thirty dollars and thirty-one cents," she said. "That includes coffee and sweet rolls in the morning."

He was about to close the door behind him when she said, "Drove a stake through his heart right behind your room. Sleep well."

On unlocking the door he detected the aroma of fresh paint and the synthetic smell of new carpeting; he judged the flowered spread on the bed to be a recent acquisition as well. The TV looked up-to-date and in the bathroom a white, plastic shower unit had been installed. He didn't bother to unload the car or unpack his bag; he undressed to his underwear, fell into bed, and went to sleep.

The sun woke him early but he lay in bed for nearly an hour without moving to get up. When he went to the car to get his toiletries, a small kitten no more than a few weeks old sat on the gravel. When it saw Smelzkoff it started to meow hysterically and tried to follow him back into the room, but he shut the door before it could gain entry.

After showering and shaving, he remembered the complimentary coffee in the office, and when he opened his door, he found the kitten still there; on seeing him it cried and followed him for a few yards across the parking area, then stopped and retreated to the concrete pad in front of his room again when Smelzkoff broke into a trot.

The motel, constructed of concrete blocks, was located in the middle of nothing and nowhere. Little vegetation survived in such the surrounding scrubby earth, and he couldn't imagine enough traffic in the area to support even a modest motel and then there was the issue of the remodeling.

The woman who had let him in the night before sat at the desk watching some television morning show. "No marks on your neck. I trust you slept well?" she said, when he opened the door.

Smelzkoff grinned and walked to the coffee pot. He tore open a pack of artificial creamer and emptied the contents into a Styrofoam cup. He topped off the cup with coffee and when he looked up the woman was staring at him. She smiled again, and then looked back at the TV.

"There's a brindle kitten outside my room," said Smelzkoff.

"Yeah?" she said. "There was an old striped stray with a litter of four. I think a snake got the others. Might have got the mother too. Haven't seen her for a few days now come to think of it." Smelzkoff looked at her without speaking. She kept her eyes trained on the television.

"How did a stray get out here?" he said at last.

"Car. People dump unwanted animals by the highway all the time," she said. "It's outside your room? Someone must have fed it. We had an elderly couple in there the other night."

"Do you have half and half for coffee?" said Smelzkoff.

"We just got what's out there," she said, still not looking up.

"Where can I get some breakfast?" he said.

"Down the road, back on the interstate, there's the Why Not? restaurant. As good as you'll get in these parts." When he stood in the door, with his back to her, she said, "You look familiar. Have I seen you on TV?"

Smelzkoff shook his head and left before she could follow up. The kitten ran out to greet him when he approached his room; Smelzkoff looked in both directions, and then stooped to pet it. It immediately clasped his hand with its paws and bit at his fingers with its small, sharp teeth, but as soon as it realized that the fingers weren't yielding any milk, it stopped sucking and resumed its agitated meowing. Smelzkoff tried to soothe it by his petting it but it was far too hungry to be distracted from its misery. Its eyes were still blue, and under the soft fur he felt the detailed outline of the kitten's ribs.

Stanley Smelzkoff remembered the cat that had come to their back door when he was a child. He had convinced his grandmother to let him feed it and it stayed for a couple of months before it got run over in the alley behind their house. His father, during one of his rare visits, had belittled him for crying about it. Smelzkoff knew that Teddy Williams had been responsible for the kitten's death; the high school hood tore up and down the alley at an excessive speed in his hot-rod, 1950 Mercury. It was guys like Teddy that had made Smelzkoff want to be a cop.

He put the kitten down and its mouth opened and closed in weak screams. He brought it some water in an ashtray and went to pack up his things, and when he came back out to put his bags in the car, he didn't see the cat anymore. He got in the truck and drove onto the highway in the direction of the restaurant. The sun beat, relentless and hot, against the side of the motel; with no shade around, he wondered if the kitten could survive much longer.

The waitress brought the coffee pot when she saw he him sit in the booth by the window. This coffee was only slightly stronger than that at the motel. She placed the menu on the table.

"Biscuits and gravy," he said, when she came back a minute later with her pad. Somehow, ordering egg whites seemed out of place and somewhat un-masculine in this part of the country. When she set the plate of floury, white food in front of him, he picked up his fork and began to eat, slowly and thoughtfully, unable to shake the image of the starving, striped kitten. After he had finished every morsel, he took his spoon and scraped the surface of the plate to collect the remaining bits of gravy. When the waitress came back to pour him more coffee, he said, "I'd like an order of the biscuits and gravy to go too."

"Good, ain't it?" she said.

"Tasty," he said. "I like the chunks of sausage, like my grand-mother made on Sunday mornings."

In the truck, he put the sack of biscuits and gravy on the passenger seat next to him and started the engine. He drove onto the highway again and headed back toward the Valley Winds Motel.

ಟಟಟ Twenty-Two: Taking the Show on the Road

DENISON HAD DONE WHAT HE COULD. Bobby thanked him and then broke the news to The Dame and Flo in his dressing room office the next morning. "Daniel's friend says the orders came from the very top; they won't even send anyone out to re-inspect until the end of the week. Daniel says we need a good lawyer."

"Does the very top mean the Mayor or the Chief-of-Police or what?" said Flo.

"The friend traced the paper work back to the Public Works Department, Building and Safety Division. But Denison's friend thinks someone one higher put the idea in their head," said Bobby.

"Any theater built before 1940 would have the same problems. This never came up when I closed on this place five years ago," said Flo.

"It's clear, someone thinks this will hurt their chances in the fall elections," said The Dame. "It's government sponsored censorship if you ask me. The land of the free and the home of the brave indeed."

"Daniel has made arrangements to have an engineer friend look into what it would take for us to comply and he's putting an attorney friend in touch to buy us more time, but the week is probably shot," said Bobby. "Maybe the whole production. I feel like I got you all in this mess and I don't know how to—"

"Girls, let's take the show on the road," said The Dame.

"Do you realize how much work it would take to get even the most minimalist production moved to another theater? And where is a such a place anyway?" said Bobby. "We'd still lose a week or two."

Flo tried to sit up in the overstuffed chair, but he ended up slumping lower in it. "This chair is probably a violation of some city code," he said. "There's an outdoor theater in Topanga Canyon. It's not very big though."

"You bloody Americans," said The Dame. "You had the Boston tea party and resisted Vietnam and you still don't get the essence of how to express dissent." She shook her large head. "Does anyone here remember Stonewall? Flo, you're old enough."

"When the drag queens protested in Greenwich Village," said Bobby. "Against the police who were raiding the gay bars. I don't remember Stonewall, but I know about it."

"We'll get the cast and every drag queen from a hundred miles and we'll picket right out in front on the street," said The Dame. "Call your boyfriend and have him get his DOGS group out here too."

"He's not my boyfriend," said Bobby.

"Right," said The Dame. "And I'm the Queen Mum. Just call him. Okay? Or do you want me to?"

"I don't know," said Bobby.

"Are you committed to *Salami* or are you going to accept this injustice lying down?" said The Dame.

⋙•⋘

When Bobby finally called Denison, after prodding from The Dame and Flo, he was surprised at the writer's enthusiasm for the demonstration. For the first time since arriving back in Los Angeles Bobby found himself following orders and not giving them. The Dame and Flo manned the telephones, immediately after shooing Bobby from his own office. "We'll need placards, and you're the artist here," said The Dame. "Frederick and Rex can help you."

The idea of rebellion bothered Bobby and he tried hard to understand the reasons for his reluctance to participate. He'd never been successful at challenging authority; with Poppy his ultimate solution had been to move away. When he was confronted by disagreement or conflict he usually withdrew; he wasn't much of a fighter.

When Denison showed up at the theater late in the afternoon with the news that he expected at least fifty members of DOGS to show up for the sidewalk demonstration, Bobby expressed his concerns. "That's great, but what if it all gets too big? Drag queens have a lot of anger. What if they turn violent?"

"That sounds rather homophobic," said Denison.

"Well you know. One minute they're carrying candles and the next they're smashing out store windows," said Bobby.

"I don't believe I'm hearing this," said Denison. He stood and came over to Bobby. "Get up. We need to talk in private."

Bobby sat on the floor astride a banner in the making, paintbrush in hand. Rex and Frederick sat nearby making their own signs but they had stopped work and were listening to the exchange.

Denison reached down, took Bobby by the arm, and pulled him to his feet, and then he pushed him to the wings and behind the stage set.

"This isn't fair and you know it. These people are your friends and they've invested a lot of their time and energy in this production and you can't just walk away from them. Don't let these petty city officials intimidate you."

"If you'd grown up with my father "

"This isn't just between you and your father anymore," said Denison. "Maybe you should talk to him."

"I can't talk to him. He's the enemy. He started all this."

"I'm not so sure."

"What do you mean?"

"He's not really a general. He's a sergeant. A pawn."

Denison put his arms around Bobby. "My friend says he's sure the shutdown of the theater didn't originate with him. As a matter of fact he says your father has been suspended, or at least he's not at the Pacific Division headquarters." Bobby stepped back and looked at Denison. "After my friend told me what he found out, I called the station and said I was a reporter. 'Could I please talk to Sergeant Smelzkoff,' I said. The receptionist told me that he was on leave. Gloria Deacon and someone higher is really responsible, I think. It sounds like they don't know what to do with him."

"Wow," said Bobby. "Just like in *Salami*. Life imitates art. Herod's real influence was Herodias. She was the one speaking out against John the Baptist. She, not Herod, drove the plot." He narrowed his eyes and stared at Denison for a moment. "Thanks. Seems like I'm always thanking you. I'm going to try to reach Poppy at home."

ॐ • ॐ

The first protesters, mostly members of the cast and crew, appeared on the street at about four o'clock in the afternoon. The marquee now announced: *Performance Cancelled by Order of the City of Los Angeles*. And even though the theater was a block off of Hollywood Boulevard, traffic on the street had grown progressively heavier, which probably meant that word had spread that there were a collection of strange people picketing on the sidewalk. Cars in both directions slowed almost to a halt, as they drove by the theater marquee. Despite Denison's review the play wasn't well known, and Bobby couldn't help thinking that if they could get reopened this publicity would be a godsend.

Rex wanted to wear his Herodkoff costume as he carried his placard, but Bobby vetoed that idea. "On stage is one thing, but it isn't Halloween," he said. "We don't want to send the message that we were cancelled on the basis of obscenity. We want to rally people behind us. We don't want to polarize the community," said Bobby. "Can I march naked?" said Frederick.

By five o'clock, many of the DOGS members called by Denison had showed up; by Bobby's conservative estimate at least fifty or sixty protesters strolled the sidewalk. Indeed, they were so many people it was difficult to read all the signs and banners. STOP CENSORSHIP. STOP POLITICS. LA UNFAIR TO ART. CAST MAYOR OUT. DEACON HATES DOGS. DAUGHTER OF SODOM. VOTE NO ON DEACON. KISS MY MOUTH. NO ON PROP 1134. NO NEW POLICE. FREE SPEECH. KISS THIS. BLACKMAIL. AND IN A WEIRD TWIST: PREPARE TO DIE. THE END IS NEAR. DON'T EAT HERE.

The Dame had a hand-held bullhorn and had turned the protest into a performance. "Ladies and Gentleman, do not be fooled by Proposition 1134. We don't need new police. We need to properly use the ones we have. Instead of worrying about dogs, they should fight real crime. They closed us down because we exposed their ineffectiveness. We challenge the wisdom of this administration." The drivers passing honked their horns in agreement. "One-one-three-four," he yelled into the speaker, "we don't need no more."

At seven, with the rush hour still in full force, the total number of protesters had swelled to about one hundred and thirty people. Bobby walked through the crowd, as though in a nightclub. (The ratio of drag queens to ordinary citizens was about two to one.) Many of the people he'd never even seen before. Unfamiliar faces smiled when they saw him; strangers slapped him on the back. "Good show, Bobby. It's about time someone resisted the fascist bullying of the bureaucracy."

Legally, Bobby was at a loss. What if there was legitimacy to some of the violations? What if some were valid, particularly with regard to the electric and structural problems? He knew that they could raise the money for some of the needed corrections, but what if they were required to do major refitting? They couldn't raise unlimited cash, after all. Denison told him that they were trumped up charges, that the codes for new theaters were undoubtedly stricter than for existing theaters, but that it was only sensible to allow owners to comply on a schedule, over time. "Yeah," said Bobby, "They shouldn't come in and destroy an existing business by making them close down to make repairs."

And then Denison reversed himself. "They do that sort of thing all the time. Unfortunately. They drove the tanning industry out of business over pollution. They close restaurants until they clean up and make repairs. But we've got an expert looking at our case." All the mess and clutter had been cleaned up, and Denison restated his belief that the real thrust of their predicament was political, not safety or any other issue. "My review worked," he said. "Too well. Someone from the city came to see this production, went back and issued a warning to the higher-ups. In their hulking, elephantine way, they reacted the only way they knew. By force."

Camera crews from all the television and radio stations had arrived and attempted to get interviews. The Dame sang one song, "I believe in miracles, you sexy thing " and looking directly into the bank of cameras, went right into another. "Oh we got trouble. Right here in Sleazy City." After he finished this number, he said, "I want to bring our producer and director, Bobby Smelzkoff, to the microphone." Confused for a moment, Bobby then realized the Dame had called the bullhorn a microphone, probably because he was so used to being on stage that he often used certain canned phrases and words. He took the device from him and was about to speak when he saw the flashing lights and heard the sirens from the arriving LAPD squad. The crowd joined hands, formed a circle, stretching from one end of the block to the other. "We shall overcome," they sang. "We shall overcome, someday."

৪০৪০৪০ Twenty-Three: Awakening

SMELZKOFF ARRIVED AT THE EDGE of Death Valley at midday, with the sun high overhead, casting no shadows. The park covered an immense area, stretching more than a hundred miles along or near the California-Nevada border. Stanley Smelzkoff felt calm in the heat, with his windows down, driving past the markers: Jubilee Pass, Funeral Peak, and Dante's View. He smiled at the sign that identified the lowest point (282 below sea level) in the U.S. "Do we feel low?" he said aloud. "Yeah, I'd said this is where we should be. Are we below sea level?" Then he began to whistle softly.

Only the hardiest ventured out in these conditions, and rarely did he pass another car. He kept the windows open and his speed moderate. There were apparently few park visitors in this the off-season, other than the Europeans who didn't usually come here in the winter, and he guessed that the temperature exceeded 110 degrees. Gradually as he got deeper into the park the scenery became more beautiful, which is to say the vast, rolling terrain gave way to more mountainous and colorful vistas, a surprise to him because like most people he had only seen the edges of the park that abutted Interstate 15 on the way to Las Vegas. If the Furnace Creek Inn, in the center of the national park, was booked, he would keep driving and find a motel outside the boundary.

After a couple of hours, he saw the sign pointing to the lodge. Smelzkoff parked in the visitors' lot and shut off the engine. Backtracking to Barstow on his special mission cost him several hours and he knew that had he arrived before lunch as originally planned, his chances of securing a room would have been better. Stretching across the seat, he lifted the moist towel off of the kennel carrier. The kitten was sleeping and didn't move so he replaced the towel, now nearly dry, and opened the door of the truck. In Barstow at the pet store he had purchased a carrier, several cans and bags of food, cat litter and a box, and some toys, though the cat was far too undeveloped and weak to be interested in toys.

The inn, located in a palm-treed oasis, raised Smelzkoff's spirits. He had a view of the grassy lawn and the grove of palms; since the day was so hot, it was at present quiet and still outside. One had no choice but to slow down, relax, and accept the heat. A decade earlier he might have enjoyed this chance to be alone, this chance to meet new people in the restaurant or at the bar or out by the pool. When the desk told him there was a vacancy, he hadn't told him about his companion. He settled in the room, fed the kitten, and waited till it slept again before he crept quietly out and closed the door.

He checked his map of the park and set out toward Telescope Peak, which rose above the valley floor to an elevation of over 11,000 feet. Remarkable considering that less than twenty-five miles directly east was the low point in the United States, which he had passed on his way to the inn.

The drive back after sunset had been slower and tedious without the surrounding scenery as inspiration. The temperature fell rapidly after dark; Smelzkoff shivered as he stepped from his truck and hurried to the room. If the cat had awakened and started to meow it might have aroused the interest of a housekeeper.

After tending to the kitten, which seemed a great deal stronger, he showered, shaved, and dressed for dinner. The little creature was calmer now that it was getting more frequent feeding and it surprised Smelzkoff when it batted at a crumpled piece of paper that he had tossed on the bedspread where it lay. He sat on the edge of the bed and flicked the paper with his thumbnail at the kitten and it batted it back again. He decided that the thing must be older than he had first thought. Its emaciated condition had made it seem more tentative and more helpless.

When he tried to put it back in the kennel carrier it began to meow loudly again. He put towels over the top to muffle the sound and put it in the bathroom and left for supper. He stood in the hallway for a while to convince himself that it couldn't be heard, and then he suddenly thought about Violet. She would be very good with the kitten.

Smelzkoff, irritated with himself for thinking of her, resolved to persevere with self-sufficiency. After all, he hadn't come here on vacation; he had chosen these harsh surroundings in order to take stock of his existence. To sum it all up. A look back, so to speak. He had hoped to arrive at some sort of understanding about life. His life. Where he had been and where he might go if he chose to continue. He didn't have a plan, though he had considered suicide as a concept.

From childhood he had dreamed of being a cop. To be sure his notion of being a cop had been defined by the types he had known or interacted with back in the Midwest, where cops walked beats, joked with people, stopped in the neighborhood diner to have a cup of coffee with friends. Cops were people, respected by others. In Los Angeles they were barricaded in cars or motorcycles and isolated on the free-ways. True there had been changes in recent years. Put a cop on bicycle or horseback and he suddenly became less threatening.

Most of the time, when people obeyed the law they got along fine with cops. Why did dog owners have to be so belligerent? He didn't make the laws. There were good reasons for dogs not be allowed on the beaches. And he firmly believed that if they were allowed to sneer at even those laws, crime overall would increase.

Bobby had been obedient as a child. What had happened? Carol had raised him more or less after the divorce; she was the one responsible.

The bartender stood with his back to the room, watching the news on television. "What do you have on tap?" said Smelzkoff to the bartender. The man turned.

"Sorry, I didn't see you," he said. "Michelob."

Smelzkoff nodded and moments later accepted the iced mug of beer. "What's happening?" he said, when the man turned again to the television.

"Some sort of altercation in Hollywood got the asshole police out in force," said the bartender. Smelzkoff winced, but said nothing. "Mind if I turn the sound up?" said the man. He looked around the empty room, and then aimed the remote control at the set.

It was that ingénue reporter who had covered The War on Dogs for one of the local stations. "The streets are clear now," she said into her mike, "after the clash earlier this evening between police and pro-testers outside the old Olympia Theater here in Hollywood." She stood in front of the entrance on a trash-strewn sidewalk. "A production of *Salami*, an opera spoof of *Salome*, had opened recently, playing two performances before being shut down by the city for alleged safety vio-lations. The production, a satire, sharply critical of police efforts in the recent War on Dogs, lampooned many of the main figures in the con-flict. Protestors, who included members of the opposition organization knows as DOGS and the cast and supporting staff of the theater, pick-eted here earlier, maintaining that the violations were trumped up in an effort to censor their political message. With Prop 1134 on the ballot this November (a measure to provide funding for the hiring of an additional ten thousand police) the protestors maintain that closing the theater was politically timed and motivated. We have footage from earlier which we're going to roll now." There was a pause; the reporter stared, motionless and silent into the camera, blinking occasionally until the tape was cued.

And then Smelzkoff saw the woman he had arrested on the beach with Bobby's mutt, a bullhorn in her fist, standing outside the theater, surrounded by a crowd. "I want to bring our producer and director, Bobby Smelzkoff, to the microphone," she said.

The demonstrators had linked arms and formed a circle. "We shall overcome some day," they sang.

"I'm a great admirer of Martin Luther King," Bobby began, "and I hear our friends the police approaching in the distance. When they get here, after they've run cars and innocent bystanders out of their way in their rush to arrest us for unlawful assembly, or protesting without a permit, or civil disobedience, or whatever regulation or law they can cite, let's remember the lesson of The Reverend Martin Luther King and his inspiration Gandhi. Refrain from violence. Violence solves nothing."

The tape had been cut and spliced here. The spectacle changed instantly, from Bobby's calming words, to a full-scale, violent confrontation. His references to Gandhi and King, hadn't been heard by the police, or if they had been heard they were ignored, and despite the attempts of most of the protestors to sit on the sidewalk and continue singing when the law enforcers arrived, the tape showed Smelzkoff's fellow police officers dragging and shoving demonstrators off the sidewalk to other cops who waited by the opened doors of a half-dozen paddy wagons to receive the wrongdoers. Many on the sidewalk appeared to be female impersonators, who triggered especially rough treatment. The jostled cameraman focused unsteadily on the transvestites, who screamed, yelled, and swatted at the police with open hands while the officers kicked and swiped at them with truncheons to prod them to their feet. One woman officer, as tall and wide as an elm, knocked the bullhorn out of Bobby's hand. He fell to the sidewalk and was immediately trampled by several cops trying to wrestle other protestors away from the theater entrance doors. Smelzkoff sat forward on the bar stool, as if by positioning himself differently he could see what was no longer revealed on screen. Seeing his own blood and flesh treated in such a brutal manner, indeed seeing all of this as an observer, and not an organizer and participant as he had been at the beach, sickened Smelzkoff and filled him with shame. Suddenly it was like one of his planned operations at the beach: helicopters flew in circular patterns overhead, their flood lights illuminating the streets in zigzag patterns, police manned their own bullhorns, truncheons rose and fell like hammers on anvils. It was a pandemonium of noise and confusion, with people running in all directions to evade the mayhem.

"Jesus," said the bartender. "It's Chicago in '68."

To Stanley Smelzkoff it was a bizarre and surreal movie premier. "*Day of the Locust*," he said, almost under his breath. Now he saw. In his desire for order he had become Colonel Nicholson in *The Bridge on the River Kwai*.

His son had pleaded for calm (in a self-assured and elegant way he had to admit) and it had all meant nothing to the peacekeepers.

After a few more scenes of the police slamming victims into the facade of the theater next to the sidewalk and throwing them across the hoods and trunks of parked cars, after countless images of protestors with bloodied faces and heads, attempting to shield themselves with their hands and arms, yelling in fear and agony, as they were thrown, tossed, beaten, dragged, kicked, and clubbed into the street, all of which lasted no more than thirty seconds but represented time endless and infinite in its sadness and brutality for Stanley Smelzkoff, the tape concluded and the broadcast was live again. "After the confrontation, more than fifty of the demonstrators were taken to jail, and another twenty-five have been admitted to area hospitals," said the reporter, her voice strained and strident. "Most of the twenty-five have been treated and released but apparently three of the demonstrators are in serious condition. The producer of the show, Bobby Smelzkoff, we are told suffered a concussion and is being held for observation in an area hospital. This is Beverly Black, reporting from Hollywood."

Smelzkoff felt as though he might never again have an appetite. The bartender puckered his lips and made a clucking sound with his tongue. "Another beer?" he said.

Smelzkoff stared at the screen without moving his body or shifting his eyes. He was afraid that if he tried to talk before he regained his composure, his voice would fail. Finally he swallowed and looked up at the bartender, who was waiting for him to respond. Smelzkoff looked at him and said, "Bobby Smelzkoff is my son."

৪৩৪৩৪৩ Twenty-Four: Violet Doesn't Live There Anymore

VIOLET AWOKE EARLY in the new apartment and began to unpack boxes after Bradley Zieman left. She walked barefoot to place the etched, crystal vase on the mantelpiece and decided that she would light a fire after the sun set. It shone now, directly through the front windows, warming the bleached, hardwood floors. Dr. Zieman told her that he had bought the six-unit building more than ten years ago as an investment, and if she liked the vacant, one-bedroom unit he'd let her have it for a reasonable price, on a month-to-month basis.

Whiskey strolled in from the kitchen after he had eaten some of the fresh food poured generously into his bowl by Violet: her way of saying this is your new home; there'll be plenty to eat here. Violet put the litter box in one corner of the bathroom, and immediately showed the cat where it was. Whiskey didn't seem at all upset by his new surroundings; Violet wondered if he sensed her relief to be out of Venice and in this roomier and better-maintained flat. After a while, it would cost her less. Eventually, it would cost her nothing.

Telling Bradley Zieman of her plans to move had been a wise and time saving decision. He had taken her to see the place; she had immediately said *yes*, and that had saved her a week of uncertainly over searching for a new home. He had even hired two day laborers, outside Home Depot, and rented a U-Haul truck for her, but Violet waited until dark to have them load her furniture and clothing into it. The whole move had been accomplished in four hours. Her luck had held. Poppy hadn't stopped by, and none of the neighbors had said anything either—but then she'd never encouraged the people on either side of her to get friendly. She had the telephone disconnected, had the utilities shut off, and left no forwarding address or phone number. Today would be the second day that she hadn't gone to work at the Mansion. She knew she could be found, certainly by someone as determined as Kent, but she hoped she made it difficult enough to allow her the time to solidify her relationship with the ripe Dr. Zieman

Whiskey sat in a rhomboid of sun and cleaned his paw; Violet went to the kitchen for a cup of hot tea and lemon. Bradley had hooked up her CD player and speakers before he left for his office; she opened another box to unpack and then put in the classical selection that Bobby had given her. Something called *the War of 1812 Overture*. "Tschaikovsky is great for beginners," he said when he gave it to her, "and full of energy." She missed spending time with Bobby. She missed Poppy too.

The morning and afternoon passed quickly. She listened to the overture twice (it did give her energy and made her feel that her decision to start over had been the correct one) before shutting off the player and turning on the television to watch "Oprah".

At four o'clock, when the first news of the evening came on, she saw the reporter on the street in Hollywood, but she paid scant attention. She had never been too interested in the news. She found world events completely beyond her comprehension. Bosnia, Serbia, Belfast, Tanzania, and Pakistan: I mean who knew where any of them were? As for the national scene, it was all politics: lawyers and politicians pissing on each other like dogs. But no question, local news was the worst: murders, rapes, abductions, and drive-by shootings. Incest. Who needed to hear of that?

Once she realized that the protest in the street involved Bobby and his opera, she didn't leave the floor in front of the television. Seeing The Dame with that loud speaker was what first caught her attention. With most drag queens it was easy to tell. But The Dame seemed like a real woman no matter what she wore. Violet recognized several others too. The one who called herself Sally Monella wore an outfit of eggplant-colored Capri pants and a pink, ruffled off-the-shoulder top that reminded Violet of those pictures of Cheryl in high school. Georgia Bush, in a tank top and shorts and not dressed as a woman, let Violet see what an attractive man the boy was, with his wide shoulders, small waist, and shapely, thick legs. Frederick and his muscular friend (she couldn't recall his name) were together, carrying signs of protest, and she remembered seeing them wrestling together when she gone to the theater that time. Dressed alike, in green and black Spandex singlets with white cross-training athletic shoes, they looked so *together*. Not only together in a fashion sense, but also in a couples sense. Violet had practically forgotten about Frederick (though she found him as attractive as she had initially) and the possibility struck her for the first time that he might be gay, or at least bisexual. He and the bodybuilder boy touched each other frequently. Even now, as they marched with their signs, they socked and punched one another, each of them draping his free arm over the other's shoulder.

She watched events unfold, from the peaceful marching to the violent and bloody thrashing that followed after the police interceded. She saw Bobby go down, she saw Frederick and the friend being dragged away, she saw the bewildered and frightened faces of the other protestors, and she felt something she had never expected to feel. Guilt. Bobby, she knew, had tried to help her. He had volunteered to make her part of the production; he had wanted to be her friend; he had given her the chance to be part of something. There was something inspiring about such a large group all wanting the same thing, all committed to expressing themselves as one. That was something she'd felt in the beginning with the girls at Fantasy. They were a family. Like Bobby and this group. A family.

Violet stood, looked at herself in the mirror over the mantelpiece, then went to the bathroom and ran a brush through her hair. She wasn't quite sure what she could do to help, but she couldn't just sit by at home and watch when Bobby needed help.

Twenty-Five: What's Going On Here?

TIME PASSED QUICKLY on the way back to Los Angeles. The night traffic consisted primarily of tractor-trailer rigs, traveling at high speed, in caravans. The kitten slept peacefully, stirring once or twice to scratch its ears, and Smelzkoff made a mental note to check for fleas and mites after they got home.

But first he needed to stop by Violet's. Once in Venice he headed south to Washington Boulevard, and turned back north on Dell to enter the canals. The sky lightened; the sun would be up in another half-hour. If she had worked the late shift she should still be in bed, but her car wasn't in her allotted space, as he pulled up. He parked, nevertheless, and looked in his glove box for a pen or pencil and something to write on. He held the pen to his teeth in an effort to compose something with the proper tone. *Dear Violet,* he began, and then he put the pen to his teeth again. *Why haven't you called?* No. He crossed that out. For all he knew she had tried and simply hadn't left a message. He was the one who had disappeared. *I went away but came back when I heard about Bobby. I'm going to see how he is. I miss you and have a lot to tell. Call me. Love, Poppy.*

When he approached the front door he noticed that her potted plants and two chairs were missing from the porch, and the barbecue grill, which she kept at the corner of the house, was gone too. He looked in through the window next to the door. The front room was empty. Smelzkoff went around the other side and checked the bedroom. Empty. But the door at the rear, leading to the kitchen, was open. Inside, his investigation revealed a bare refrigerator and empty cupboards.

Back at his house he expected to find an explanation, but there was no note on either his front or back door, and the mailbox yielded nothing but an electric bill and a fistful of grocery store mailers. He put his bag in the bedroom, put the kitten's litter box and food bowls in the kitchen, and picked up the phone. "Dolores, I need to find out what hospital the injured were taken to last night in Hollywood. Is Lieutenant Portman in?" Smelzkoff stood poised with his pen over paper and waited. "You know who's calling," he said. "Is he in or not?"

❞•❝

It took several telephone calls and a measure of persistence for Smelzkoff to find out which hospital Bobby and the others had been sent to after the battle. Lieutenant Portman had referred him to the precinct with jurisdiction over Hollywood and when he telephoned and identified himself he had been put on hold, kept waiting, and finally disconnected. He considered putting on his uniform and driving to Hollywood to go into the station house in person, but then he was uncertain of the reception he would get. The news coverage he'd seen mentioned his name as one of the early leaders of The War on Dogs (if not the creator and organizer) but they seemed uncertain about whether or not he had played an active role in recent events. Hell, arresting people and chasing them off of beaches was one thing, but he hadn't beaten up any people for walking on a public sidewalk.

When at last he arrived at Hollywood General he checked with patient information and found that Bobby Smelzkoff had been transferred to Midway Hospital in West Hollywood. So he got back in the truck and drove west. At Midway the receptionist told him that Bobby Smelzkoff was on the fourth floor. No one to this point would give him any details as to why Bobby had been transferred, and he feared that his son's injuries might be serious.

Down the hall he passed a young man in a wheel chair and through an open door he saw a patient being helped by a nurse into his bed. He knocked, then opened the door to room 452, and found Bobby dressed, sitting in a chair by the window, staring at a magazine in his lap.

"I was afraid I'd find you in traction or all bandaged up," said Smelzkoff. "They're releasing you?"

Bobby, in profile, closed the magazine and dropped it on the floor, next to his chair. He spoke without turning to face Smelzkoff. "Friend picking me up," he said.

Smelzkoff could understand that his son would be reserved after such an ordeal, even traumatized, but he barely opened his mouth when he spoke and his tone conveyed no emotion of any kind. Neither contempt, nor disgust, nor fear, nor relief.

"I had nothing to do with it, you know," said Smelzkoff. Bobby nodded. Smelzkoff crossed the room and stood in front of his son. "I was in the desert and I came home as soon as I saw the evening news," he said. Bobby nodded again. "You could call your friend, tell them I'm taking you home. Who is it? Is it Violet?" Bobby shook his head this time.

"No, it's not Violet, or no you don't want to call your friend?" said Smelzkoff.

"Not Violet," Bobby said, out of the corner of his mouth.

"What's wrong with your face?" said Smelzkoff.

And then the door opened and someone came in. "How are you doing?" the man said, as he closed the door behind him, but Bobby didn't answer him either. The man came over, glanced briefly at Smelzkoff, stepped past him, and put his hand on Bobby's shoulder. "Ready?"

"I'm Stan, Bobby's father," said Smelzkoff.

"Yes, General, I know who you are," said the man, bowing slightly.

At first Smelzkoff hadn't placed him. The posture (he stooped a bit like tall men and women often did) the silver hair at the temples, the man's confident air. And then he remembered the gym. And that prompted him to recall standing in the writer's living room, looking at the photos of him with younger men. What was he doing with Bobby? Smelzkoff cleared his throat. "Did the detectives ever get back to you on your break in?" he said.

"Right," said the man. "Wouldn't that make history?" Bobby stood and immediately put his hand to his head.

"Could someone please tell me what's going on here?" said Smelzkoff. "Bobby, are you all right?" He saw then. The two sides of his son's face didn't match. Only one eyebrow arched, one lid blinked, one cheek twitched—and when he spoke the left side of his face stayed slack and inflexible, as if he had suffered a stroke or something. Smelzkoff looked away from his son and into the writer's eyes.

"Bell's palsy is a common facial paralysis, usually temporary," said the writer, "a result of the head injury he sustained I suspect—when your colleagues went on their spree of violence yesterday."

"Are you a doctor?"

"He needs to get some rest. Why don't you leave him alone for a while? Visit him at home later."

"You're not his father, even if you are old enough."

"Daniel, please," said Bobby. "Poppy, enough."

Smelzkoff chose not to walk out with them. Seeing his son's obvious discomfort convinced him to put his pride aside. Bobby didn't need support to walk. He didn't call for a wheel chair or limp and, as far as Smelzkoff could tell, his son wasn't in pain. Once he had figured it out though it had been hard not to stare, to try to make some sense of this palsy thing. Facial paralysis was something he associated with the aged and the infirm.

He looked out the window onto the parking lot below until he saw Bobby and the man appear. They walked close together; the man, Daniel, had his arm around Bobby's shoulder.

ಬಿಬಿಬಿ Twenty-Six: Phantom Of The Opera

"**Y**OU'RE CAUSING QUITE A STIR out there," said Brandon. "Are you all right?"

"How did you hear?" said Bobby.

"I've been reading the *LA. Times*," said Brandon. "I have to be in Sacramento on Friday. State business."

"My spirits are pretty low, but except for the fact that I look like the phantom of the opera, Dr. Manna says I'm fine," said Bobby. "I'm not sure what's going to happen with *Salami*. I have a friend with a contact in city hall."

"Phantom of the opera?"

"My face is paralyzed. Bell's palsy. A reaction to getting hit on the head by a dyke cop," said Bobby. "Phil says it should go away in week or two. I don't know how things got so carried away. All I wanted to do was put on a show."

"The theater's still closed?"

"We only got in three performances," said Bobby.

"I made some calls," said Brandon. "I'm coming down to LA after my Friday meetings, to spend the weekend, if you're up to having company. I'd like to meet your friend. The one who's helping. What's his name? Phil? I have some questions for him."

"I'd love to see you. No, Phil's my doctor. My friend who's helping is Daniel Denison. What questions?"

"Daniel Denison, the writer?"

"You've heard of him?"

"I've seen his reviews in the *LA Times*. He's no Pauline Kael, but he's got a lot of insight. I'd like to ask him when the last time was that the theater was inspected? And were there any violations then, and what prompted this one? It's clear from the coverage that the timing of the inspection was politically motivated. We could threaten legal action, get them to take another look at things. Ultimately there's always a political element to these things," said Brandon.

"Have you seen Jason? Does he know?" said Bobby.

ॐ•ॐ

Bobby put on gym shorts, took a towel from the shelf, and walked outside to the hot tub, with Ginger trailing. If only he could feel optimistic about one aspect of his life, he could cope, but nothing about his current situation gave him hope. His health was precarious, he had no partner, his play had been snuffed out, and his parents were unavailable for support. He had friends (and so many were eager to help) but he doubted their resolve. He put his foot in the recessed tub to test the temperature of the churning water. Gradually, he stepped into it, sat down, and leaned back against the side. Ginger stood with her front paws at the edge, looking down on the foamy surface. Pleased to have Bobby at eye level, she licked the lifeless side of his face. He couldn't eat or drink properly, chewing with the teeth on one side of his mouth, sipping through a straw to drink coffee and juice. The timpani thundered, drawing his attention to the music. Rachmaninoff, *Isle of the Dead.* Perfect for the moment. He closed his eyes and sunk lower to let the steaming water froth over his shoulders and under his chin.

And opened them when Ginger barked, to find Poppy standing at the edge of the tub, looking at him from the other side.

"Do you feel like talking?"

Bobby nodded. "I guess," he said.

"Mind if I turn the morbid music down?"

"The receiver's in my room, inside the armoire."

Poppy came back out, stripped off his shirt, pulled off his shoes and socks, and stepped out of his trousers. Then he got into the tub and sat across from Bobby. "Like I said at the hospital, I was in the desert and came back when I saw the news. I'd like to help." Ginger jumped up on the closest lounge chair and lay down.

"I appreciate that, but I've got all kinds," said Bobby. His father seemed so young and sturdy in his tight-fitting uniform, but his arms looked smaller now and his chest muscles drooped. Never had Bobby seen him so restrained. No doubt, the paralysis freaked him out. "A friend has a contact at city hall "

"That writer guy from the beach?" said Poppy. "You must really hate me."

"And a lawyer friend from New York. He's coming in town this weekend." Bobby closed his eyes. "And you don't despise me?" he said. "Daniel's a great guy."

"The proudest day of my life was when you were born. I didn't start out with anything but love. You're the one that—"

"Turned out to be a fag?"

"I've accepted that."

"Have you?" Bobby opened his eyes to look at his father. He steadied his palms on the bottom of the hot tub and rose up higher in the water.

"It's just, I mean, well, why do you have to be—"

"Such a girl?" said Bobby, leaning forward.

"I wanted a kid to play hoops with; not a ballet dancer," said poppy. "I felt cheated."

"Looks like we've both been cheated," said Bobby, leaning back again. "It would be nice if I had a father to share a performance of *Sweeny Todd* with."

"So we don't have much in common. Your mother and I didn't either. But I'm still your father and you're the only kid I've got," said Poppy. "It's not too late to find some things we can do together, is it? I could go to your opera. And you could go to see the Dodgers with me."

"You'd be too embarrassed to be seen with me," said Bobby. "And there may never be another performance of *Salami*."

"I guess you had a lot of fun with your old man," said Poppy.

"I was infuriated when you put Ginger in the pound. The whole fucking War on Dogs was so foolish."

"So, you made a fool out of me," said Poppy.

"Not you. What you had come to symbolize. You don't think spending all that money and time to arrest people for having dogs off-leash is a waste of time?"

"I think that there are plenty of people who resent all the dog crap in the grass and on the beaches and I think there are plenty of dog owners who think whatever their pets do is perfectly fine. They don't give a shit. They don't deserve to have pets. Pets are a responsibility. I don't have nothing against pets."

"Oh, come on, Poppy," said Bobby.

"Can't you admit that there's at least a bit of truth to what I'm saying? I only ever wanted to be a cop for good reasons. Some drivers drive drunk and kill innocent people. Some people steal from other people. Some people take drugs and steal to pay for them. Being a cop is a good and honorable thing and I'm sorry if you don't respect me for being one."

"Don't give me that singsong: a cop's business is to know the haunts and habits of felons and to foil as much roguery as possible. Good police work depends on the consent and cooperation of the public too, and cops should be civil and courteous to those who empower them. I don't appreciate excesses and I think they often concentrate on the wrong things," said Bobby. "Remember when you told me about the partners who would pick up gang members and drive them to a rival gang's territory and drop them off. Can't you admit that is wrong?" Poppy didn't say anything at first, and then he nodded. "We may never see eye to eye but at least maybe we can develop some respect for each other's position," said Bobby.

"It'll take some time I guess, but—"

"I don't know how much time I have," said Bobby.

"What does that mean? It has something to do with your face, don't it?" said Poppy.

"Doesn't it," said Bobby. "I'm hot. I have to get out," said Bobby. Wet as he was he didn't want to take a chance that there were tears.

"No, I don't want you to get out, unless we keep talking," said Poppy. "There's more to this than you're letting on. And I deserve to know. You don't have AIDS, do you?" Bobby sat transfixed. "I saw those men in the hospital where you were. They looked like they had it. That was the AIDS ward, wasn't it? For Christ's sake. How long have you known?"

"It's not the death sentence it used to be," said Bobby.

"Does your mother know?"

"I'm on so many meds and I get tired."

"How long?" said Poppy.

"Almost five years."

"And your mother?"

"She doesn't know either."

"You kept this from us all this time?"

And then the interrogation ended. Poppy sat quietly in the hot tub, his head bowed, his shoulders slumped, without further comment.

Bobby made no move to get out of the water nor did he speak; he tried a few times to say something to relieve the tension but no sound emerged. The truth is he could never have predicted his father's reaction to the knowledge that in addition to being a big sissy his son was also a sick sissy. If only The Dame and Frederick and Rex would come home and distract Poppy from this psychodrama.

Finally, after the Rachmaninoff started to play for the third time, after Bobby stood and reached for his towel and went in to turn it off, after he put on his clothes and returned to find his father pitched forward in the water, his shoulders heaving in silent grief, after he had placed his hand on his father's burr head and left it there, he found the courage to speak.

ಬುಬುಬು Twenty-Seven: Death and Deception in Venice

THE EVIDENCE HAD BEEN THERE in front of him all the time. How had he missed it? Why hadn't he allowed himself to consider the possibility that Bobby was sick? For a while after Bobby revealed his AIDS, Smelzkoff had plodded forward trying to amass details that served only to distract him from the truth.

And just when they were getting along so well, actually discussing their relationship, Bobby dropped his hideous news. Smelzkoff maintained his gaze as his son's bony shoulders and flat chest came up out of the water. And then he thought of that damned kitten with its protruding ribs and pathetic, wobbly attempts to follow him that morning at the motel and he could no longer hold back the feelings. He appreciated the fact that Bobby left him alone and went into the house to change and he wasn't even conscious of his son's return until Bobby placed his hand on his head and left it there.

"You could teach me to lift weights," said Bobby. "The doctor wants me to put on a few pounds. And you can go with me to Yoga.

It'll make you more flexible and I bet it would improve your workouts with weights too." Smelzkoff wiped his face with the back of his hand and stood to get out. "Wait. I'll get you a towel," said Bobby.

"Does Violet know?" said Smelzkoff.

"Not unless she guessed," said Bobby. "I haven't seen her for over a week."

"I'm curious, that is, maybe you don't want to say," said Smelzkoff, "but do you know how you got it?"

Bobby hesitated. "You mean, do I know how I got infected?"

Smelzkoff looked at his son and waited. When Bobby started to speak his voice was low and hesitant. "It's funny I've been asked before, but I haven't discussed it much. Except for the doctor, when I found out I was positive, and Jason." He cleared his throat. "But I know. I know all too well."

"Do you feel like talking about it?"

"I'm not sure," said Bobby. "I'm better off knowing how, I suppose."

"It's up to you. If you don't."

"When I first moved to New York, I met this guy. I hadn't had any experience, and I was pretty uncomfortable about the whole idea of sex." Bobby rubbed the immobile side of his face with his hand, as if by massaging it he could make it work again. "He was a big guy, from New Zealand I think, and he had a funny sense of humor and was quite charming. He told me that he had been married twice and that hadn't had sex for a couple of years. I thought he meant he was straight and when he said he hadn't had sex for a couple of years, I guess I assumed he was HIV negative. He wanted to have anal intercourse," said Bobby, hesitating to glance at Smelzkoff for a second, "and he tried several times to put it in, but I told him it hurt too much. He got extremely aggressive and kept insisting, and I had to fight him off. Finally when he realized that I wasn't going to give in, he pinned me down with his knees on my shoulders and came on my face. I got semen in my eyes. It burned like crazy and scared the shit out of me." Bobby stopped and looked at Smelzkoff again. "Does this upset you too much?" said Bobby.

"No, it's all right," said Smelzkoff. But he was lying. He sat rigid and unmoving while Bobby continued.

"I never saw him again and then I met Jason. We'd been together about a year and a half and I met someone from Florida at a party who had gotten AIDS from a man who had told him the same story (about having been married and not having had sex for a long time) and when he said he still could hear that accent, I had a mortifying feeling that somehow it was the same guy. The boy from Florida and I compared notes and sure enough it was the same person. He said he was a rugby player and even joked with the guy that he had put it in after he went to sleep. He said the same thing to me. 'I slipped it in after you went to sleep,' he said. 'And you loved it.'

"Jason and I had been planning to get tested, but we were afraid and had been putting it off. Then I knew I had to. When my results came back positive I wasn't really surprised. Somehow I had come to expect it. It explained the rashes and the mouth sores that kept coming back. And yet at the same time I couldn't believe it either. Simon, my doctor in New York, said there were a few cases of a person getting AIDS through eye contact. And gee, guess what? I was one of the lucky ones."

"I'm sorry," said Smelzkoff, at a loss. "What a sicko. Do you know where he is?"

"The kid from Florida tried to find him and found out he had died," said Bobby.

"No telling how many people he gave it to," said Smelzkoff.

"It ruined my relationship with Jason; we were afraid to even have safe sex after that. Lying about HIV is pretty common in the gay community. You have to be safe, you have to ask, and then you have to assume they might be lying," said Bobby.

Smelzkoff couldn't bear to hear any more. "Did Violet tell you she was moving?" he said. Bobby looked at him as if puzzled. "I went by her place and it was cleaned out, like she never ever lived there."

In a bluesy voice, through fixed lips, Bobby sang, "She lied to him; she lied to you; and now she's gonna lie to that man too. I'm sorry," he said. "I don't mean to make light of things. I like Violet. I really do. But she's a mystery."

☙•❧

The next morning, after his shower, Smelzkoff took out the wool pants and designer shirt that Violet had given him months ago. He dressed, glanced at his watch to note the time, and then slipped on the square-toed shoes that she had also purchased for him, and which he had never worn. As he sat on the edge of the bed tying them, the kitten raced from under the chair in the corner and jumped at the laces, sinking its tiny, sharp claws into his moving hands. He laughed, picked up the baby, and stroked the soft fur, prompting a burst of trancelike purring from the puss.

After telephoning The Deaconess's office to make sure she would be in, he had decided to dress in sporty attire to indicate that his was an unofficial visit, and off-the-record. He had convinced Gloria Deacon to talk to him only after promising her secretary that it was of the utmost importance, a dire emergency in fact.

"Smelzkoff, I'm real busy," she said, in the fake southern accent that she used to convey annoyance.

"You're gonna be a whole lot busier, Miss Deacon, ifin y'all don't see me as soon as possible," said Smelzkoff, affecting a less-refined version of the same accent.

Naturally, he insisted that the matter was too confidential to discuss over the phone and hinted only that it had to do with the recent, critical developments in The War on Dogs. As he got in behind the wheel of his truck he had no idea what he was going to tell Gloria Deacon when she received him in her downtown Los Angeles office in less than one hour's time.

☙•❧

At first, Bobby's tale about Violet's disappearance in New York (and the fact that she had met a boy named Frederick) surprised Smelzkoff. Then it angered him. His anger hadn't lasted long though, because he knew, had always known, that a girl as beautiful as Violet, working in a strip joint, met men—lots of men. It did please him that Bobby repeated what he knew, not to make him think less of Violet, but to make sure that his father didn't have unrealistic expectations. "I don't want to see you get hurt," said Bobby. Then he had gone on to say that he was sure Violet and Frederick were no longer seeing each other. "But she may have met someone else," said Bobby, "and I think Frederick might be gay." When Smelzkoff asked what Frederick looked like, Bobby said, "He was the one with Ginger. You arrested him on the beach." When Smelzkoff remembered the nearly naked, powerfully built young man, blood pulsed suddenly through his temples.

Gloria Deacon was sitting at her desk reading the newspaper through half glasses that rested uncertainly on the end of her nose, when Smelzkoff entered her office, carrying a shopping bag and with Ginger on-leash. Bobby had told him what was going on from his end and Smelzkoff's challenge was to use a mixture of truth and fantasy to win over the woman's trust.

"Smelzkoff, what the fuck is *that?*"

Ginger strained at the end of the leash to explore the room with her nose. Smelzkoff dropped the leash to release her, and she limped excitedly around, sniffing at the chairs, in the corners of the room, stopping now and then to spend additional time on certain stains in the carpet.

"Don't let her appearance fool you. She's a trained member of the city bomb squad," he said in a hushed voice, glancing surreptitiously left and right, up and down. Gloria Deacon rolled her eyes, not making a connection between Smelzkoff's presence with the dog and her office.

Cringing, and with a look of disgust, the councilwoman finally looked away from Ginger and over at Smelzkoff, who had taken a chair in front of her desk. "Don't you look festive," she said. "What's the occasion? What's so urgent?"

Smelzkoff leaned in toward her. "I'll get right to it. We shouldn't talk here, though," he whispered. Stretching across the surface of her desk, he took a gold pen from its holder and pointed to her writing pad. Gloria Deacon's eyes grew wide and her lips parted. She glanced down for a moment, tore off the top sheet, which was filled with her handwritten notes, and then slid the now blank pad over to him. *I have reason to believe your office is bugged*, he wrote, and then pushed the pad back over to her.

"Oh now really, Smelzy, I hardly think—"

Smelzkoff coughed and put his hand up to silence her. He stood and walked over to the credenza against the wall that ran perpendicular to her desk. A picture of a cat in Elizabethan costume hung above it; he ran his hand around the edges of the frame. Finding nothing (as he knew he would) he walked briskly back to her desk and ran his hands similarly underneath the protruding edges. Ginger followed him (since he had a piece of beef jerky concealed in his palm) and after a moment or two of studied concentration, Smelzkoff withdrew the listening device, no larger than a hazelnut, which he had purchased at Radio Shack one half hour earlier and which he now pretended to find affixed to the undersurface of Gloria Deacon's desk. Ginger barked, for another treat, and Smelzkoff patted her on the head. "Good work, girl," he said.

Then he walked in long strides, to the window behind her desk, peered anxiously through it, and twisted the wand to close her miniblinds. He put his index finger to his lips, took her arm, and motioned for her to follow him out of the room. Gloria Deacon stood and looked first over her shoulder, then around the room and followed him obediently.

Outside on the sidewalk, Smelzkoff said, "I like your hat. Leather? L.L. Cool J wears a hat like that, doesn't he?"

"Smelzy," said The Deaconess, suddenly without even a trace of authority in her voice, "please tell me what's going on."

"Here, take Ginger," said Smelzkoff, thrusting the dog's lead into her hand. "But L.L. Cool J's hat is black, isn't it? And yours is red."

"I don't want this mangy mutt," said Gloria Deacon. "You're scaring me, Smelzy."

"What do you call that kind of hat?" said Smelzkoff.

"It's a goddamned, porkpie hat. Is my life in danger?"

"I've been able to infiltrate the opposition by pretending to be sympathetic to their cause," said Smelzkoff.

"DOGS? Have you forgotten what that stands for? Why are they after me?" said Gloria Deacon. Despite her arthritis, Ginger strained at the end of the leash and although The Deaconess wore an exasperated expression she said nothing, allowing the curious dog to pull her along. When they arrived at the intersection, they were forced to wait for the walk sign among a group of about ten people, some of whom Smelzkoff noticed looking at her hat.

"Sit, Mutt," said Gloria Deacon, jerking at the leash.

The light changed and they crossed the street. "You know you might as well wear a bull's eye on your back," said Smelzkoff, pointing to her hat. "I mean I know it's your trademark and all, but until the danger passes "

"I can't take it off." Gloria Deacon glanced around.

"When we start your campaign for mayor, it'll be just the ticket; now it makes us sitting ducks," said Smelzkoff.

"How did you—"

"I'm not completely stupid," said Smelzkoff, "I know ambition when I see it. The important thing is, you can win. You're good."

"And I suppose you would expect to be my Chief-of-Police." Gloria Deacon's voice was saturated with sarcasm.

"First things first." Smelzkoff set a faster pace, which caused Ginger to trot, and The Deaconess struggled to keep up in her heels. When they arrived at the Dorothy Chandler Music Pavilion, Smelzkoff said, "By the fountain. The noise of the water will drown out our conversation."

Gloria Deacon's face glistened with perspiration and she struggled for breath. "Sit down, damn it," she barked at Ginger. "It's your fruity son, isn't it? That's how you know, isn't it?"

Smelzkoff ignored the slur and said, "He's merely a puppet."

"They claim it's genetic," said Gloria Deacon. "Are you a fruit too?"

Smelzkoff took a deep breath, and winked at her. "Don't make me prove to you that I'm hetero," he said. "Business first, though. The opposition has help from insiders at City Hall," he said, in a grave tone. "I hope there aren't any skeletons for them to unearth."

Gloria Deacon smiled weakly, averted her eyes, and focused on a spot to the right, just above his head. "Certainly not. Though, I would expect that everyone has had a youthful indiscretion or two in his past." She looked at Smelzkoff again. "What in heaven's name are they planning?"

"To ruin you in case things backfire." And here he decided to take a leap. "They know the inspection of the theater was instigated by you."

"The mayor signed off on that." Gloria Deacon grabbed his sleeve and stared at him.

"And what does that tell you?"

Gloria Deacon let go of him, shoved Ginger's lead at him, walked to a nearby bench, and sat. "So the son of a bitch isn't quitting. The bastard's going to run for reelection. Again. All that talk about me being his successor was nothing but smoke and mirrors up my ass." Gloria Deacon stood suddenly. "But why has he aligned himself with—"

"The mayor is into cross-dressing," said Smelzkoff.

Gloria Deacon sat again. "Now you've completely lost it."

"There are Polaroids," said Smelzkoff.

Gloria Deacon bounced back to her feet and grabbed the front of Smelzkoff's shirt. "Get them," she said.

"Yes, of course. In time. But we can't take a chance of being seen together. Take off your hat. Put it in your purse."

Smelzkoff reached out to take it and she stepped back and ducked. "I can't," she said.

And after much cajoling and pleading, after reminding her that it could mean the end of her political career, after stressing the need for secrecy, Gloria Deacon took off her red leather porkpie hat, with the wig sewn into the lining and exposed the patchy sprouts of gray hair that dotted her shiny, lumpy, head.

"I can't go back to my office like this," she said.

Smelzkoff stifled his urge to laugh. "I have a hard hat in my shopping bag," he said.

•

Smelzkoff didn't know whether or not, short of convincing the contentious woman that she was in danger, he had accomplished much during their encounter. Perhaps he'd bought some time or at best convinced her that she was swimming in shark-infested waters. "Why on earth would—? Never mind. I don't want to know," said Gloria Deacon. They took a taxi back to City Hall. The driver kept looking in his rear view mirror, no doubt wondering why this woman wore a mid-calf dress, high-heeled shoes, and a red hard hat.

Smelzkoff walked from Deacon's office to the lot where he parked his truck and set off for home. Time to find Violet.

ಬಿಬಿಬಿ Twenty-Eight: East of Eden

WHEN VIOLET ENTERED Dr. Young's office she detected a mood, and naturally her first inclination was to blame herself. He had kept her waiting in the reception area for ten minutes past her scheduled appointment time; she heard him in the next room, on the telephone, his voice shrill and feisty, and when he finally opened the door his eyes were red, the skin around them bloated and purple. But really, how could it be her fault? She hadn't done anything to him. True she hadn't been in for an appointment in some time now, but that was not sufficient justification for him to complain with salty tears to someone else.

Odd, but he knew everything about her (well not every little thing) while she knew nothing about him—except for what she saw. His life remained a mystery. Did he drink or do drugs? Did he like kinky sex? Did he get along with his family? Did he collect Fiesta Ware or prefer watching the Kings? Violet resented Dr. Young, not only for what he knew about her, but also for what she didn't know about him.

"You'll have to excuse me, Violet," he said. I have allergies, and with these Santa Ana winds—" He gestured toward the sofa and sat in his wing back. "So, how are you?"

"I moved," she said, "to a new apartment."

"Well, that's nice. When did you decide to move?"

"I haven't gone into work for a week."

Dr. Young nodded. "It appears you're making some changes," he said.

"Kent's trying to get me to do films," said Violet. This time Dr. Young exhaled, with his mouth open. Without pause, Violet told him, in rapid succession, about meeting Bradley Zieman, how he was taken by her, how she moved into an apartment he owned, how she had slept with him a few times, and how she knew immediately that he wanted to marry her.

"Do you want to marry him?" said Dr. Young.

"Cheryl says, 'people in Hell need ice water.'"

"Do you think you're in Hell, Violet?"

"I think I'm somewhere east of Eden," said Violet.

"That's amusing. Have you read *East of Eden*?"

"I saw the movie on cable."

"It's a fabulous film. Jo Van Fleet's performance is breathtaking."

Violet smiled as if she knew about Jo Van Fleet and waited for Dr. Young to get back to business. "You know she was a New York stage actress and *East of Eden* was her first film. Elia Kazan directed her. An auspicious debut one might say." He peered silently at a spot somewhere above her head, lost in the world that she didn't share, his mouth puckered, his nostrils flared as if reliving the actress's performance. Violet feared that Dr. Young might begin to cry, but then the pucker became a sneer and he said, taking a deep breath and looking directly at her, "I could have been a damned fine film critic."

"Uh huh," said Violet.

Young shook his head, violently, as if to rid himself of anxiety. "So what happened to Poppy?" he said, drumming his fingers.

"What happened to Poppy?"

"Yes, what did he think about you moving?"

"Nothing, I guess."

"Nothing?"

"I didn't leave a forwarding address."

"Really. Why's that?"

"I don't know," said Violet. "Bradley Zieman wants me to go to Moscow, Russia with him. On vacation."

"Well, that could be a nice opportunity for you. You sound undecided. How do you feel about going to Russia, with someone you just met?"

Was this criticism? She had just mentioned the word marriage in conjunction with this man and Young hinted that it would be unwise to go on a trip with him. The irony wasn't lost on her. But then maybe that was Dr. Young's point. Violet shrugged.

"Did you discuss your plans with anyone?"

"I was on my way to see Bobby "

"To tell him that you were moving?"

"There was this riot at the theater where his play—"

"You know the LAPD is really out of control," said Dr. Young. "They're nothing but thugs and homophobes. I for one am sick to death of their brutality." Dr. Young slapped his hand on the chair arm. "Is he all right? To have such an ogre for a father must—"

"Poppy loves Bobby," said Violet. Dr. Young blinked. "I can tell," she said. "I was on my way to see him, but I had to turn around. Bobby is one of the reasons I came to see you. When I saw him on the news I missed him and I wanted to talk to him. I felt sad. Because it's like he has a family that cares about him and—"

"I'm sorry, Violet, but I think you're romanticizing the situation a bit. Poppy is hardly the ideal father."

"Not Poppy. Everyone in the play. Terrible things are happening but they're still together, they're helping each other out, and I think they're lucky to have each other."

Dr. Young adjusted his hips in the seat of the chair, crossed his legs. "It's nice to see you express such strong opinions," he said. "So, I'm confused. Did you, or did you not, see Bobby?"

"I stopped to get a sandwich and got sick."

"I'm sorry," said Dr. Young. "Food poisoning? There's a lot of flu going around. When did this happen?"

"No," said Violet. "It wasn't the food or the flu."

"But you're all right now?"

"It was two days ago," said Violet. "I'm pregnant."

Dr, Young blinked several times. "Pregnant. I see. When did you find out?"

"I did a home pregnancy test." She was often late with her period (that in itself hadn't concerned her) but two weeks was longer than ever in the past. And she realized she had been so extremely tired, which she had attributed to the stress of dealing with her move and getting to know Bradley Zieman. The first bite had made her nauseous. She got back in her car, after vomiting in the restaurant bathroom, and turned in at a pharmacy to buy the home test. She kept it in her purse and, after Zieman left for the office the next morning, she took it into the bathroom and saturated it with her urine. Unlike other occasions when she had used one, this time the indicator came up *plus*.

"How far along are you?"

"About three weeks," said Violet. "In *East of Eden*, James Dean grew up not knowing who his real mother was. I want my baby to know his parents. Both of them. His father too."

"And," Dr. Young paused, as if to choose his words carefully, "That would mean that—"

"Poppy's the father," said Violet.

❧•❧

Masks frightened Violet: when Bobby first turned around she put her hand to her mouth and let out an involuntary scream.

"Where did you disappear to?" he said.

"Please take that creepy thing off," said Violet.

"My own face is creepier," said Bobby, slipping the Phantom, half-mask over the top of his head. "I'm half-paralyzed. Sort of like being half-nuts or having half a mind to throw in the towel. From a head injury. But the doctor says I should regain movement in a week or two. I know what you're thinking: Oh, poor Bobby; he finally had one too many facelifts."

Despite his shocking appearance, not quite disfigurement, but eerily disconcerting nonetheless, Violet stepped forward to put her arms around him. "I need a hug," she said. "I've really messed things up."

"So have I, Sweetie. Where on Earth have you been?" he said, squeezing her tight. "I'd kiss you but I just washed my hair."

Violet nestled her head on Bobby's shoulder and didn't move until she felt the tear travel down her cheek and onto his T-shirt. She let go and brushed another one aside with her fingers. "Do you have any tissue?" she said.

Bobby nodded. "Sure, Honey," he said. "Would you like some tea? I could use a cup of tea." He reached to touch her hair for a moment, and then let go and went into the kitchen. Violet sat in a lounge chair by the edge of the pool, not knowing where to begin and feeling a little selfish about burdening her friend. Obviously, he had problems of his own.

"Kettle's on," he said, coming back outside and taking a seat across from her. "Now tell me. What's so terrible with you?"

"Where's Ginger?" said Violet.

"This you won't believe. Poppy took her, and wouldn't tell me why; he just said he needed to borrow a dog."

"What do you suppose that means?" said Violet.

"Maybe it's his way of reaching out. We had a good talk; maybe for the first time we really talked. He was upset about what happened in Hollywood."

"I saw the news," said Violet. "I was on my way to see you, but I had to turn back. Everybody's upset with the police and the city. Dr. Young was spitting mad. Are the others okay?"

"I guess I got hurt the worst. Some got away with just scratches and bruises, and at least a dozen others were treated and released. The Dame and Frederick and Rex weren't hurt; they've been on a party binge ever since the show closed. They're still in bed." He gestured toward the front house. "Probably the same bed. To each his own, I guess." Bobby lowered his voice. "Probably a good thing you didn't pursue Frederick. I think he's in the middle of a major life change."

Violet smiled. "I sensed."

Bobby got up when the teakettle began to whistle. "I'll get our tea," he said, and went to the kitchen.

Unsure about the proper way to tell her story, Violet attempted to organize her thoughts, to choose the least disgraceful way of unraveling her tale. Bobby returned with a tray that held two cups and two spoons, several packets of sugar and the creamer, and set it on down on the glass table. "If you want lemon, I have lemon," he said.

"Sugar is fine," she said. Bobby sat again and took a sip of his tea. "I can only drink out of the right side of my mouth," he said.

"I had an accident in the Beverly Center garage," said Violet.

Bobby set down his cup. "You're okay, right?"

She nodded again. "And I met this man "

"God, if I met men as fast as you do Excuse me," he said, when the telephone rang. "Hold that thought. I have to get this; Brandon is supposed to call. You remember Brandon," he yelled, over his shoulder. "We stayed at his house in New Jersey." Bobby disappeared into his room and was gone for about five minutes. Periodically, Violet heard his excited voice.

When he came back out by the pool, he clapped his hands together, and smiled crookedly. "Remember what a brilliant lawyer I said Brandon was? His firm does tons of legal work for the city of LA, and he had a meeting with the mayor at home and is coming over to tell me about it."

Bobby apologized again, and when he took a sip of his tea and set down his cup and looked at her, the one side of his face alert and poised, and the other inflexible and illegible, Violet decided to cut to the chase. "How would you like to have a little brother or sister?" she said.

ಬಿಬಿಬಿ Twenty-Nine: Quid Pro Quo

B OBBY THREW HIMSELF, not enthusiastically but cautiously, on the pro-choice side of the argument, and so it surprised him that, when Violet delivered the news of her impending motherhood, he didn't consider termination of the pregnancy (he couldn't bring himself to use that other word it so repelled him) as an option. And, happily, it appeared that Violet felt the same way. Sure, she was concerned about Poppy's reaction (who wouldn't be?) and sure there were any number of reasons to make one think that she might not have the necessary mothering skills at this stage of her life, but perhaps a child would be a good thing for her—and she for it. The girl had a lot of love in her heart.

She spoke frankly to Bobby: she'd made many mistakes and had promised herself never to fall back on the dancing. As for what Poppy would say? Even if he didn't want to start a second family, Violet told Bobby she would still want the baby. And yes, she was sure: Poppy was the father.

Bobby wondered now if she'd want to have the child if it belonged to this new man, the man she would now have to confront as well with her news. Bobby didn't envy Violet. She got herself into one jam after another and now she'd have to do what she was unaccustomed to doing: deal with the consequences. Well, they were Poppy's consequences, too. Poppy, a father at sixty like Cary Grant, but of course Cary Grant had had enough money to see that any child of his would be well cared for after he was gone. Bobby hoped that Poppy's child would be as fortunate.

"I could lose it though," said Violet "It's early yet. Maybe I should wait to tell Poppy."

"I don't think I'd advise that," said Bobby. "It would amount to postponement of too too many important issues, which you know you have a tendency to do." He wagged his finger and, embarrassed at his condescension, quickly withdrew it. Violet told him about Kent too, and how she'd left Fantasy, and her apartment, and how she might have made a commitment to Dr. Bradley Zieman

"That name sounds familiar," said Bobby.

He sat at attention, involved with the details of her story, and had forgotten that Brandon was on his way—till he heard him at the side gate.

"Back here," said Bobby, "with Violet."

Brandon wore deck shoes and Bermuda shorts and a lemon yellow polo shirt. "Whoever said gays all have a sense of fashion, hasn't seen you," said Bobby.

"Easy," said Brandon. "The mayor dresses just like this. Hey you," he said to Violet. "Get up and give me a hug. You look radiant."

Violet smiled and stood, evidently pleased by his warmth and familiarity.

"Interesting word, *radiant*," said Bobby, winking at Violet with his good eye.

"So, I'm dying to give you the scoop, but I'm on vacation. Got any beer?" said Brandon.

"I'll get it, and you two can talk," said Violet. "In the house, or the mini-fridge in your room?" she said, looking at Bobby? He pointed to the house.

"There's a scandal brewing in city hall," said Brandon, taking Violet's chair. "Nothing's been picked up by the newspapers yet, though. There have been complaints of building inspectors taking bribes. Accepting bribes to give owners a clean bill is commonplace, but these guys are actually soliciting the money and making it clear that the money can make bad inspections go away. The city is using their internal auditors and has hired my firm as well to look into the extent of the problem and their liability if the charges prove true. For us, for you, the timing is perfect. The mayor pretty much admitted that the inspection of the Olympia Theater was triggered by a request from an elected official. He wouldn't say who, and I didn't press. Your friend Denison was able to show me the two prior inspections, which the Olympic passed with flying colors."

"So Daniel was able to help?" said Bobby.

"Yeh, yeh, yeh. Absolutely. He's a hottie too. Anything up with you and him?" said Brandon.

When Violet appeared with the beer and Brandon got up to pull another chair close for her, Bobby took the opportunity to ignore the question. "Get off your feet, Violet," he said. "Sit and relax."

"I don't want to intrude," said Violet.

"We're all family here," said Bobby. "Please, sit down. It's important that you take care of yourself." He waited until she settled in the chair, then he looked at Brandon.

Brandon took a swallow of beer and continued. "Daniel pointed out that of the four pages of violations, some of which are total creation, most have already been taken care of. Snags in the carpet runners have been covered with duct tape and the back hallways have been cleared of clutter to eliminate fire hazards and such. The big hang-up is the wiring. It needs to be modernized but there's no immediate danger. An earthquake, well that's another matter altogether." Brandon took another sip, withdrew a pack of cigarettes from the pocket of his shorts, and pulled out one to light. He took a puff, tilted back his head, and exhaled up into the air. Bobby watched until satisfied that none of the smoke would blow in Violet's face.

"So here's what we got," Brandon went on. "If you promise to get the wiring modernized within six months and if your cohorts promise to make no further sidewalk protests over Proposition 1134, the show can reopen immediately—provided that the new inspection verifies that the improvements we discussed have actually been made."

"We can reopen?" said Bobby.

"Quid pro quid," said Brandon.

"When?" said Bobby.

"Inspectors will come tomorrow. Provided things are the way Denison described, you can put on a Saturday performance," said Brandon.

Bobby let out a sigh. "I guess I should be pleased."

Brandon swallowed the last of the beer, set the empty on the table, and inhaled on his cigarette. "But?" he said.

Bobby looked down at his feet. "And I am pleased, Brandon. I am." He looked up. "It's just that, how about our civil rights? What about my friends who were beaten? What about my face?"

His friend took a final puff and then put out his cigarette. "You could sue," he said, exhaling, "if you want. But I have to say it wouldn't be an easy or short process." Brandon suddenly began to sound like a lawyer. "They need something from you now, but for you to claim that your civil rights were violated, when you didn't have a permit to demonstrate on public property, when after all is said and done your injury might be more a result of your existing state of health, rather than your injury at the hands of the police, well, you'd have to dig in for the long haul and after the wait, after the stress of appearances and continuances and procedural delays, the results might not be what you want."

"Why don't you bite my head off?" said Bobby.

"I think I saw the other side of your face move," said Brandon. "See, you're improving already."

"I'm still going to wear the mask at the theater; I think it's a fairly stylish touch."

"Uncle Collie used to wear a mask," said Violet.

ೞೞೞ Thirty: Basic Police Work

STANLEY SMELZKOFF LEFT GINGER in his truck and went to the entrance of Fantasy Mansion, looking for Violet's car in the parking lot as he walked. Inside, he waited for his eyes to adjust to the darkness and then he glanced around to see if he recognized one or another of Violet's acquaintances. "You're the first, the last, my everything," crooned Barry White. The girl on main stage, ghostly white with hair the color of straw (and from the looks of it, with the texture of straw as well) was new, but then every time he came in there were any number of fresh faces, meaning simply that they were new in the club and not that there was anything really fresh about them. Stanley Smelzkoff walked over to the bar and ordered bottled water from the male bartender whom he recognized. "I'm looking for Violet Carlisle," said Smelzkoff.

"Hasn't been in for several days now," said the bartender. The man glanced around the room and then wiped down the area in front of Smelzkoff with a rag. "You're her friend, aren't you?"

"Any of the girls she was close to here now?" said Smelzkoff.

The bartender dried his hands on his apron and looked around again. "Last I heard Michelle moved to New York. They spent time together," he said. Then a dark Polynesian-looking girl, wearing plastic coconut shells on her breasts and a synthetic-looking grass skirt over a G-string, came up to the service area with a tray of empty glasses and put in an order for beverages. "Debbie," said the bartender, "this here's a friend of Violet's. I was just telling him we ain't seen Violet for a while and we're getting somewhat worried."

Smelzkoff nodded to her and said to the man, "Any particular reason why you're worried?"

"You're a cop, right? You're Violet's cop friend," said Debbie, the barmaid. She looked around, set down her tray at the service area, and began removing the dirty glasses while she spoke. "Don't say I told you, but go see Kent and make sure he knows that you're watching out for Violet."

"The manager? Does he know where she is?" said Smelzkoff.

She looked at Smelzkoff. "Three Cokes, two crans, and a coffee," she said to the bartender. "I don't think so, or he wouldn't be questioning all of us every day." The bartender looked at the girl, raised his eyebrows, and began to fill her order. "And don't say I said nothing," said Debbie.

"Is he in the office now?"

Debbie glanced furtively up above his head, at the high-mounted security camera, and nodded. "You know where the office is?" she said. Smelzkoff pointed in the general direction. "Up the stairs and down the hallway," said Debbie. "First door you come to, on the right."

"Much oblige," said Smelzkoff. He took a large swallow of his water, went behind the stage and up the stairs.

When he knocked on the door, he heard, "Just a minute," from inside. Moments later the door was pulled open, and Kent's reddened face appeared. "Who are you ?" he said. He choked briefly on the smoke swirling from his palmed cigarette and stood blocking Smelzkoff's view of the room.

Smelzkoff took out his badge and showed it to him. "Sergeant Stanley Smelzkoff," he said. "Can I come in?"

"What do you want with me?" said Kent.

"Nothing yet," said Smelzkoff. "I'm inquiring as to the details of Violet Carlisle," said Smelzkoff. Then it must have hit Kent: a glimmer of recognition flickered in the man's darting eyes. "Can I come in," said Smelzkoff again.

"Sure," said Kent. "But I ain't seen Violet for days now. And she ain't called and she's in deep shit. I'm trying to run a business here." He took a quick look over his shoulder and stepped back from the door.

Smelzkoff walked around the room and stopped in front of the wall of autographed pictures. In addition to dancers' pictures, there were signed, headshots from several male television and movie personalities; he recognized a few of the faces but had no idea of their names. He honed in on one thick, black signature on the photo of a bald man with airbrushed teeth. The first name appeared to be Fred, but the last name (a slash of ink that ran off the picture edge) was undecipherable.

"Why's Violet in trouble?" said Smelzkoff. "People can quit their jobs, can't they?"

"Yeah, they can quit, if they give proper notice."

"So how does she hurt anyone other than herself if she doesn't give notice?" said Smelzkoff, keeping his eyes fixed on Kent's.

"I got to replace her in the line up," said Kent. "You don't know where she is either, do you?" he said, sneering.

"You seem a little strung out," said Smelzkoff. He glanced at the coffee pot on the Formica table behind the man's desk. "Ought to watch your coffee intake. Caffeine attaches to your prostate and all. Man's got to be careful of his prostate at your age. Did you get your PSA this year?"

Kent shook his head, snuffed his nose.

"Allergies?" said Smelzkoff. Kent grunted, reached for a cigarette, and lit it "How's your heart. Do you get an annual EKG? Cigarettes are bad for your heart you know. Too much caffeine, too much nicotine. They may be legal drugs, but that don't mean they aren't bad for you."

Smelzkoff reached in and took out his wallet and handed Kent a card. "Give me a call if you hear anything." He went to the door.

"Right," said Kent, "I'll be sure to call you first thing."

Stanley Smelzkoff turned back around. "How about illegal drugs? Ever fool around with illegal drugs, Kent?" he said.

Kent made a snorting noise. "Nah," he said, looking uncomfortable.

Smelzkoff exited without further comment and went downstairs. He left a twenty-dollar bill with the bartender, and on his way to the entrance the waitress, Debbie, emerged from behind a Grecian column and took hold of his arm. "Listen" she said, balancing her tray on her hand and leaning in close. "I maybe shouldn't say anything, but Violet told me that she had met a guy, a doctor. That's the last any of us heard from her. I didn't say nothing to Kent. I mean it's only been a week, but—"

"Thanks," said Smelzkoff. He reached into his pocket and handed her his card and his last twenty. "Call me if you hear from her," he said.

At the truck Ginger had moved over and was sitting in the driver's seat behind the steering wheel.

๛•๖

When he had gone into Bobby's room to get Ginger's leash, Smelzkoff had seen the photograph, lying atop a stack of books next to his son's bed. The larger of the three individuals, in the center of the picture, Smelzkoff recognized as the behemoth he had mistaken as a woman during the night raid at the beach; the gender of the two flanking and smaller female impersonators would however be a mystery to no one, so broad and muscular were their shoulders, so striated and masculine were their jaws.

Smelzkoff had held the enlarged photo in his hand and studied it: the trio wore only tiny G-strings, leaving their breasts, their bellies, and their legs uncovered. The two boys on the outside (one black, one white) had massive ripped abdominal muscles, and reminded him of the freaky women at Gold's who went too far in their attempts to build muscle, but it took an abundance of imagination and complete concentration for Stanley Smelzkoff to picture the nearly-naked giant in the middle as a man, so fleshy and pendulous were his breasts, so pale, round, and swollen was his stomach—which hung so low that it practically obliterated his G-string and looked like some prize-winning squash at a Wisconsin county fair.

The whole idea of the three posing unashamedly as naked women disgusted Smelzkoff, but he had palmed the photo and slipped it inside his shirt, and decided then and there that there was no need to tell Bobby of his plans. First he went to his own house and rummaged through his desk drawers until he found that picture of the mayor, presiding over a recent police awards ceremony, (the size of the figures in the two photos was not exactly the same, but close enough he hoped to accomplish his purpose) and then he drove to the crime lab. Randy owed Smelzkoff big-time, because he had gotten the man's girlfriend, Denise, out of a jam with Officer Perez, after she sassed Perez unapologetically when he pulled her over on Washington Boulevard for speeding. "I don't like that mouthy bitch," said Perez, "even if she is a knockout."

"Then do it for Randy," said Smelzkoff. "He deserves a solid. He has enough grief with her."

Today Smelzkoff would see how successful Randy had been in his efforts to realize what had been Smelzkoff's concept. He made his way through the corridors, entered the lab area, and saw the computer geek at his desk at the back of the room. Randy looked up when he approached. "How'd we do?" said Smelzkoff.

"Is this going to get me in trouble?" said Randy.

"It's a joke," said Smelzkoff. "Your name won't be mentioned. Let me see."

Computer equipment covered every inch of Randy's desk: processing units, scanners, monitors, printers, and enough programming manuals Smelzkoff imagined to encircle the globe if put end to end.

The man nervously unlocked and pulled open a lower drawer to extract a file folder, then handed the folder to Smelzkoff and waited.

When he saw the finished product, Smelzkoff laughed so loud and so long at the eight by ten photo, that Randy repeatedly looked toward the door as if afraid someone would come in unexpectedly and demand to be let in on the joke. The mayor's head had been put in place atop the 300-pound body of the English transvestite so expertly that Smelzkoff doubted that anyone could tell that the photograph was a composite with the naked eye.

"I used a pixel program to match the hairline," said Randy, now smiling himself. "His honor looks good as a redhead."

"Did you reduce the size of his head?" said Smelzkoff.

"Very slightly. The body is so large on the middle figure that it actually looks less real now than before," said Randy. "Are those implants?"

"I don't think so. They sag too much," said Smelzkoff.

He thanked Randy, slipped the photograph back in the folder, and said goodbye. On his way to the parking lot Smelzkoff checked his watch. On Valentine's Day, when Violet handed him the small white box with the red ribbon that contained the wristwatch, she had said, "Think of me every time you look at it, Poppy."

𖠿•𖠿

At the telephone office, the woman, Shirley, made a copy of the bill and handed it to Smelzkoff. "You know I'm not supposed to do this without proper authorization," she said. "What are you going to do for me?" She leaned back in her chair so that her sweater stretched tight across her chest.

Smelzkoff had dealt with the woman, probably forty years of age, several times before on police work; he was well aware of her flirtation. "Dinner for two at Koo Koo Roo?" he said, smiling.

"Fine, Stanley," she said. "When do you want to go?"

Smelzkoff saw his own telephone number several times at the beginning of the month, and Bobby's, and that of Fantasy Mansion. "Run this through, Shirley" he said, pointing to an unfamiliar one.

Shirley pecked out the numerals on her keypad and waited for the information to come up on the screen. "Williams Sonoma in Santa Monica," she said.

"And this," he said pointing to another.

Seconds later. "Bed, Bath and Beyond," said Shirley. About two-thirds of the way through the month, the familiar numbers disappeared; there was little activity for several days. Then, repeated six or seven times over the last three days of the billing period, a heretofore unseen telephone number.

"Try this one," said Smelzkoff.

"So when are we going to dinner?" said Shirley. She typed in the numbers again, looked at Smelzkoff, and waited for his reply.

"Won't your husband be upset?" said Smelzkoff.

"Who says he has to know?" said Shirley.

"What does it say?" said Smelzkoff, stretching to look at the monitor.

"Bradley Zieman, MD, in Beverly Hills," said Shirley.

"There's a mistake," said Smelzkoff. "That's my—" Smelzkoff stopped and tried to reason it out: he must have made these calls himself, during the time when he was seeing the good doctor but the timing was wrong and he had seldom used Violet's telephone.

Shirley consulted her note pad. "You asked for 305-5555," she said.

"Who does this one belong to?" said Smelzkoff, trying to convey an air of nonchalance, though the stout woman had already detected his change of mood and made no further attempt to flirt.

"Bradley Zieman MD, again," said Shirley. "This one in Brentwood. I'd say from the street address it's his residence."

Smelzkoff had a sudden bitter taste in his mouth and his heartbeat accelerated. He looked at the dates again, asked Shirley for a calendar, and she pushed a loose-leaf desktop issue over to him. He quickly confirmed that he had been in the desert when these calls (and there were several of them) had been made.

How was this possible? He had never mentioned the doctor he was seeing, although he had complained mightily about his discomfort during the period when Zieman was treating him like some medical experiment at Dachau. Then Smelzkoff remembered Debbie at Fantasy Mansion and what she said about Violet meeting a doctor. A frantic urge to evacuate his bowels, prompted from all the coffee he had consumed, overcame him. Shirley handed him a key attached to large piece of Plexiglas and he made a dash for the door.

ಬಬಬಬ Thirty-One: A Farewell to Arms

B OBBY HAD BELIEVED that he wanted a relationship again. Many in the community treated those without partners as incomplete human beings, as something less than whole—at least that was the message he'd gotten. He knew that he still mourned the loss of Jason, but after meeting Daniel Denison he'd been so thrilled to find someone attracted to him that he'd lost sight of a few facts. Standing at the bathroom sink, he swallowed the last of his evening pills and took a breath.

Over the past few days he had repeatedly asked himself: Was he ready to start dating?; Was he ready to make someone else number one or at least number two?; Did he want to commit to waiting around for someone to call, compromise on what restaurant to visit, and agree on the same television show? True, no one said a person had to give up his identity, but that was the way he did things: a complete dedication to the other. And that was the best argument for not getting involved at this time. How ignoble to use someone as fodder for one's ego.

Bobby pulled on his khaki trousers, buttoned up the fly, and took down the navy blue sweater from the shelf. He didn't know how to love without losing himself; he'd already found himself waiting for Denison to call, and when the call didn't come at the expected time, he got that empty feeling again. He sat on the bed and laced his shoes. Sex would be tricky, too. So far their interaction had been flirty and affectionate, with lots of touching, but no sex. How could he gnaw at a man's lips with a face half-frozen?

He took his keys, stepped outside, and locked the door behind him. Passing the pool and the hot tub, he walked alongside the front house and opened the gate. Oh sure, Doctor Phil said he would recover; he already felt the sensation returning in his cheek and chin. But now was the time to take care of himself. The promise of improved relations with Poppy lingered, although going to that gym where giants inflated their bodies intimidated Bobby.

And then there was Violet. Even if Poppy rejected the idea of having another child, Violet's decision, which she seemed secure with, had been made, and Bobby was determined to help her. The idea of a little brother or sister exhilarated and encouraged him.

He stood waiting for the light to change, distracted for a moment by The Venice library with its postmodern skylights and exposed beams. The show would reopen: he had that to contend with and, with the reopening, there were bound to be snags. He had just summed it up. Health and work. Friends and his family.

Maybe he'd write, too. He'd done a fair job with *Salami*. Maybe he'd try his hand at an original screenplay or teleplay. Bobby turned left at Grand. Trouble was he liked Denison. If he didn't like him, he wouldn't be going through this process, having all this doubt.

So here he was on a trek to the beach and Denison's house in the cool evening air of October.

"Come over for the sunset," Denison had said. "It's directly off the balcony this time of year."

The water level in the canals was high, ducks peeped, geese squawked, but Violet's house stood empty and dark. A moment of incertitude. What if she chose to disappear next time with a child he had come to love? Nothing was certain. She had this history; so much about her remained an enigma.

Bobby crossed the last pedestrian bridge, walked the path between the houses, and crossed Pacific Avenue, a bit short of breath. Now that he was a mere block from the beach and the writer's house, he was having second thoughts and feeling more than a little timid.

෯•ෂ

"Where's Ginger?" said Denison when he opened the door.

"My dad has her," said Bobby.

Denison's face registered surprise, but he made no comment as he closed the door behind Bobby and reached out for a hug; Bobby moved easily into his grasp and held on tight.

"Thanks, first of all, for your help," said Bobby. "You and Brandon were terrific. We reopen tomorrow. He's going to stay for the performance before he goes back to New York."

"I'm glad I could help and I'm glad things turned out for the better, because it's a great show and Brandon's a good friend. He thinks very highly of you. We all do."

Bobby let go, moved away, and looked out onto the silvery water of the Pacific Ocean. "I'm parched," he said.

"I have juice and sodas," said Denison.

"Water's fine," said Bobby.

Denison came back in with a bottle of Perrier and said, "What's so urgent?"

"I never thought I'd develop feeling for anyone so soon after Jason," said Bobby.

"Your face is getting more animated," said Denison.

"That's what Brandon said. I really like you, you know. If I didn't, I wouldn't have to have this conversation. We'd just go our separate ways and that would be the end of it."

"Thank you, I think. I like you too," said Denison.

"But—and it's a big but." Bobby smiled and Denison smiled with him.

"Let's go out on the deck and sit down," said Denison. He opened the sliding door, went outside, and sat down in the love seat.

Bobby followed, but rather than take the empty spot on the settee next to Denison, he chose the wicker chair adjoining. How should he start? Even though he and his father had moved closer to each other, even though the show would reopen, even though his face was healing, he simply didn't feel good enough about himself.

"I need to concentrate on *me*, on getting and staying healthy. My medicine makes me feel rotten and even though Doctor Manna says there are at least a dozen therapies that I haven't tried, I'm not sure I can take the stress that dating brings with it. That was me talking and not Phil. He says I'm going to be around for a long time. My viral load is below 50. It's not undetectable but it's low. But I don't want to put that kind of burden on another person. And I feel like I have time to develop a relationship later. It's not so urgent."

"I'm glad you like Dr. Manna," said Denison.

"It's more than that. I trust him. You know how important it is to find someone who supports you, someone who isn't just out for the money, someone who doesn't just want to feel powerful. Phil works to find ways to save me money and explains things and asks for my input and suggests bulletins to read and encourages me to know as much as I can about my situation. He says those who get involved in their own treatment have far better results. He even stopped by one night to see how I was doing after a change in my medicine. Who knew? A doctor who makes house calls. He said he would still work with me if I wanted to try homeopathetic medicine. That's what he calls it."

"Maybe he's attracted to you," said Denison.

"I don't get that from him. I get that he's interested in his patients as people. And I'm not ready for a relationship. I'm not in a good enough place to date yet. If I were, you'd fill the bill. But I have to be honest."

"I see," said Denison, who now seemed at a loss for words.

"Who's to say I won't call you in three months and ask you out on a date? Though I realize you may not be available then," said Bobby.

"I'm not going anywhere," said Denison. "I appreciate your honesty. And as much as I hate to admit it, it's probably the right thing for you. I spent too much of my own youth with a lover, instead of finding out who I was. Now that I'm alone I find it's not so bad. Friendship is not out of the question, is it?"

Bobby looked at him. Green eyes for him represented intelligence, not jealousy. Bobby nodded. "We should be friends," he said. "Definitely."

❧ • ❦

Bobby hurried through the dark chilly night to his father's house. Skipping up the two steps and onto the porch, he peeked through the glass of Poppy's front door. A candle on the coffee table provided the only light in the room; his father sat on the sofa, his back to the window, Ginger at his feet. Poppy had something resting on his lap, something of considerable interest to him from the way he looked down at it and seemed to stroke it, and something of great interest to Ginger as well. Poppy had music on so Bobby tapped loudly on the glass, saw his father's head turn to look at him, and realized that whatever he held on his lap was alive, because he saw it jump to the floor when Poppy got up to unlock the door. Ginger ran to Bobby, her tail whacking the base of the couch. She sniffed his shoes and limped into the middle of Poppy's living room and took a rubber chew toy in her mouth, then she ran back to Bobby and dropped it at his feet.

"Trying to steal my dog, eh?" said Bobby. "Buying her expensive gifts." Poppy smiled, rather self-consciously, and stepped back from the door.

"Let me turn the music down. I was getting ready to bring her back," said Poppy.

"I didn't know you liked Leonard Cohen. What's wrong?" said Bobby. Despite the darkness of the room, Bobby detected something in Poppy's face: muscles slack; forehead and eyes lined with sadness. "What ran into the kitchen?"

"Nothing," said Poppy.

"Nothing ran into the kitchen?" said Bobby.

"Nothing's wrong," said Poppy.

Bobby strode through the front room and looked in the kitchen. The light from the ventilation hood above the stove was on, dimly, but it provided enough illumination for him to see, next to the back door, a litter box and two bowls: one with water and the other containing dry pet food. A kitten raced from under the table and attacked his shoe, before darting into a space between the refrigerator and the built-in cabinet adjacent.

"A cat? You've got a cat. Is it yours? Where did you get a cat?"

Poppy came into the room behind him. "It was starving. I rescued it from the desert."

"Are you getting soft on me?"

"I'm not keeping it."

Bobby crouched, reached out, and called to the kitten. "Is it a girl or a boy?"

"It's just till I find it a home," said Poppy.

The cat came to Bobby and allowed it to pet him and then it rolled over suddenly to bite and claw at his hand. "Ouch. He's got your disposition," said Bobby.

"Ha ha," said Poppy. "So what's up?" When he turned and went back into the front room, Bobby picked up the kitten and followed, with Ginger running and jumping in circles around his legs, clamoring for her share of attention.

Bobby stood in the doorway looking at his father. "What's up with you, Poppy? You look like you lost your best friend. Are you burning incense? Candles and incense? Kittens and dogs? Leonard Cohen? Next you'll tell me an alien spaceship hovered over the back-yard."

Poppy slumped down on the couch again. "I saw Buddha in my kitchen making pancakes," said Poppy.

"That's funny," said Bobby.

"So how are you? You feeling all right? Your face seems better," said Poppy.

"I think it is," said Bobby. "I just went over to Daniel's house."

"And?"

"I told him I wasn't ready for primetime," said Bobby. But it seemed wrong to provide the details: he could see that his father was suffering, and he wanted to help. "You look—I don't know—tired or sad or something," said Bobby.

Poppy sank lower on the couch, rested his head against the back cushion. Bobby sat down across from him in the matching lounge chair and put the kitten on his lap. "What's his name?" said Bobby.

"I went looking for Violet," said Poppy.

"That's one reason I came over," said Bobby. "She stopped by the house."

"You saw her? Did she tell you?" said Poppy.

"She told me some things. What do you mean?"

"She's got herself a doctor."

"How do you know that?"

"It doesn't matter. I found out. He's a quack."

"You know him?" Bobby pulled gently at the cat's soft ears with his fingers and listened to it purring.

"He was the ghoul that ran me through the wringer over my prostate. He's a money-grubbing freak."

"That's why that name sounded so familiar. I must have heard you mention him," said Bobby. He paused. "Maybe Violet was attracted to the stability. She meets a lot of men and from what she tells me you never seemed willing to commit."

"I didn't realize how much I cared, I guess."

"She's done with the doctor," said Bobby, knowing he had to be careful about how much he said to his father.

"Then there will be someone else," said Poppy.

"I don't think so. Wait till you talk to her. You have to decide what you want too. If you gave Violet a reason to feel confident… "

"I told her I loved her."

"When was that?"

"I left it in a note, one morning."

"Go see her then," said Bobby. "I have her new number and address. She needs to talk to you."

Poppy buried his face in his hands, massaged it vigorously for a while, and then looked up.

"I don't know—if she could take up with a nut like Zieman "

"Don't be hasty. Hear what she has to say," said Bobby. "Will you do that?" The cat had fallen asleep and was no longer purring.

Ginger sat in front of Poppy and put one paw on his knee. "She loves sensitive people," said Bobby.

ဆဆဆ Thirty-Two: The Parent Trap

S MELZKOFF DIDN'T CALL VIOLET after Bobby left. His son had shifted somewhat in his position toward her, but Smelzkoff chose not to press. He brushed his teeth, swallowed his nightly dose of aspirin (for his heart), and retired shortly after Bobby hugged him and disappeared with Ginger, into the darkness with the sound of the surf hammering the shore two blocks away.

Stanley Smelzkoff felt worthless without sufficient rest and so went to bed early. Unable to sleep, he became progressively more frantic as the night went on, waking each time the living room mantle clock chimed the hour. At two o'clock, three o'clock, four o'clock, and five, he sat up in bed with the memory of Violet's betrayal pressing on his chest and struggled to banish his grief. The kitten settled in the hollow at the back of his knees. Flattered by its desire to be near him, he tried to lie fixed in position so as not to disturb the animal. At five-thirty A.M., with the anemic light of dawn made weaker by a drizzling mist, Smelzkoff got out of bed for the last time, giving up on the idea that he could face his situation refreshed.

At six o'clock his telephone rang. He took his coffee with him to answer it, perplexed as to who might be calling at such a time of the morning, especially since he wasn't scheduled to go back on duty for another three days. The cold, wood floor groaned under his feet as he rushed to pick up before the fourth ring. He took the receiver from the cradle, answered, and listened.

"I can't sleep," said Violet.

"Me either," said Smelzkoff, his pain alleviated for a moment.

"Bobby came by last night, after he left you," said Violet.

"I see," said Smelzkoff.

"I'm sorry, Poppy," said Violet. "About the doctor. About Dr. Zieman. I didn't know."

"We can't continue like this," said Smelzkoff.

"Can I come over?" said Violet. "I want to explain."

Smelzkoff hung up, lit a stick of Siesta Under The Trees incense, stuck it in the base of his only potted plant (a corn plant), and went to the bedroom to dress. The kitten was curled in a ball, sleeping on one of his pillows. Smelzkoff pulled on workout pants and a sweatshirt, left the bedroom, shutting the door behind him, and went to the kitchen. He quickly gathered the kitten's dishes and put them outside on the back steps.

It was still dark outside when Violet arrived. They embraced, but he pushed back. The sight of her filled him with such a mixture of emotions: he was relieved to see her in good health, but was angry that she had disappeared and taken up with Zieman. He wanted to scold her, but he wanted to hold her.

"I panicked," said Violet.

In the kitchen they sat at the table by the back window and drank coffee. While the sky lightened outside, Poppy listened as the girl (why did she have to be so beautiful?) explained about Kent's plan for her to meet a filmmaker.

"I don't think he'll bother you again," said Smelzkoff, telling her of his visit. "But you can't go back there." Violet nodded in agreement.

The mist now turned to rain, increasing in intensity and forming puddles in the back yard, Smelzkoff gave his full attention while Violet described how she had met Dr. Bradley Zieman. There wasn't a scratch on his Bentley, but she could see that he planned to make trouble and so she flirted and agreed to have drinks. Kent was the one she was running from: that's why she moved, without telling anyone, to an apartment owned by Zieman. "It was a big mistake," said Violet. "He's so weird. I'm not going to see him anymore."

Except to pay the rent, thought Poppy. Whatever that entailed. "And where does that leave us?" said Smelzkoff.

"I know what I want. I'm not sure if you know what you want," said Violet.

"What do you want?" said Smelzkoff.

"To be with you and our baby," said Violet.

"I guess I want—"

Violet sat back in her chair, smiled, placed her hand on her belly, and rubbed.

Smelzkoff paused. He inferred that she meant marriage and family, and that was where he'd always had problems. All those different emotions stewing in the same pot again. How could a person think clearly? How could a person know what to do? The matter of his age hadn't gone away. And he was in the midst of a career crisis, too. "What kind of father would I be at sixty?"

"Are you really serious? Do you know what a fucked up childhood I had? It's hard for me to believe that my real mother could have been as indifferent as Cheryl. You're so decent, Poppy," said Violet. "Besides, you can be whatever kind of father you want to be. I personally think you're going to be very tender."

"I'm not so sure I want to find out," said Smelzkoff. "Cheryl's not your mother? You were adopted?"

"Cheryl said my real mother didn't want me; she said I was damned lucky she took me in, because my real mother gave me up when I was less than a month old to be a lawyer. Cheryl said that girl didn't want to change my shitty diapers; she wanted a life.

"You don't have a choice, Poppy," said Violet. She smiled again, leaned forward, and reached out to put her hand on his arm, which rested on the table. She looked solemnly into his eyes. "I hope you'll be as happy as I am," she said.

A flash of light. "Mine?" said Poppy.

Violet nodded, squeezed his arm.

"And not?" he said.

"We never had intercourse," said Violet.

ಜಲಜಲ Thirty-Three: Another Opening

O N SATURDAY WHEN THE CURTAIN came up again, thanks to Daniel Denison's laudatory column in *The Los Angeles Times*, thanks to the full page ad taken out by Brandon in the *Calendar* section (paid for by the city of LA as part of the agreement he had hammered out), thanks to all the media publicity the show had received when the police went on their rampage against the protestors, there was hardly an empty seat in the Olympic Theater.

Bobby watched from the wings in his Phantom mask, pleased at the performance, which came off without a single glitch. It was as nearly perfect as anyone could expect, almost as if the layoff had done them all good, given them time to ponder their roles, while the unconscious parts of their brains worked to refine their interpretations. The Dame added a short rendition of the twist to her dance for Herodkoff; it went over quite well with the full-house crowd, as did practically every trill, every ascent and descent of her voice, as she soared, plunged, and warbled her way through the Strauss score. Seeing Poppy in the box that he had provided made Bobby nervous; though his face was in the dark, Bobby saw his father's rigid posture in silhouette. He had laughed when Salami first came on stage, but since Herodkoff's interaction with her was such an important part of the comedy he kept watching for Poppy's response afterwards and, regrettably, saw him sitting straight and unflinching.

The mayor attended too with his wife (they had front row seats) as if to say, *Hey, this is all in good fun, fellow citizens!* and perhaps to signal a shift in his administration's policy regarding the LAPD. When Herodias, costumed in red and capped in her red, silk stovepipe hat, first came on, the mayor laughed long with enthusiasm, his body shaking in spasms, though who could tell with these politicians whether their emotions were sincere or mere posturing. If the man had been allied with Gloria Deacon, it wasn't apparent from his enjoyment at the parody of her in the opera.

In addition to Brandon and Denison, who sat on the two chairs in front of Poppy in the box, there were a great many celebrities across all age groups. The ones Bobby recognized from film were liberals, known for their support of social causes and animal rights—and at the same time he noticed that the aging actor who had done those Biblical epics (he couldn't recall his name) and who had become president of NRA was not among them.

The only empty seat was the chair next to Poppy in the box, the seat Bobby had intended for Violet. He wasn't sure what that meant. Surely by now his father had a chance to see Violet and hear her news, but unfortunately Bobby had been so busy getting the show back up and running that he hadn't had a chance to call and find out his father's response. He hoped Poppy would support Violet; it seemed a way for the two people he cared about to improve their lives. Assuming that after this performance Poppy didn't pull back in horror from the both of them.

The Dame had planned an after-play party for the cast and friends at Bobby's house. Poppy already said he would attend; in a way Bobby was anxious for the performance to end so that he could find out what had happened between his father and Violet.

The music ended, the curtain descended on cue after Salami's demise and the crowd jumped immediately to their feet. But Poppy was no longer in the box. The audience clapped and roared their approval as the cast made their appearances back on stage. When the curtain dropped for the third time, The Dame ran over to grab Bobby's hand and pull him to the center of the stage; then the lights came up and the crowd thundered their approval even more exuberantly. They stomped, hooted, whistled, and applauded till hands must have surely bled. It warmed Bobby's heart, but it embarrassed him, too. That was one good thing about the mask he wore. It covered the tears that ran unrestrained down the impaired side of his face.

ಔಔಔ Thirty-Four: A Dangerous Liaison

VIOLET HAD BEEN READY to leave the apartment to meet Poppy at the theater when Dr. Bradley Zieman showed up in her hallway. He had used his master key to gain entry while she was in the bathroom putting finishing spray on her hair and dabbing Poppy's favorite perfume on her neck and elbows.

"I didn't hear you come in," said Violet.

"Why haven't you called me back?" he said, blocking the doorway.

"I was going to, first thing tomorrow. I'm seeing my friend Bobby's play tonight," said Violet.

"First you're too sick for company, then you're too busy with castings, and now Bobby's play. I'm beginning to think you're a lot of hot air," said Bradley Zieman.

Violet tried to walk past him and out of the bathroom, but he took hold of her arm, just above the elbow, and stopped her progress. "Can't we sit in the living room?" she said. "I don't want to miss Bobby when he stops by."

"Call him," Zieman said. "Tell him you're sick, tell you can't make it, because you're not leaving this apartment until we settle a few things."

"What's the matter with you? You're hurting my arm," said Violet, trying to stay calm.

"For one thing I found out where you've been acting, Sabrina," said Bradley Zieman. "Now get on the phone." He led her roughly by the arm down the hallway and into the bedroom and shoved her toward the telephone on the night table.

"Can't this wait till tomorrow?" said Violet, sitting on the edge of the bed.

Zieman moved forward until he stood above and in front of her. He took her head, covered both of her ears with his hands, and said, "I don't appreciate being led down the primrose path, you little trollop."

"I'm wearing posts. You're mashing them into my neck," said Violet.

"Pick up the phone," said Zieman.

Violet rubbed her ear lobes and neck. Then she dialed Poppy's number, waited until the voice mail recording played through, and said after the beep, "Bobby, this is Violet. Listen, I hope you haven't left yet for my place. My landlord came over. There's a problem with my rent check and I'm not going to be able to make the play. Call me later. Love you. Bye." She hung up.

"Love you," said Zieman, mocking. "Just a friend, right?"

"He's gay," said Violet. She stood and walked past Bradley Zieman to the door. When he didn't attempt to touch or stop her, she said, "Would you like some wine? I could use a glass."

"Yeah, I'll have wine. If that's what it takes for you to tell the truth, get us some wine and come into the parlor," said Zieman.

In the kitchen Violet took a bottle of Chardonnay out of the fridge, and chose two wine goblets from the shelf. Unbalanced, she thought. Bradley Zieman was not dealing with a full deck. That's how Cheryl would put it. Violet peeled off the metal foil that covered the mouth of the bottle and stuck the sharp prong of the opener into the cork. Kent could be squeezed and fingered like an accordion, but Zieman was educated and arrogant. Arrogant enough to believe he could have whatever he wanted. After withdrawing the cork, Violet poured the amber wine into the glasses.

One could stall Kent; bluffing was a part of his game, but she sensed that Bradley Zieman seldom bluffed. She slipped the opener into the flapped pocket of her Navy blazer, picked up the two glasses and went to the living room. Dr. Bradley Zieman of Brentwood was dangerous indeed.

ಬಿಬಿಬಿ Thirty-Five: Cracking the Code

THE STAGING, COSTUMES, and performances were professional and polished, and a part of Smelzkoff saluted Bobby for having put together the production. He loved his son (seeing him attacked and beaten made him realize how much he loved his son) but a stage full of so many strange people disturbed him; men with breasts and women with penises and body builders with erections. It disgusted him. Like a sideshow of lizard men and 1000 pound, conjoined twins in a carnival. Like those grizzled bodybuilder women at Gold's—and the men who took so many steroids that their skin turned purple. Stanley Smelzkoff had stood for order and uniformity. No, everyone didn't have to be exactly alike, but what was with those who wished to be so drastically different?

Perhaps if Violet had showed up, perhaps if she'd been beside him in the box, he could have relaxed and been swept away with the laughter. Heaven knows everybody else in the Olympic Theater seemed to love the show. How could he have allowed Violet to disappoint him yet again? After half an hour of the performance, when the writer and Bobby's friend from New York were convulsed with laughter and applause, he slipped silently from his seat and stole down the steps to the theater exit.

He had promised to go to Bobby's party but without Violet he didn't have the desire or courage. He drove south to Sunset Boulevard and turned west. He picked up his cell phone and dialed his voice mail number. Violet had made it clear that she intended to have the baby with or without his support and she swore it was his and not that pervert's. Would he always doubt her? Was it too late for him to believe in her? He had to find a way to protect his feelings. Perhaps in Venice he would drive up Abbot Kinney and stop in Hal's for a drink. He rejected the idea. He didn't feel like talking to anyone except Violet. The knowledge that he was going to be a father again made him smile despite his apprehension.

First message, sent at 7:55 P.M. Bobby, this is Violet. I hope you haven't...Smelzkoff listened to the entire message, looked at the clock on the dash, and pressed *1* to hear the message again. My landlord came over...my rent check...Her tone? Was this a message she meant for Bobby? Or was something brewing? She seemed to be speaking in code.

At the next light, Smelzkoff reached in his pocket and took out the note with Violet's address. After a moment to consider the fastest route, he swerved south in front of traffic and sped toward Santa Monica Boulevard. He pressed hard on the accelerator. Whatever the reason, if her landlord, A.K.A. Dr. Bradley Zieman, was there, it was time for a showdown. Violet didn't have a checking account. She dealt solely in cash.

ಹುಹುಹು Thirty-Six: Celebration

BY THE TIME BOBBY ARRIVED home the bartender (a waif of a girl with cropped henna-colored hair and black makeup) and servers (twin blond boys in acrobatic tights) that Dame Ethel had hired, were making drinks and distributing hors d'oeuvres from silver trays. Thirty-five to forty guests already mingled outdoors on the patio and in the areas surrounding the swimming pool and hot tub. Frederick and Rex stood facing each other at the edge of the pool in crouched wrestling stances, each man poised to clasp the other in a hold that would lead to his capitulation and subsequent introduction to the cold water. Sally Monella and Georgia Bush sat in lounge chairs sipping margaritas, smiling, or rather smirking, and uttering comments to each other as they watched the two beefy boys at play.

The Dame, dressed in kimono and with chopsticks perforating her up-hairdo, glided easily through the crowd, nodding to this one and that, stopping occasionally to check on a friend's cocktail, chatting for a few minutes when a guest took hold of her sleeve or offered a comment. Dame Ethyl had already mentioned to Bobby earlier in the afternoon that she simply ached to play Butterfly.

Daniel Denison and Brandon sat close to each other on steps that led to the back porch where the outdoor bar had been set up. Bobby sensed that their interest in each other was more than platonic: Denison brushed a leaf—which had drifted from the potted ficus tree that sat above them on the porch—off of Brandon's sweater; Brandon touched Daniel's hair with his fingers and Bobby overheard him say, "Salt and pepper hair is so sexy."

Seeing their intimate behavior stabbed at Bobby for a moment, but he recovered quickly. He, after all, had brought everyone together; these were friendships and romances that he had inspired. This creative family, here because of him, was something to be proud of.

Ginger and Crab followed whichever of the servers currently had a full tray of food, as they offered edibles to the guests. Occasionally a dollop of sour cream or sprinkling of caviar fell from a pastry puff and onto the ground as it was taken from the plate, and unless Ginger worked fast it usually went to the sour-natured and more aggressive Crab, who didn't hesitate to snarl and show his teeth.

So far the guests appeared to be comfortable, enjoying their drinks and food. The owners of *Playa de Jaime*, Jaime and Ned, took several appetizers at once from one of the servers, and smacked their tongues against the roofs of their mouths after each bite as they attempted to analyze the ingredients. Each time a server walked away, Jaime pinched him on the ass. At least no one seemed drunk (goosing was expected behavior from Jaime) and no one was naked in the pool. Even Rex and Frederick had stopped skirmishing and sat at the edge of the hot tub with their bare feet dangling in the froth of the simmering water. Bobby looked at his watch from time to time and searched the growing crowd for some sign of Poppy and Violet.

Bobby started for his room to call both their places in an attempt to locate them, and then he saw the figure enter the back yard from the side of the house. Bobby ducked behind a palm, adjusted his mask over his eye, and looked closer. He had packed on more muscle and his buzzed hair had been peroxided, but Jason still poked his head forward like a turkey when he walked.

৩০৪৩০ Thirty-Seven: Doctor Strange Love

NINE-FIFTY-FIVE. Exactly two hours since Violet's message. Smelzkoff slowed and strained to read the address numbers on buildings. The deciduous hardwoods, which lined the avenue, retained their leaves longer in this climate, blocking much of the illumination emitted by the streetlights. "There are two griffins on the front steps, Poppy," said Violet, when she told him about her new place, though Smelzkoff didn't know what griffins were, and didn't ask. Later, he consulted the dictionary.

After seeing the two statues, Smelzkoff pulled over and parked in the first available spot. Since the area was restricted to permit parking, he put a police business placard on his dash before getting out of the truck. The street was relatively quiet, with little passing traffic, but he saw evidence of a Saturday night party at one Spanish-style stucco as he stepped onto the sidewalk: smiling people visible through the living room bay window; others standing and smoking outside on the front stoop. There were six units in Violet's building; hers (number 3) was on the first floor, at the back and on the right, she had said. He approached the complex with caution, wondering what he would find and how he would react to what he found.

The door to the entry corridor had been kept ajar by the use of a rolled-up newspaper, wedged between the door and frame. Smelzkoff pushed it open, crossed the threshold, and journeyed down the hallway, past the stairs that led to the second floor, past the row of mailboxes, past the fake potted rubber plant to the end, where he found the door with a 3 on it. To his surprise this door was also unlatched and cracked open.

Instinctively Smelzkoff reached for his holster, before he remembered that he was in civilian attire and unarmed. Her message had emphasized the word *problem*—and Bobby wasn't supposed to pick her up. Smelzkoff considered going back to his car for his gun. Zieman struck him as eccentric at best, a deviant at worst.

Smelzkoff stood to the side, pushed the door to her apartment open until the space was wide enough for him to look inside. Violet, with her back to him, stood in front of a fireplace, a portable telephone pressed against her ear. Smelzkoff couldn't see all the room so he opened the door wider and looked around. Satisfied that she was alone, except for Whiskey, who lay sleeping in a corner of her sofa, he stepped inside and said, "Honey, are you all right?"

"Poppy," said Violet, turning around. "I was just trying to call you. Thank God you're here." She turned off the phone, put it on the mantle, and ran to him. Her upper lip was swollen, she had a small cut above her right eye, and her mascara and lipstick were smeared. And either her lipstick had smudged against her front teeth—or that was blood.

Smelzkoff held her and stroked her hair. She didn't cry but he could feel her body trembling. "Who did this," said Smelzkoff, pushing back to look at her face again.

"I was on my way out to meet you at the theater when he showed up," said Violet. "He got rough right away. I had told him that I was an actor, but then he found out about Fantasy Mansion."

Smelzkoff thought about the baby. He took her by the hands and led her to the sofa. "Does he know you're pregnant? He didn't punch you, did he?" Smelzkoff tried to stay calm, so as not to upset Violet any further, but the idea of Zieman striking her triggered a nerve above his right eyelid, and it began to flutter until he put his fingers up to stop it.

"I pretended to like it. I thought if he doesn't believe I'm an actor, I'll fool him. I told him I'd been waiting for him to take charge. I made as if it was one of his sex games. I said that I liked it when he took control."

Smelzkoff felt the hair stand out on the back of his neck. "You had sex with him?"

"He likes to be dominated. I've never had sex with him," said Violet.

Smelzkoff sat without comment for a moment, trying to reconcile such disparate statements. He must have had a look of astonishment or total disbelief on his face. Tongue-tied. He was tongue-tied. "I'm confused. If—"

"He's impotent," said Violet. "He's totally into dildos. We've never ever even had intercourse. He liked me to use a dildo on him. That, and the timing of things, is how I know he's not the father. We've never done the deed."

Violet was massaging his hand with hers. He stared at her in silence. It seemed unbelievable. And yet, from his own experiences with Dr. Bradley Zieman, it seemed oddly and strangely believable. Something about the way he had perspired when he administered the various tests, something about the way his pupils enlarged, the way his irises were surrounded by white, the way he never quite made eye contact all of this seemed to say that Violet was telling the straight, dead-on, unmitigated truth about the salacious Dr. Bradley Zieman.

"When I find that piece of low life scum, I'm going to make him wish he'd never—" Smelzkoff stopped himself. "So how did you finally get rid of him?" he said.

"I haven't yet," said Violet. "He's in the bedroom."

৪৪৪ Thirty-Eight: Reunion In Venice

NOT ONE TELEPHONE CALL or letter from Jason in the six months since they had separated. Once Bobby dreamed that he saw him in a pottery store and another time he actually thought he saw him ordering crullers in a donut shop on La Brea. Although he didn't quite pinch himself when Jason first walked into the yard this night, he did consider for a speck of time that this too was simply another dream. But of course it wasn't, and the real question was: why had Jason come?

If only Bobby could get across the room to Brandon to ask a few questions. Jason hadn't known his address or telephone number, and for him to show up at a time like this, he simply must have been coached—by the only remaining connection between them. How could Brandon think he would want to be seen in this state of semi-paralysis. These were not the circumstances that made one plan a reunion. And he couldn't hide or leave: it was his party.

Although, why not? A word to The Dame, the real hostess anyway, and out the door. The mask isolated him from others. He could dash across the patio, disappear inside, and exit through the front of the house. Bobby perspired beneath the mask and heard clearly the thump-thump thump-thump of blood as it coursed through the veins in his temples.

Then it was too late. Jason saw Brandon on the steps, who in turn pointed to where Bobby stood in the shadow of the palm. In an instant Jason came toward him. Bobby took a breath and then two steps forward. Jason smiled and reached out with both arms to embrace him, but Bobby merely extended his hand and accepted the kiss on the cheek without returning it.

"I saw *Salami*," said Jason.

"Where's your boyfriend?" said Bobby.

"We're not together anymore," said Jason. "It was amazing. Absolutely amazing."

"You're so muscled, but then I suppose I've changed too, haven't I?" said Bobby.

"Brandon told me," said Jason.

"Brandon's awfully free with his information."

"Don't blame him. When I heard he was coming out, I hassled him until he told me where you were living. It was all my idea. I wanted to apologize."

"You could have written or called."

"Can I see your face?" Jason reached toward the mask.

Bobby tilted his head back and away. "So you like my mask. Don't change the subject," he said.

"Come on, Bobby. It's me. Brandon says your face is better."

"It's me? You didn't even come to my going away party. It's fairly obvious that I didn't know who you were."

"All right, so I have a lot of explaining to do," said Jason. He reached out again, this time for Bobby's hand, and Bobby allowed him to hold it. "After you hear me out, I hope you'll see my side of things," said Jason. "But later. In a more sober environment. Your friends seem cool. Introduce me?"

His hand felt at once familiar and strange. Jason clasped his hand over the fingers and caressed the back of Bobby's hand with his thumb. But Jason's hand was thicker now and slightly calloused, which served as a reminder that time had passed and that things were different. "I'm sorry that I'm not all giggling to see you, but I'm still hurting. You threw me aside and now show up here uninvited. What gall."

"Do you want me to leave?"

"I cared about you," said Bobby.

"I cared about you. Why do you think I freaked out when you got sick? Remember that movie where the woman learns that her husband has been killed in the war and she sleeps with a boy from high school to celebrate his memory?"

"*Summer of '42*," said Bobby.

"It was kind of like that," said Jason.

Certainly whatever Jason had to do to get through the days he should do. But it all sounded so familiar. Please understand me. Please empathize with me. Please sympathize with me. Please. Please. Please. Me. Me. Me. Bobby was the one who was sick, but it was Jason who pleaded for compassion.

"Poor Jason," said Bobby, "you have the emotional temperament of a fifteen-year-old."

"What does that mean?" said Jason.

"Did you say hello to Ginger?" said Bobby, when his dog, the dog they had picked out together, walked over. Ginger sniffed Jason's shoes and pants cuffs, and wagged her tail to acknowledge his presence. "Apparently a bad mother is better than no mother," said Bobby.

Bobby didn't know what made him look toward the front house, but he did—and that's when he saw his own mother and Tom, home from Greece, standing on the back porch and looking out over the party that was taking place in their yard.

"I think my mother's calling me," said Bobby.

He brushed past Jason, weaved through the guests, and approached the steps to the back porch, only to find The Dame bowing in welcome to Bobby's astonished mother and stepfather.

ଓଓଓ Thirty-Nine: Another Reunion

SMELZKOFF HAD NO IDEA what he would find as Violet led him to the bedroom. He wanted to rush in and pummel the doctor with his fists; he wanted to punch him till his teeth littered the floor; he wanted to drag him by his bushy hair to the roof and then toss him off of it. No, he wanted to slap him, simply, with an open hand: far more appropriate treatment for a coward. Violet pushed open the door; light from the hallway revealed the silhouette of a figure lying motionless on his back, on the bed and in darkness. Was he asleep? Or unconscious? Dead?

Violet had refused to give Smelzkoff additional details. Once she finished telling how she had turned the tables on Dr. Bradley Zieman, she insisted instead on taking him to see for himself. She reached around, just inside the door, and flipped a switch to light the room. Smelzkoff entered and approached the bed. Zieman, naked except for the mask over his eyes, and with a florescent green tennis ball jammed in his mouth, had been handcuffed to the headboard.

"My God, isn't it hard to breath?" Smelzkoff stopped at the edge of the bed; Zieman turned his head toward him, his eyes darting left and right, up and down, through the slits of the mask. He began to thrash about and made moaning noises through his nose. "He's not hurt, is he?" said Smelzkoff.

"Only his dignity," said Violet.

"Come here," said Smelzkoff to her. "Stand next to me. I want him to see what he did to your face." He reached down and pulled the tennis ball from Zieman's mouth, abruptly, which caused the doctor's teeth to clack together.

"Watch it, I've got veneers," said Zieman.

"You're an asshole, Doctor," said Smelzkoff, through his own clenched teeth. "Or, I should say, you're an asshole doctor."

"Who are you? Get me out of these cuffs," said Zieman. "Bitch, you're going to regret this."

Smelzkoff reached down to unfasten the mask, and Zieman recoiled. "I won't hit you," said Smelzkoff. "But I may have to catheterize you with a garden hose."

With the mask removed, Zieman could apparently see better. "You're a patient. How did I don't—"

"So, we meet again. Small world, isn't it? Violet's going to press charges. That should make your world even smaller," said Smelzkoff.

౭౦౭౦౭౦ Forty: Time for the Family

S MELZKOFF HAD CLUNG TO VIOLET throughout most of the night. Though he usually rolled over to sleep unencumbered after a brief period of lying with her in the spoons position, he had on this particular night allowed her to, indeed had insisted that she, stay close.

And when they awoke, Violet put her head on his chest and ran her fingers through his hair. Neither of them made a move to get out of bed until they heard Whiskey and the kitten romping through the front part of his house. "This I've got to see," said Violet. "I still can't believe you've got a cat."

Smelzkoff kissed her on the cheek and swung his legs over the side of his bed to get up and make coffee. "We have to see Bobby and explain why we didn't make the party last night."

Violet put on her robe, stepped into her slippers. "What about his face? Will he really get the feeling back?"

"Does anyone know with AIDS?" Smelzkoff looked at her for a moment before averting his eyes. "It's not my place to talk about it, but I'm going to go full crazy if I don't tell someone," he said. And when Violet didn't gasp or cry out in horror, he said, "You knew?"

"I figured it out in New York," said Violet. "He mentioned his medicine, and he's so thin."

Smelzkoff pulled on his trousers. "How can two cats make so much noise?" He walked into the kitchen, and Violet followed.

"I don't know how to say this," she said. "but how long—"

Smelzkoff sighed. "I got to get involved. I really don't know nothing. He asked me to train him, since the doctor wants him heavier." Smelzkoff smiled. "Here's my chance to beef him up," and then more seriously he added, "He's been gutsy, keeping this all to himself; he hasn't even told his mother."

"Let's go now," said Violet. "We can have coffee at his house." She turned off the faucet, took the coffee pot from Smelzkoff's hand, and placed it back on the burner. Then she put her arms around him and rested her head on his chest again. "If anything were to happen to him and he couldn't see the baby " she said. "He was so excited when I told him."

"Oh I don't reckon he's in any immediate danger," said Smelzkoff. "Do you think?"

"Poppy," said Violet. "I think I'd like to try to find my birth mother."

❧•❧

They parked in the driveway, got out of the car, and made their way alongside the house. The back yard and pool area were surprisingly tidy, considering that there had been a party the night before.

Smelzkoff went to the guesthouse and tapped on Bobby's door. Ginger growled and barked, rather halfheartedly, Smelzkoff thought, and then he tried the knob and found the door unlocked. Violet followed him into the room. "I'm sorry," said Smelzkoff. "I thought you were alone."

"Poppy, this is Jason. We lived together in New York," said Bobby. Jason sat up in bed and reached across Bobby's prone figure to extend his hand. "Jason this is my father. And this is my friend, Violet. What happened to you two last night? You hated the play, didn't you, Poppy?"

"There's so much to tell you," said Violet.

"Ditto," said Bobby. "Mother and Tom came home last night."

"They're here?" said Smelzkoff.

"They arrived in the middle of the party. Mom's fine now, but Tom's still in shock."

And then Smelzkoff realized that Bobby no longer wore the mask. "Your face is working," he said.

"But I was in the mask at the party," said Bobby. "I gave Mother the sordid details. At least it took her mind off The Dame and Flo and the rest of the girls. She pretends, but she's no more liberal than you, Poppy."

"Will you cut me some slack?" said Smelzkoff. Here he was, standing in his son's bedroom, with him sick and lying in bed with another man, and who knew what had transpired between them? Although the friend looked pretty robust at that. Still, Smelzkoff thought, with so much new information and so much unknown, he deserved some time to get used to things, didn't he?

"I'll get your mother up and we can all have coffee," said Smelzkoff. "We brought a coffee cake to go with. Violet and I made some decisions last night."

❧ • ❦

Smelzkoff stood on the back porch waiting. Carol came to the door wearing a bathrobe. Her hair disheveled; her eyes swollen and red. She suffered, no doubt, from a combination of jet lag and stress, but she smiled when she saw him.

She opened the door and moved back to let him enter the kitchen, and started to cry even before she spoke. "Stan, what are we going to do?" she said.

Smelzkoff took hold of Carol's shoulders. "We're going to learn all there is to learn about AIDS and we're going to support him and love him. That's what we're going to do. And I'm going to put some weight on him at Gold's. He needs us—and we need him."

They talked for about fifteen minutes. Smelzkoff reassured Carol again and again that if Bobby said he was going to be all right then they had to take his word for it. But privately he wondered. When Tom came into the kitchen, Smelzkoff said, "I came to tell you to put the coffee on. I want you to meet my fiancée. Where are your other houseguests? You know how they separate the men from the boys in Greece, don't you, Tom?"

છ•ન્

Everyone sat at the kitchen table. They'd been exchanging stories for almost two hours now. Carol related how Tom had turned red and practically kicked at imaginary clumps of grass when The Dame pinched his cheek and called him a *fercrimptepunum*. Smelzkoff, with coaching from Violet, told about the evil Dr. Zieman and how she had managed to outsmart and overpower him. Violet's lip was still swollen, but she had covered the other scratches and abrasions with makeup. Hearing this, Bobby became very concerned and wanted assurances that she hadn't received any blows to the abdomen. Smelzkoff didn't know quite what to make of his son's friend Jason, who stayed close to Bobby, holding his hand and watching him whenever he spoke.

At one-thirty, after Carol had exhausted them with tales of Greece, Tom looked at this watch and turned on the television on the counter, saying he needed to check the market closing quotations. Before he had a chance to use the remote to click off of the local station and onto the cable business channel though, Smelzkoff saw Gloria Deacon at the podium, addressing the press.

"Don't change it," he said. The Deaconess wore the red hard hat that Smelzkoff had given her, after convincing her to expose her bald head.

"It is with a great sense of destiny and a commitment to victory that I announce today my intention to run for mayor of our great city of Los Angeles," said Gloria Deacon. "My hat is not an homage to fashion, but a symbol of what our great city can be if we're not afraid to get our hands dirty. We can make LA an orderly place to live. For too long now, we've been a place that deviants call home." Then she went on to tell how her life had been in danger, and warned that if anything happened to her, it would be no simple accident. "There are those who wish to shut me up," she said. A banner behind her proclaimed: *Yes, on Prop 1134.*

And the moment that the press conference ended, Gloria Deacon ran her first campaign spot. The doctored photo—which Smelzkoff had provided, with the mayor's head on the transvestite's fleshy body, flanked by two other transvestites, came on screen. The nipples had all been censored with black rectangles, which served only to make the snapshot more lascivious, but there was no mistaking the identity of the face in the middle. It was the mayor's.

Raucous, striptease music (blaring horns and percussive drumbeats; one could almost see the garters flying) accompanied the photograph, loud at first and then subdued when the somber, documentary-style tone of the voice-over began: "Don't let him strip away LA's dignity any further," intoned the narrator.

"That's the picture I took. In the *pose plastique* tradition," said Bobby. "But someone has altered it."

The photograph faded to black and was replaced by one of Gloria Deacon in her red hardhat and red coveralls. She stood in the middle of a jail construction site on a heap of rubble, blueprints rolled up in her hand and pointing with the other to a spot on the horizon. "It's time for a change," droned the announcer. "Time for order. Time to lock away perversion. Time for the family. Time for Gloria Deacon."

Then she turned to the camera, removed the hard hat to reveal her glistening, shaved head, and smiled.

"That didn't take long," said Smelzkoff.

"She gives new meaning to the term bull dyke," said the Dame, who had come out of the guest room and into the kitchen undetected until he spoke.

"Poppy," said Bobby. "Have you and Violet been tested?"

꙳꙳꙳ Forty-One: Anniversary

A WARM, SPRING SUN MELTED the winter snow in the mountains of the Angeles National Forest, turning this tranquil brook into a thunder of water coursing over deposited rocks and fallen tree limbs. Birch grew up to form miniature islands in the stream and filter the sun's overhead light. Cool vapors from the spray of water colliding against rocks misted his hair and face and purified Bobby's spirit. He had come here today because it was an anniversary of sorts: exactly one year since he had left New York to live in Los Angeles.

Ginger enjoyed it here too. The terrain was rocky and uneven but not so treacherous as to keep her from following Bobby down the slope, through the growth, along the banks of the stream. The trees had started to bud; it was a miracle that the smaller of them could maintain their hold in such a mad rush of water.

Bobby used a walking stick to advance over the mossy ground and he crisscrossed from one side to the other when there was a rock large and anchored enough to use as a stepping stone. Even then he occasionally miss-stepped and slipped, with one or both feet ending up in the frigid water. Neuropathy from his medicines caused his feet and legs to ache, but like Ginger, he pushed on. Both of them were doing rather well these days, he thought. Considering.

He spread his blanket on a level, dry spot, next to a large boulder, sat, and opened the wicker basket. He tossed Ginger a piece of turkey jerky then took half of a tuna sandwich out of its foil and nibbled at it, though it was more the idea of a picnic than voracious hunger that made him stop to eat at this time.

With Ginger lying next to him on a bed of leaves, he began to think about how his life, and indeed so many other lives, had changed over the last year. Poppy and Violet had married, a simple-hearted ceremony by the pool at his mother's and Tom's house. Bobby, the best man, made the toast and read a poem by Daniel Denison, entitled "Lemons", which wasn't really about lemons, but passion. After the back-yard ritual Stanley and Violet Smelzkoff had left for a short honeymoon in Lake Geneva, Wisconsin, where Poppy had gone with his grandmother as a boy. The baby, a girl, was due in three months, and Poppy was now busy putting on an addition to his house on 25th Avenue, while Violet prepared the nursery. The new room, an L extension at the rear of the house, with bathroom, would become the new master suite, and Poppy's old bedroom would become a nursery for Marigold.

After Gloria Deacons's victorious campaign for mayor, Poppy had chosen to retire with full pension from the police force, saying his heart was no longer into the enforcement of misguided laws, and had started his own business, as a personal trainer at Gold's. After certification, his first two clients were Jaime and Ned from *Playa de Jaime* restaurant. Then his client list grew rapidly he even trained several celebrities (one a cranky woman who dispensed legal advice on network television; another an effeminate man who hosted a home decorating show on cable) but he was never too busy to call Bobby at home and say, "I've got an hour at two-thirty; we'll train legs today." Thanks to his father's attention and insistence he had put on fifteen pounds, fifteen important pounds according to the doctor, in case he came down with an infection in the future. The biweekly shots of testosterone had helped him gain the weight, he knew, but when people commented on how good he looked, he gave his father the credit.

After a successful run of more than six months for *Salami*, Bobby had decided to close the show. Jason had convinced his father to back a production of the show in New York, and had begged Bobby to direct it, but after only a few minutes he had decided against returning to New York. Life was good in Venice and he had come too far in reconciling with his father to leave now. Dame Ethyl, Rex, Frederick, Sally Monella, Georgia Bush and the rest of the cast and crew had already left and were in rehearsals with the new director for their off-Broadway opening.

Sure, he found it difficult to be alone when the entire world seemed paired-up, but relationships took work too. Jason had initially said he wanted to try again, and though a part of Bobby was flattered by the change of mind, he knew that he himself didn't want to. He was smarter and stronger now, and Jason wasn't the one for him if indeed there was really anyone for him any more. Not that he didn't trust Jason All right, so he didn't trust Jason. That didn't make Jason a blameworthy person just not an appropriate mate for Bobby. Even Poppy and Violet had problems. But their love overcame. That was the one thing he did know. Neither of them talked about their situation with him, except to say that they saw a counselor together, Violet's therapist, Dr. Young. (Poppy complained to Bobby that the doctor could barely bring himself to make eye contact.)

Rex and Frederick were open lovers now, Daniel and Brandon were involved in a long-distance relationship, and Jason already had a new boyfriend. Bobby had Ginger, and that was okay. His numbers were good, there were all kinds of new medicines they could try, Doctor Phil said, if his viral load increased or his T-cells dropped. Bobby was content as never before.

Work on his memoir was going well. Daniel Denison was a constant source of inspiration and encouragement. What a different world it was to write a book and not a play. One worked with others on a play—the cast and crew for a start. A play was a social enterprise. But not a book. A book was hour on top of hour, alone at the computer. Isolation. He couldn't go back stage and interact with others. And he was a perfectionist. He wanted to do the best he could.

At least in Venice he could go outdoors and see others, year-round, thanks to the closeness of people's houses and apartments, and thanks to the mild weather.

After the news of Violet's experience with Dr. Bradley Zieman hit the papers, several other women and a couple of men came forward (immigrants from Russia of all places), to register complaints of abuse. Things were progressing slowly, but it was beginning to look as if the strange and offensive doctor might be involved in some sort of white slavery ring and, as a result, would lose his license. Poppy said the situation encouraged him. "Hopefully, the system still works," he said.

"You mean you are hopeful that the system still works," Bobby corrected.

A truce in *The War on Dogs* was in effect. Who knew for how long? Though the populace had elected Gloria Deacon to the mayorship—despite the news uncovered by a zealous press that, in her twenties, she had given birth to a child out of wedlock, then subsequently chosen a career in law and politics over motherhood and given the girl up in a private adoption, and despite the fact that her campaign picture of the mayor in drag had been proved a fake, they had at the same time defeated Proposition 1134, the proposal for hiring 10,000 new police. So, with no new manpower, Gloria Deacon had to abandon her plan to prosecute and punish litterers. Another slogan during her campaign had been: *Pick it up, or stick em up!*

Poppy had grumbled with disgust on election night as the returns came in. "What else can you expect from people who make an ex-wrestler their governor?" he had said.

Bobby smiled now, thinking about Gloria Deacon. In a Charles Dickens' novel, she would have turned out to be Violet's mother, but this was real life and such a revelation would embody too great a coincidence to be within the realm of possibility. Life didn't always imitate art. Violet had made some initial attempts to locate her birth mother, but the trail had vanished in Kansas, and after that she forgot about finding her, for the time being, and began to prepare for the arrival of hers and Poppy's own offspring.

Flo, by the end of *Salami's* run, had gotten all her money back with enough left over to modernize and update the Olympic Theater. Bobby had given Flo parts of his memoir to read and he had been wildly enthusiastic. "It would make a dynamite screenplay," he said. "It's so visual and I love the way you jump back and forth from the past to the present."

For his part, Bobby didn't understand why everything had to be conceived as a screenplay. Although recently, after a trip on Friday morning to the Farmer's Market in Venice, he imagined a movie which took place entirely within the confines of the market on a single day. Like classical Greek theater, the time elapsed during the performance would equal the time of the action of the drama. He decided thereafter to spend every Friday morning at the market, listening to the muffled chatter of the masked flower growers, recording the complaints of the egg lady, who offered green eggs from Chilean chickens, observing the obsequious pandering to customers by the owner of the coffee cart, witnessing the competitive jostling for fruit by the woman dressed in purple with matching eye shadow, and perhaps even engaging in banter with the bread man and his regulars. Everything one wished to know about social interaction could be observed at a Farmer's Market.

Bobby wrapped the remainder of his sandwich back up in foil and lay back on the blanket. Ginger stretched forward on her front legs, licked his face, and let out a contented groan.

Tomorrow was Friday. Bobby resolved to get to the market early, right after it opened. The butter boy had bristly brown hair with blond highlights, white teeth with one incisor slightly overlapping, and the most mischievous, hazel eyes Bobby had ever encountered. For several weeks now, when he saw Bobby approach his stand, he had rested his hands on his hips, cocked his head to one side, smiled deliciously, and said, "Morning, handsome. How about some fresh, sweet butter."

About the Author

The author, as a boy, with his first dog, Topsy.

RONALD ALEXANDER is a Pushcart-nominated author whose fiction, poetry and essays have appeared in journals including *The Chattahoochee Review*, *Confrontation*, *Columbia*, and *The James White Review*. His work has been performed on "Word Theatre," his novella *Romanze for Martha* was a finalist in the St. Andrews Novella competition, and his novel *The Final Audit* was published by Hollyridge Press. Mr. Alexander lives in Venice, California with his Labrador retriever, Cub.

About the Illustrator

NATHAN GEARE will receive his Bachelor of Fine Arts degree from UCLA in June 2008. His painting and sculpture has been shown at Arena 1 Gallery in the Santa Monica Airport, Upstairs at the Market in Los Angeles, and at the UCLA Wright Gallery. For more information on the artist, please contact Hollyridge Press.

Acknowledgements

For reading the early drafts, I am grateful to my friends Jack and Annie Wilder, Nancy Lamb, Jamie Branda, Chris Harvey, Victor Archuleta, Petr Hiemer, Phil Arlen and Maylen Dominguez-Arlen. My thanks to Edward Gunawan and David Maurice Gil for their creative video promotion, to Nathan Geare for his clever illustrations portraying dog-life at the beach, and finally, for their editing, encouragement, and enthusiasm, I thank my friends at Hollyridge Press: Ian Wilson, Jack Straub and Richard Williams.

www.ingramcontent.com/pod-product-compliance
Lightning Source LLC
Chambersburg PA
CBHW031202020726
47499CB00002B/448